Paradise Misplaced

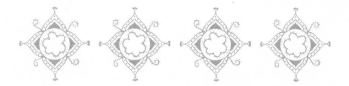

PARADISE MISPLACED

BOOK 1
of the
MEXICAN EDEN TRILOGY

Sylvia Montgomery Shaw

Swedenborg Foundation Press
West Chester, Pennsylvania

Library of Congress Cataloging-in-Publication Data

Shaw, Sylvia Montgomery.
Paradise misplaced / Sylvia Montgomery Shaw.
p. cm.—(Mexican Eden trilogy ; Bk. 1)
ISBN 978-0-87785-341-1 (alk. paper)
1. Young men—Mexico—Fiction. 2. Metaphysics—Fiction. 3. Mexico—History—
Revolution, 1910-1920—Fiction. 4. Psychological fiction. I. Title.
PS3619.H3945P37 2012
813'.6—dc23
2011041258

Edited by Morgan Beard
Design and typesetting by Karen Connor

Printed in the United States of America

Swedenborg Foundation Press
320 North Church Street
West Chester, PA 19380
www.swedenborg.com

*To my parents, who gave me
my Mexican years*

If the skies did not storm,
causing unlike elements to scatter,
the air would never clear; destructive forces
would amass and wreak havoc.

EMANUEL SWEDENBORG

Embody me.
Flare up like flame
And make big shadows I can move in.
Let everything happen to you: beauty and terror.
Just keep going. No feeling is final.
Don't let yourself lose me.

RAINER MARIA RILKE

Part 1

THE GENERAL'S HEIRS

1

DEATH IN SAN ANGEL

THE PLAN WAS simple and well intentioned. So, too, was the murder.

A few kilometers from the outskirts of Mexico City, the village of San Angel slept loose limbed. Afternoon rain had washed the faces of its colonial churches and mansions. By midnight the sky had cleared, shining muted moonlight on the one man in the deserted plaza. He walked briskly. His long cassock fluttered behind him, a black sail on a darkened sea of stone.

Bougainvillea blossoms shaken loose by the storm carpeted the cobblestones, muting his footsteps. No one stirred in the houses with grated windows and walled gardens. San Angel slept peacefully, unaware of the catastrophic earthquake that would literally jolt it and all of Mexico City at dawn. The young man was just as ignorant of the internal upheaval that awaited him. In time he would come to know that the destruction of an inner landscape is no less devastating than the physical collapse of buildings. But the time was not yet. Unaware, he walked on, deluded into thinking that intentions, like the ground under his feet, are solid and predictable, and that rationality can always prevail over passion.

He stopped in front of a massive stone wall. The front door rose tall as the portals of a cathedral. Masons had carved the name of the house and the year of its construction into the lintel of *cantera* stone: *San Justín de los Moros*—Saint Justin of the Moors. 1568. For a few seconds the priest was acutely aware of the scent of wet trees and moist earth. A church bell tolled 1 a.m. The wind picked up. Reaching for the ancient door knocker, he hesitated. Towering eucalyptus trees and cedars trapped within walled gardens shook their heads.

You can still turn around, they seemed to warn the priest.

No. I have no choice.

Yes, you do.

The knocker struck the brass plate, again and again. A voice syrupy with sleep grumbled, "The señor general does not receive at this hour!"

"Eufemio! Open up! It's me!"

Eufemio Rosarito hastened to obey, for he knew the voice well. Yet even after he drew aside the last of the three bolts, the door remained reluctant, its ancient hinges whining plaintively. The old porter, eyes sharp as obsidian, stood on the threshold with a lantern held to one side so that he could look into the visitor's face. He stared with the familiarity earned by years of service. In his grin he wore his badge of honor—the front teeth knocked out by French troops many years ago when he refused to reveal his master's escape route. No man of mixed loyalties, Eufemio Rosarito.

"Father Samuel! How good to see you again! Your dear father will be so pleased!"

"How are you, Eufemio?" The young man embraced the servant with genuine pleasure. Then he pulled back as if to study the features he knew so well: Eufemio's eyes, narrow slits that almost disappeared under shaggy brows; the thin cloud-wisp of a beard; the solitary mole that rose prominently on the left cheek.

"I wouldn't have come so late, but I know the odd hours my father keeps, and how he hates being disturbed during the day."

"True enough, sir. True enough. While the sun is up, we all walk around silent as cats so as not to disturb the general. Right about now he should be finishing evening prayers."

"Good." He walked slowly beside the old servant. "So tell me, how are the ghosts treating you these days?" the visitor quipped, remembering Eufemio's penchant for the supernatural.

Eufemio's eyes narrowed ever so slightly. Then he gave a short laugh. "They make it clear they're here to stay, Father. Pardoning, sir, but I think they have better things to do than to trouble themselves over an old Indian."

"And my father? How is he?"

"Not well, sir. As I explained to your brother the other night—" Again, the eyes flickered slightly.

"Which one?" *Benjamín the apostate or Rodolfo the illegitimate?* the young man had to refrain from adding.

"The captain, sir. As I said, the señor general is not well. Not well. He sleeps little and spends his days and nights in prayer and fasting—not normal fasting, but the kind invented by the devil to destroy saints! A street dog has more flesh on its bones! Pardoning, sir, but I don't know why he keeps a cook!"

"Why, to feed that father confessor of his! Is Father Casimiro here?"

"No, sir. He left yesterday for Oaxaca." Eufemio spoke in his energetic manner as he fastened each of the bolts on the door, his words crisp and clear almost to the point of exaggeration. The effect was of a solid efficiency and dependability. "That just leaves me—and the cook and her daughter—to look after your father. But Father Casimiro promised to be back in a week or so."

"*Deo gratia!*" The priest smiled benignly.

The servant led the way through a tunnel of thick masonry to an enormous central patio. There wasn't a single light anywhere—not because of the lateness of the hour, but because fanaticism had banished it. Even in the tenuous glow of the lantern, the priest could see the desolation of his childhood home. It still affected him deeply. No matter how often he visited his father—the last time had been just over a year ago—he always felt ambushed. Old wounds tore open. The fact that the courtyard had been stripped of all plants and that the lush gardens behind the house had reverted back into wild tangles stung him with the raw power of betrayal. He hated the perversity that had deliberately allowed everything in San Justín to either fall into chaos or to wither away, even the ubiquitous bougainvillea. He knew without seeing them that the once-brilliant vines hung like cadavers from the upper terraces.

So this is how the richest man in Mexico lives! he marveled bitterly.

The porter handed the lantern to him. "Keep the light with you, don Samuelito," he said with a wink, using the diminutive form of the name, as if the priest were still a child who rode on his strong shoulders. "I know my way around this house."

"No, Eufemio. You keep it, in case one of your ghosts tries to trip you on the stairs! No! I insist. I'll sit right here by the fountain. Go."

He watched Eufemio and his light ascend the courtyard stairs and vanish after the turn on the first landing. Left in the dark, the visitor worked his way cautiously to the edge of the fountain that once sang of water and sunlight. Like everything else in San Justín, it had long since been strangled into silence. He needed no light to tell him that the Talavera tiles, once so vibrant with color and water's varnish, lay buried under thick layers of dead vegetation. The young man gazed up at the terraces that encircled the courtyard, invisible in the darkness, and thought about the glory days of that house, the sun- and moon-coated days.

He listened in the stinging silence and wondered where it had all gone—the lights that once spilled into the central courtyard and throughout the house when his parents entertained the mighty of Mexico, when mariachi music and Strauss and Lehár waltzes soared into the sky, and women in silk gowns and men in black-tie formal wear danced till dawn. He listened intently, as if sheer willpower could bring back echoes of sparkling trumpets and violins, tenor voices singing love songs, fireworks embroidering the night sky, women in fragrances that made him heady with desire in his adolescence. Above all, he listened for his father's voice, loud and convivial before mortality frightened it into submission, cheery and passionate before he traded his wife and children for asceticism and salvation.

The priest sat in the dark casting for ghosts. Instead of the happy ones that he sought, he remembered his mother's voice, sharp with terror and disbelief.

"Lucio! What are you doing?"

In the lightning flash of memory the priest was a child again, clinging to his mother while his father stoked an enormous bonfire in the courtyard.

"It's vanity! All vanity!" his father raved as he burned furniture, books, draperies, paintings—everything that he could order the frightened servants to bring to feed the ravenous appetite of the flames.

The visitor's hands began to shake. To still them, he gripped the scalloped edge of the fountain hard, hard to remind himself to focus, to not forget why he was there and what he had to accomplish. The wind moaned his mother's sorrow in that cavernous emptiness. *It won't work,* the air itself seemed to warn him. *Leave!*

"Don Samuel! Your father will see you now," Eufemio called down.

The young man hurried up the stairs, taking the steps by twos as he had done since childhood. Eufemio met him on the upper landing and led him along the north veranda. As they drew near his father's room, the priest began to breathe unevenly.

Never mind, Eufemio. I'll return tomorrow, he suddenly wanted to say.

Servant and visitor stopped outside the general's bedroom. Eufemio handed over the lantern and muttered advice cloaked as a blessing. "Speak calmly, and may the saints be with you."

The priest stared after the departing figure. He was alone now. The wind blew just then, setting dozens of doors and windows rattling. In the sickly light of the lantern he became aware of eyes that watched him—men and women the color of ash. These were his father's heroes, martyrs of the church garishly painted on the walls by the untutored, unskilled Father Casimiro. Every one of the murals depicted with a voyeur's glee the torments of the martyred. Men and women with bodies graphically tortured stared through expressionless eyes. Rendered empty of pain, joy, or fear, they were barely human.

Like Father, damn him! How has it come to this? he railed inwardly.

Fifteen years after his parents' separation, he still could not understand or accept his father's metamorphosis. How had the splendid General Lucio Nyman Berquist—El Vikingo, as fellow officers called him, not simply in reference to his Scandinavian heritage but in tribute to his courage and boldness as a warrior— how had the Viking become so hopelessly ossified? How had his father, who used to ride a horse as if he and it shared the same skeleton, the same spirit—a glorious centaur—how had such a man become so utterly joyless? How had he come to believe that life and salvation are mutually exclusive? And why, why, had the family come to mean as little to him as objects that he could cast into flames?

The young man felt the impulse to pound his fist on his father's door so that all of San Angel would hear his rage. Taking a deep, slow breath, and then a second one, he knocked softly. Then he entered the lair.

The room smelled as if it had been shut up for months, perhaps years. He could see nothing beyond the circle of light cast by the lantern. Setting it down on the floor, he penetrated deeper into the room, squinting into the feeble light of a candle, the only other source of light in that cavernous darkness. The room held a table and a chair. He remembered what he could not see:

the cot with a horse blanket of the coarsest wool and a log for a pillow. Then something stirred just out of sight, a figure that was melded into the darkness and stale air. A face cadaverously pale looked up from under a monk's cowl, and the young man knew he was staring once again at the shade of a departed hero.

I'll never fool him.

I have to—for Isabel.

METEORS

THE RUMORS FELL like meteors—brief, spectacular flashes of light across Mexican skies.

Everyone in the capital city was talking about it. General Lucio Nyman Berquist, reputedly the richest man in the country, had been murdered. Not that that mattered per se. What was gruesome, what made for such animated conversation and sold so many newspapers, was the fact that the accused murderer was none other than his son Samuel Nyman Vizcarra. More astonishingly, the young man was a newly ordained priest!

The scandalous murder would vanish soon enough from the public eye, as surely as Halley's Comet of the previous year had disappeared without a trace. But for a few weeks in 1911, during Francisco León de la Barra's uneventful interim presidency, during those anticlimactic weeks when the euphoric Francisco Madero ran his presidential campaign, urging others to run against him when everyone knew it was no race at all—given the adoration of the masses for the hero of the revolution—only the Nyman Vizcarra trial offered the complacent citizens of Mexico City true suspense and ardent drama.

The older members of the exclusive Jockey Club smoked cigars, swapped stories about El Vikingo's exploits in love and war, and speculated about why he had become so reclusive. Had it been fourteen or fifteen years now since anyone had last laid eyes on Lucio Nyman? What had impelled him to withdraw from the world? And what had possessed that poor young man to murder his own father?

"Gambling debts, no doubt."

"Yes, but remember, he's a priest."

"So? Do priests not eat and live and spend money too? And then there's the issue of Nyman's last will and testament. Now there's a story!"

Ladies in mansions along Reforma Avenue and the new Colonia Juarez read the newspaper accounts as they sipped coffee from Limoges cups. They gathered in the homes of friends to commiserate on the fall of a great family. Even those who had never been particularly fond of the widow pitied her.

"Poor Manuela! First she's had to cope with the bizarre change in her husband all these years! Then the elopement of her son."

"Not to mention that debacle with the will! Think of it! Every last penny went to some American girl, a nobody with a pretty face!"

"Not exactly a nobody. They say she was Rodolfo's mistress or, more likely, Lucio's! And now Samuel accused of murder! Samuel of all people! It's unthinkable!"

Monogrammed tongs dropped sugar cubes into the delicately painted porcelain cups. Afternoon sunlight polished silver coffee services. Servants in livery replenished pastry trays. Rumors swooped from house to house.

Then someone would inevitably remark, "Do you know that it was Manuela's idea to have Lucio's body exhumed?" And then all gossip would stop long enough for the sudden jab of empathy, intense in the fleeting silence. "However will she endure it?"

Everyone followed the trial and added to the collective musings of the city. Shopkeepers, seamstresses, school teachers, bureaucrats—petty or otherwise—all read the newspaper accounts with avid interest. For those who couldn't read, there was hearsay and the *Semana Ilustrada* with its predilection for photos over text. The illustrated weekly managed to convey the essence of the matter: the grieving widow who had unwittingly set in motion the downfall of a beloved son. The photos captured a small woman draped in black crepe and sorrow. The photographs also let people gape unabashedly at the fashionable Countess Eva Nyman de Comardo Tejada del Renglón, sister of the accused priest. Her beauty and sadness heightened the sense of pathos. Prostitutes on the seamy east side of town studied the pictures. Perhaps they yearned to emulate the countess with her French haute couture. Yet most of them focused on the photos of the young priest, marveling at the beauty of his symmetrical features, the lightness of his eyes—apparent even in black-and-white newsprint—and the broad shoulders. Or perhaps they noted the openness of his gaze, the innocent candor, and felt a twinge of pity.

A reporter for the *Heraldo* waxed literary.

> For sheer drama, the trial of Samuel Nyman Vizcarra promises to rival *Don Juan Tenorio!* The accused would seem proof that rakes and devils appear in comely form. Samuel Nyman Vizcarra is a man in his midtwenties, gifted with wealth, social prominence, and the attributes of classical male beauty generously bequeathed him by his Swedish father and his Mexican mother. What he seems to lack is a fair Inés to redeem him. But then given his chosen profession, it is highly unlikely that he would have such feminine intercession available to him—or we would hope as much!

A reporter for the English edition of the *Heraldo* was no less melodramatic in his coverage for the city's Anglo-American readers:

> We would remind our readers that patricide, though heinous, is not of itself an unusual crime. But when it comes from a noble house, the very gods take note!

In Father Samuel Nyman we may have a tragedy of classical proportions. As we witness the fall of the noble and the mighty, we are reminded of the tragic Oedipus and the fatal encounter with his father. If the accused is found guilty, whether of first degree or of second degree murder, our analogy will have been apt.

For the benefit of our readers, we hereby offer a brief summation of the facts that led to the shocking arrest and arraignment of Father Samuel Nyman:

General Nyman's body was discovered by his servant, Eufemio Rosarito, moments after the earthquake that struck the city early on the morning of June 7, 1911. It seems that a large bronze crucifix that hung over the general's bed had been dislodged by the severity of the quake, crushing the back of his skull. An apparent act of God. A funeral followed, highly publicized and attended by the city's first families, including Interim President Francisco León de la Barra.

Readers may well wonder what led the family to question such an obvious cause of death. Herein lies a bitter irony:

On July 7, 1911, General Lucio Nyman Berquist's last will and testament was read in the presence of his heirs. To everyone's astonishment, it excluded them all—all but the general's daughter-in-law. We have it on good authority that said young woman, who had eloped with one of the general's sons a few months prior to these events, is an American—now doña Isabel Brentt de Nyman. Curiously, the heiress to the Nyman Berquist fortune has absented herself from the proceedings. Understandably, her absence has set off a barrage of speculation. However, this reporter will confine himself to the facts known at present.

When the general's widow, doña Manuela Vizcarra de Nyman, suspected foul play and had her husband's body exhumed, a team of forensic specialists reported the following: (1) that the victim died within a five-hour period prior to the earthquake, and (2) that the general was not killed by one blow, but by two distinct blows to the back of the head.

Furthermore, when the police conducted an investigation of the premises and reported that nothing else in the victim's room had been loosened by the earthquake—neither ornaments on the wall, as there were none, nor bits of masonry nor chunks of plaster—and as traces of blood were found on the brass crucifix, it was deduced that the crucifix had to be the one object that had inflicted both blows. Hence, as the quake could no longer be blamed for the death of General Nyman, the matter was now a criminal investigation that led inexorably to the last man known to have been with the victim in the early hours of June 7. By a cruel twist of fate—cruel from the perspective of the woman who launched the whole investigation—the path led to none other than her own son.

The sidewalk outside the courthouse was packed with curious bystanders who wanted to catch a glimpse of the patricidal priest. The corridors and outer lobby were just as crowded. Inside the large courtroom every seat had been taken a full hour before the proceedings were to begin. The air pulsed with a sense of excitement. Finally a vehicle drew up to the courthouse. Guards jumped down and escorted a tall, young man through the central doors. In spite of the publicity the case had already garnered, the crowd still gasped collectively at the sight of the priest in manacles.

As the trial got under way, no one was surprised by the prosecution's opening statements, nor by the defense's plea for acquittal. When Samuel Nyman Vizcarra was asked how he pleaded, he spoke in a clear voice.

"I am innocent."

Witnesses for the prosecution testified that the general's relationship to all four of his children had been highly contentious, that the accused had visited him on at least two occasions in the last few months, and that Samuel had been in Mexico City on the night of the murder. Witnesses for the defense testified to the high moral character of the defendant and to his exemplary devotion to his small parish in the state of Morelos. The defense attorney called on a wide spectrum of witnesses, from the mighty of Mexico to the lowly, from bishops to humble parishioners—white-clad Indians whose sandaled feet seemed as out of place in the formal courtroom as their straw hats in that assemblage of fedoras and plumed Gainsboroughs. The parishioners spoke in the soft tones of the Morelos peasant, their glances furtive, their manner timid and courteous. All praised the young priest. When the prosecutor finally called Samuel Nyman to the witness stand, the spectators leaned forward as of one mind, craning their necks for a better look.

Samuel Nyman rose but did not move forward.

"The prosecution now calls on Samuel Nyman Vizcarra!" the prosecutor repeated.

The priest remained rooted to the spot. Standing nearly a foot taller than his attorney, he seemed deaf to the man's whispered instructions to obey the summons. The judge peered over the top of his glasses:

"Kindly take the stand."

"No. I've said all that I am going to say."

There was an audible gasp. The judge adjusted his glasses. "This is not a request. You are hereby ordered to take the stand."

EYEWITNESSES

THE PRIEST GAZED at the judge with a calmness of manner that could easily be mistaken for arrogance.

"If you do not take the stand, I will have to cite you for contempt."

"Do as you must."

Samuel Nyman sat down again. In spite of threats, fines, and the pleas of family and attorney, he immured himself in a stubborn silence. Later, when his own attorney called him to take the stand, the young man remained just as intractable.

In the end, the whole case hung on the testimony of the general's three servants—the only other people known to have been in the Nyman house on the night of the murder. The first of the servants to be called to the witness stand was Juana Villa, the cook's fifteen-year-old daughter. The girl clung to one of her thick braids throughout the proceeding, her fingers spasmodically climbing the full length, from tip to jaw, and back again.

"Miss Villa," the defense attorney began in soft tones, as if speaking to a skittish horse, "Could you kindly point out to the court Father Samuel Nyman? Thank you. And is that the man who visited General Nyman at 1 a.m. on June 7?"

She nodded.

"Please speak up."

"Yes. That is, I—I—think so."

"You need to know, not to think so. A man's freedom depends on it."

The girl burst into tears. "I don't—I don't know! It was dark. . . . We heard voices, my mother and I. We were awakened late at night."

"Can you swear before the Virgin herself that you saw—"

"Objection!" The prosecutor jumped to his feet. "Must I remind my colleague that we are in a secular court of law?"

"Miss Villa, can you swear to this court that you saw Father Nyman on the night of June 7 at 1 a.m.?"

The girl wept copious tears. When she could finally speak, she stammered, "I—I didn't . . . I didn't see him enter. I was sleeping when he arrived."

"Then what did you see?"

"Nothing. I . . . I heard loud voices . . . and the slam . . . the slamming of a door later on."

"Then you never actually saw him."

"Not until later." Glancing at the priest, she began to sob again.

"Don't be afraid. Just tell the court—tell me—what you actually saw. Did you actually see Father Nyman at the end of the visit or did you—"

"I saw him! Yes, I think I did!"

"You *think?*"

"It was dark, and I was standing behind my mother. She's a big woman."

The room burst into laughter.

Pánfila Villa, the girl's mother, walked with energetic strides and smiled expansively; once in the witness stand, she eased herself into the chair with a satisfied sigh. When asked how long she had been in the general's employ, she beamed: "Two years—almost!"

"And in that time, how often did Father Samuel visit his father?"

"I didn't see much of him the first year or so. He was away somewhere studying to be a priest."

"How about this past May and June. How often would you say the accused visited his father?"

"Once. No, twice!"

"Twice. You're certain? And did you converse with him during those visits?"

"No, sir. I had my duties in the kitchen." She smiled at the spectators.

"Then you hardly knew him."

"I knew him well enough! I swear by the Virgin . . ." She glanced at the judge. "I swear on my child's life that this is the man who woke us in the middle of the night!" She pointed to the accused.

The defense attorney locked his hands behind his back and calmly paced, taking only a few steps before returning to the eyewitness. The short excursion served as a transition.

"General Nyman was known for the severity of his piety. He hardly ate. Why would he need a cook?"

"Because as anyone who knows me can tell you, I make the best beans in the whole city!"

"And your daughter, what purpose did she serve in the general's monastery?"

"She did the wash and helped me in the kitchen."

"To pour water into the pot or to serve up the beans?"

Pánfila Villa's eyes narrowed into thin slits. "Oh, we did plenty to earn our keep, let me assure you! That's a huge house to keep clean! It has over twenty rooms!"

"Indeed. Then he must have paid you well. Could you tell the court how much the general paid you and your daughter for your hard work?"

"Two pesos."

"Each?"

"No, for the two of us."

"So that's one peso a day each?"

"No, a week."

"That hardly seems adequate compensation for two servants. Yet he was the wealthiest man in Mexico. Didn't that irk you?"

She scooped up her smile again and twisted it.

"If you think that smelly old man was the richest man in Mexico, I'd hate to see what the poorest man is like!"

The courtroom erupted in laughter.

"And if you think I killed the general, you're crazier than he was! And he was looney, as looney as they come. His son over there is no better! Who visits anyone in the middle of the night, tell me that!"

More laughter. "Kindly answer the questions put to you and nothing else. Let's just say for the sake of argument—"

"I'm not arguing with nobody. I'm telling you, that priest woke us up in the middle of the night when he had no business to be troubling people!"

"Let's assume that Father Samuel had a perfectly good reason for visiting his father so late at night. All that aside, isn't it possible that someone paid the general a visit after Father Samuel left—someone with far different intentions?"

"You mean, some other thief or murderer? That's impossible!"

"Why? Even in a city as gracious as ours, despicable people commit despicable crimes. Homes are burglarized; people have been known to be murdered in their sleep."

"San Justín is a fortress. There is only one entrance, and it has more locks and bolts than the Federal Penitentiary! Once Eufemio locks the door, no one gets in and no one gets out."

"People scale walls."

Pánfila Villa crossed her arms across her ample chest. "You've never seen the place, have you? Well, let me tell you: the general had workers install not just broken glass all along the top of the outer walls, but he also had them set razor-sharp blades into the concrete, sticking up and out in all directions. Unless you're a bird or the devil himself, there's no getting past those barriers! No one enters San Justín except by the main door. And no one gets past me! I'm a light sleeper and hear everything!" She was smiling expansively again. "I heard the general and his son arguing as plain as day!"

"Well then, can you tell us what they argued about?"

"I didn't say I heard their words—only their voices."

Eufemio Rosarito's sandals creaked as he walked across the marble floor. His stooped shoulders made him seem older than his years, as did the leather-hardness of his skin. Clutching his straw hat to his chest, the old man bowed awkwardly to the judge and to the prosecutor who was about to cross-examine him.

"Mr. Rosarito, could you tell the court how many years you served General Lucio Nyman Berquist?"

"Pardoning, sir, but I don't know."

"Well, could you give us some idea?"

"Most of my life, sir."

"And how old are you?"

"Pardoning, sir. I don't know. I only know that I've served the señor general from the time I was old enough to carry a gun. I was his adjutant." His eyes wandered to the priest and back again as the prosecutor asked his next question. "I'm sorry. What was that, sir?"

"I asked you to tell the court how you came to lose your teeth."

Eufemio tugged on the thin gray wisps of his beard as if stalling, as if assessing the tactical reason behind the question. "A French soldier hit me with the butt of his rifle." His eyes had narrowed warily.

"Can you tell the court why he did that?"

"Because I wouldn't tell him the general's escape route."

"Later, when the general retired, why didn't you do likewise and return to your own people?"

"I wanted to go on serving the general. He let me stay on as his personal servant. I also became the porter to his house."

"So the general entrusted the safety of his home to you."

"Yes, sir."

"Now, could you point out to the court the last visitor whom you admitted into General Nyman's house on the night of June 7, 1911?"

Reluctantly, the old servant fixed his eyes on the priest, who gazed back impassively.

"Would you point him out for us, please."

Eufemio seemed on the verge of tears.

"I am simply asking you to point out Father Samuel Nyman, nothing else." The prosecutor spoke gently, a reassuring hand on the man's shoulder.

Eufemio pointed to the accused with a hand that shook. Then he looked away, careful to avoid eye contact with the accused from then on. The pain of having to testify against the son of his beloved master was palpable. Even the prosecutor seemed to feel a twinge of pity.

"How long have you known the accused?" he asked gently.

"You mean Father Samuel?" The old Indian gazed through eyes glazed with pain. He cleared his throat. "Since his birth, sir."

"You'll have to speak up."

"Since his birth."

"What was your relationship to the accused?"

Eufemio scratched the back of his gray head. "I'm a servant, sir."

"We understand that. But on what terms were you with the accused? What was the nature of your interaction with him?"

"I was his first horse." The old man tried to smile, but his lips twitched.

The prosecutor paused.

"Tell me, the night of June 7, did the accused seem nervous to you?"

"No, sir."

"How did he seem to you?"

"Glad to see me and eager to see his father."

"Did you hear any of their conversation?"

"No, sir. Pardoning, but don Samuel closed the door after he entered the general's room. For privacy!" he added quickly.

"But you heard them?"

"I couldn't hear the words, only the sound of voices and scuffling."

"What kind of scuffling?"

There was a long, pained pause. The prosecutor repeated the question.

"Like a chair or perhaps the table being pushed aside. I don't know, sir. Pardoning."

"Please tell the court what you did next."

"I hurried over to the general's room."

The servant stopped as if he had reached the end of his story.

"Well? What happened next?"

"I reached the general's door just as don Samuel was leaving the room."

"Describe him. How did he look?"

The old man fixed sorrowful eyes on the attorney. "He was upset, sir."

"What did he say as he passed you? Pánfila Villa, who was listening from her room, testified that she heard him mumbling but could not make out the words. You were standing next to him. What did Father Samuel say?"

The old man cast anguished eyes on the accused and back again at the attorney. His gnarled hands shook as he gripped the railing. The prosecutor pressed a hand over his. "I enjoin you before this sacred court to speak the truth. Only the truth. What did Father Samuel mutter as he left his father's room?"

Eufemio Rosarito hung his head and mumbled the phrase that everyone in Mexico City would be repeating that day, the words that cinched the case: "He said, 'Damn you to hell!'"

The English edition of the *Heraldo* carried the story to its full conclusion:

> Father Samuel Nyman Vizcarra was found guilty of the premeditated murder of his father, General Lucio Nyman Berquist, and was sentenced to thirty years in the Federal Penitentiary of Mexico City. It is worth noting that the accused showed little emotion. His mother, on the other hand, cried out with all the pathos of Hecuba: "No! There's been some terrible mistake! You have the wrong man! My son is the kindest, the gentlest of men! This is all a mistake!"
>
> The condemned man turned around, his eyes brimming with tears. He started toward her but was stopped by the guards. She too, poor woman, was held back by another son, the esteemed Rodolfo Nyman, who was trying to comfort her. Just when the drama had reached its feverish pitch, its tragic dénouement, a tall young man flung open the doors and approached the bench, buttoning his cassock as he walked. There was an audible gasp. Before us stood a perfect duplicate of the accused! Two identical priests. The intruder, who apparently had been sitting in the back row during the proceedings, spoke in a clear voice edged with bravado and a hint of pride.
>
> "Your Honor, I am Captain Benjamín Nyman Vizcarra, at your service!"

THE SECOND BLOW

FATHER SAMUEL NYMAN was given a full acquittal. Benjamín
Nyman Vizcarra was charged with the murder of his father and
was tried before the end of the month. The second trial was
over in a matter of a few days. Cynics quipped that the prosecution had already made the iron mask during the first trial. All
that was required now was for the accused to bring it to his face
and let the authorities bolt him into it. Benjamín Nyman had
other ideas. Unlike his brother, he launched a vigorous defense.
Refusing the services of a defense attorney, the young officer
cross-examined the coroners himself, calling into question their
methods and their insistence that the general had died *before* the
earthquake. Throughout the trial, he proceeded with a sharpness
of mind and a tinge of humor that often won him applause or
laughter. One such moment occurred early in the trial when the
prosecutor cross-examined him, laying before him the grisly scenario of the crime.

"I submit to the court that the accused gained entrance into
the house by letting the servants believe he was his brother Samuel, whom they had every reason to trust. As we have all wit-

nessed to our enormous surprise, such a masquerade was astonishingly easy to perpetrate. Then he proceeded to his father's room, argued with him, loudly enough that the others in the house heard it, grasped the crucifix off the wall and struck the victim two vicious blows."

At this point the prosecutor fixed a triumphant stare on the accused.

"You were even bold enough to leave the murder weapon behind—"

"So that the earthquake could be blamed for the murder?" Benjamín Nyman crossed his arms and smiled. "I can boast of a share of insightfulness, but I have not yet learned how to predict earthquakes!"

The crowd laughed uproariously. The prosecutor reddened. And so it went until the last day, when the prosecutor painted the scenario one last time.

"Captain, you have challenged the findings of a team of experts, all of whom insist that your father died before the earthquake. You have even challenged their considered opinion as forensic experts that there were two blows to the head. You insist that there was only one blow, and that the crucifix, when dislodged by the earthquake, was heavy enough to inflict that single fatal blow. Therefore, by your logic, the crucifix is not a murder weapon at all but simply an object shaken loose in an earthquake. An act of God, shall we say. Now let's go back to the actual argument with your father."

The prosecutor stopped pacing.

"You admit that he goaded you."

"He impugned my wife's honor."

"So you've said. And since you could not get him to desist from his accusations against your wife—excuse me, Captain, but could you kindly point her out to the court?"

The young man shifted uneasily in his chair.

"No, I can't."

"Why not? Surely she's here?"

"No."

"Ah . . ." There was a pensive pause on the part of the attorney, fingers steepled and brought to his lips. "So we were saying, your father was impugning your wife's loyalty?"

"Her honor. My honor!"

"Of course. So you had to make him stop. Naturally. How did you put it . . ." He glanced through his notes. "Ah, yes. 'I grabbed him and pushed him against the wall.'"

"Only as a warning. To make him stop."

"Hard, Captain?"

"Only enough to make him realize that he could not trample on my honor."

"When was the house built?"

Benjamín squinted. "I beg your pardon?"

"How old is the house?"

"I don't know . . . 1568."

"So you do know. It's a colonial house, solidly built with walls a meter thick, no?"

The young man said nothing.

"Are the walls smooth or rough in your father's room?"

"I don't know . . . smooth."

"The police report indicates that this particular room has no plaster at all. The stone has been deliberately exposed in this one room. I believe your father was a pious man, so much so that even the trappings of plaster would have distressed him. Except for a cot, a rough-hewn table, and a chair, the room was quite bare. The only ornamentation was the bronze crucifix. But to return to the walls, they are solid and coarsely textured. Stone in its natural state—hardly a smooth surface. The police report also indicates that the nail that was holding up the crucifix did not seem strong enough to carry the weight. So you may actually be correct that the earthquake shook the crucifix down on your father as he lay in his bed."

Benjamín Nyman's eyes narrowed as he tried to race ahead to the conclusion.

"Likewise, you may be correct in your insistence that the crucifix is not a murder weapon at all, but merely an object that was knocked down by natural forces. I begin to agree with you, Captain, and I'll tell you why. Because you struck the first blow—not with the cross—but by slamming your father's head against a rough stone wall."

"No! I only pressed him—"

"The servants heard the scuffle from downstairs. It was that loud."

"No! I only pushed him to the wall to make him stop!"

"You shoved a frail old man against a stone wall that is far from smooth. What did you think was going to happen? I'll tell you what happened. You cracked his skull with that one savage attack, causing internal bleeding. You left his room cursing him—perhaps you had forgotten by then that you were masquerading as a priest—"

"No. I—"

"And you left him to stagger over to his bed, with no one to tend to his head injury. God alone knows for certain if your father died before the earthquake, or if the quake struck the second blow—finishing what you had started. But one thing is undeniable: *you* struck the first fatal blow."

The accused had dropped his stance of easy logic and ready humor. Even as he clenched both fists in front of him to demonstrate how he grasped his father merely to subdue him into silence, doubt seeped into his eyes, deeply staining them.

On August 16, 1911, Benjamín Nyman was found guilty of the premeditated murder of his father. Moments after being sentenced, he was transferred to the penitentiary. His family followed in their chauffeur-driven Phaeton. He was processed with surprising speed and efficiency. As uniforms were not required, the prisoner entered the first of a series of inner courtyards impeccably dressed in his own tailored suit. His mother and two brothers followed close behind him, their wide umbrellas shielding them from the rain, guards flanking them as if forming an honorary escort. Inmates watched the procession from upper windows.

"Who's that?" one asked with marked excitement.

"Well, I'll be damned! There's a little justice in this damned country after all! They didn't let him off the hook!" a second prisoner exclaimed with gusto.

"Let who off the hook?"

"Nyman. The poor bastard murdered his old man for the inheritance, and his wife and her attorney ran off with the loot!"

As word spread, more prisoners rushed to windows, jostling each other for a glimpse of the newest inmate. As the small group made its way deeper into the prison, the sky hailed catcalls and howls.

"Wait till you're alone!" someone yelled.

5

LA BELLE DAME SANS MERCI

MANUELA NYMAN WAS breathing heavily by the time they were admitted into Benjamín's cell. She slumped into the one chair in the cramped room. Rodolfo, the eldest of her three sons, cast about, as if searching for some way of fanning her face. Nothing in the sterility of that space offered itself. Samuel stood behind her in a gesture of protection. Benjamín got on his knees and reached for her hands.

"Are you all right, Mamá?"

"Oh, son! Why did you go to see him? What did you think that would accomplish?"

"I was desperate. After they disbanded the revolutionary army, I had no income, and the federal army wouldn't take me back. When I heard that Father had disowned me, I knew I needed to plead my cause. Who better than Samuel? But I thought Samuel was in San Gabrielín, so I had to plead my case myself, but Father refused to see me. So I had no other choice, don't you see? I knew he would listen to Samuel."

"You could have come to *me!* To me! I would have helped you in spite of everything!"

"I can't begin to tell you how sorry, how very, very sorry I am about everything!" Tears streamed down his face. "Samuel," he looked up at his twin, "it was cowardly of me to let you go through the trial. Damn it! Why didn't you defend yourself? You knew it was me all along! I kept waiting for you to speak up, you the truthful one, and I would have stepped forward. I swear it! But when you didn't, I began to hope that they would see how . . . how ludicrous it was to suspect you of all people! I swear to you, I never thought they would convict you!"

The confession spilled over the causeway, unrestrained and unstoppable. Before Samuel could respond, Manuela preempted him.

"Of course he forgives you! Oh, my son! My son!" Manuela locked Benjamín in the fortress of her arms, and he, in that darkest hour, was glad to dissolve into the black-crepe layers, to feel, however fleetingly, however impossibly, protected by her. "None of this is your fault!" Manuela spoke passionately, divining his need, transparent in the pale green of his irises. "Oh, my poor boy! None of this is your fault!"

"The hell it isn't!" Rodolfo muttered in a low voice.

"I swear to you I never meant to hurt him! He was taunting me. I just wanted him to stop!"

"I know, I know, my dear! Lucio was a wretch! He could drive the very saints into spasms of rage with his tirades! You must never blame yourself! He brought it all on himself!"

The absolution was total, her love tragic and unconditional.

They were allowed a one-hour visit that first day. A guard who was patrolling the corridor paused to observe the family from the other side of the open cell door. Crossing his arms, Calixto Contreras leaned against a pillar and stared with an openness that would have been deemed impudent outside the prison walls. He could see that all three brothers were equally tall, impressively tall, and that the papers were right. The twins were identical in every way—*except that one was a murderer and the other a priest!* But why was the oldest of three so dark-complexioned like himself, with eyes as dark as his own? Why was he not fair like his brothers, with their light skin and green eyes—or was it pale brown? Hard to tell in that light. One thing was clear from their expensive clothes: they had more money to burn in one day than he could make in a year, or ten, or fifty. He hated the bastards. As for the mother, with her fair skin, dark hair, and haughty manner, she was clearly a damn Spanish aristocrat, he decided, as Spanish as Hernán Cortés.

"Well, at least the place is clean," he heard her say.

"It's the newest prison in the whole country." The priest spoke with forced cheer. "It's a model prison, progressive and—"

Progressive! The guard sniggered, rapping his billy club against the banister as he sauntered away.

Inside the cell, Rodolfo was struggling against a mounting sense of claustrophobia. Shifting from one foot to the other, he kept glancing out the window and back at his mother, who seemed in no hurry to leave. From time to time he tugged on his kid gloves, refusing to remove them, refusing to let his skin make even the slightest contact with the prison, this tomb where they were leaving his brother. He visualized the airy spaciousness of his home here in the city just a short drive away, a world away from this place. He clung to the thought of the fine dinner that his cook was preparing for him and for the family during their stay with him; he tried visualizing the uncorking of the chardonnay that awaited them and the smooth, fiery taste of their after-dinner brandy, soon, soon, if he could just get his mother away!

"It's time to take Mamá home," he ventured with exquisite solicitude.

"No! Not yet! It hasn't been an hour yet!" She clung ferociously to Benjamín. And just as suddenly, her ferocity took a new turn, as sudden as the violent downpour that was creating small rivers in the streets. Manuela set her features into a stern repose. "Benjamín, there's something you need to know. I cannot keep it from you any longer."

He sat on the edge of the cot where he was condemned to sleep for the next twenty-five years. That he had actually gotten a lesser sentence than Samuel had been given before his acquittal was hardly a comfort. Twenty-five years felt like a life sentence. He needed to sleep, to be alone, to cry! To rage! He was only half listening now, his eyes roving over the floor, his thoughts calculating the area of the floor space, then the volume. *What is my world now? How many meters are they giving me—or should I think in centimeters? Millimeters? My God! How will I breathe in here?*

"I had a detective follow her. The woman is as traitorous as the biblical Delilah."

His eyes snapped back to his mother's face.

"That's utterly unfair. And her name is Isabel. Kindly use her name when referring to my wife."

"Wife! How can you grace her with such a title after she ran off with that man, that so-called lawyer of hers?"

"She didn't run off with him. She left with him to return to her grandfather's house. He merely escorted her back to Cuernavaca."

"And that's the action of a loving wife, is it? Then where was she during the trial?"

He dragged an unsteady hand through his hair. "I assure you that she doesn't even know I was accused, let alone convicted. Everything has happened so fast!"

"How can she not know? The whole country knows!"

"Not Isa! Remember, her grandfather is a recluse and he doesn't believe in newspapers. He won't have them in his house. I tell you, Isabel doesn't *know* what's happened, or she'd be here!"

"Listen to me, Benjamín. It's time you faced the truth about Isabel Brentt."

Reaching into her purse, she retrieved a newspaper clipping and held it out to him.

He shook his head as if to ask, why do you bother me with this just now?

"Go on! Read it and see her for what she is!"

He took it and unfolded it, his lips pressed into a thin line. The headline read: *"La Belle Dame Sans Merci."*

"What is it?"

"It's French for 'the Beautiful Lady without Mercy.'"

"I know what it means!" he snapped.

"It's an editorial from yesterday's *Heraldo.* It encapsulates what everyone in Mexico knows about Isabel Brentt except you. Read it."

Benjamín clenched his teeth in the cramped silence as he read.

> If indeed the captain is a victim of a manipulative woman, what can we conclude but that the lady in question is of a Macbethian cast, or that once again a man has fallen under the spell of a *belle dame sans merci.* For if the captain is found guilty of murder, only one person will have benefitted from the whole drama—and clearly, it is not the errant son of the late General Lucio Nyman Berquist.

"Sensationalism. It sells copy."

"Then believe this." Manuela handed him an envelope, her gloved hands steady and lethal as a wrecking ball. "Open it and see the truth with your own eyes."

He looked at the photographs taken by the detective: Isabel wearing the suit he knew to be sky blue, like her eyes. Isa with her unmistakable hair, deeply blonde even in sepia; Isa with her lawyer, Tomás Tepaneca; the two of them sitting in the arcade of the Bella Vista Hotel in Cuernavaca, their heads close together in intimate conversation. Each image dealt a blow that reverberated throughout the corridors of his denial. The deathblow, the one that finally brought down the whole edifice, was the last photograph, blurred yet unmistakable: Isa kissing Tepaneca passionately on the lips.

"They're lovers." His mother spoke unemotionally, as if ordering the gelding of one of her horses. "He's as Indian as Tlaloc. Why she traded you for him, I'll never understand!"

"Why are you doing this?" His voice had dropped to a hoarse whisper.

Manuela's eyes narrowed. "Why? To liberate you from her spell! These photographs speak the truth."

He was on his feet, shaking a finger at her. "I don't need the damn truth!" he shouted.

Rodolfo grabbed him roughly. Samuel interposed himself between the two. "Everyone stay calm," the priest urged with soft intensity. "We're all tense. We've all been through a lot."

"Don't tell me to stay calm!" the prisoner shouted.

"Rage if you must, son, but face the truth," Manuela spoke over all of them, though she hardly raised her voice.

"And how the hell is the truth going to help me survive this place? Answer me that. I have nothing now! You've taken it all! Get out! Leave me alone!"

His shouting brought guards to the door. Samuel and Rodolfo had to help their mother out, half carrying her as she sobbed hysterically.

Prisoner 243 awoke to his first morning in the penitentiary, day two of the twenty-five years he was sentenced to spend there. Nine thousand one hundred twenty-five days. He had not yet figured in leap years. Getting up from his cot, Benjamín stretched his long body on the cold, tile floor. His cell was as clean and antiseptic as the finest surgery, sterile and unpalatable as bleach. It was early, not yet time for his corridor to go to the shower room, so he focused on his long-standing routine of rigorous exercise, adapting it to the small cell. He was determined to continue his daily workouts, doing pushups to an inner prompting, monotonous as the white-throated toucan's *dios-te-dé-dé* call. Again and again, *dios-te-dé-dé*. Another push-up. *One more.*

Break last week's record. Eighty-eight. *Dios-te-dé-dé! One more, damn it!* Eighty-nine. *Dios-te-dé-dé. Another! Come on! Do it!* His arms gave out, his muscles pointedly refusing to obey. The prisoner rolled onto his back, sweat pouring off him, drenching his bare chest, arms and face. As he stared into the white ceiling with its bare bulb, a single thought fluttered through his mind: *God! How am I going to live in this cage?*

His one small window overlooked a bleak courtyard—a fragment at that—and what he guessed was another cell block. He jumped to his feet and started to run in place. He panted and sweated in the cramped floor space that had become his world, his puny world—running so that his legs and arms would not forget their purpose. Running. Jumping. Reminding himself that he was alive and needed to stay that way, strong and able, so that when he got out, when they finally released him from the cage, he could fly and search for them, search for them and find them, find them and kill them both as honor demanded.

Forget them! another voice prompted. *Don't think about them. Keep running. Think about San Serafín!*

With eyes shut tight, Benjamín Nyman Vizcarra tried to imagine he was on the lane to the family's plantation. He forced himself to imagine the tall umbrella trees that shaded the lane on both sides.

You're a boy again! his pounding heart urged. *Run with the wind, faster than the wind! See the swaying shadows! Think it! Will it!*

But there were no trees. No shadows. No lane. Only the prosecutors and the journalists who stoned him with questions. Even his mother had joined the lynching, it seemed to him. Yes, she had absolved him of his father's murder, but not without exacting a terrible price from him in the name of truth.

Keep running, the inner voice coached him. *Don't think about Isabel! Focus on San Serafín. You're home; you can see the house at the end of the lane. Picture it and see it!* But there was only the fog of sterile white walls, prison walls that crippled memory, all but the memory of the photographs that crippled him inwardly. He stopped and hunched forward, hands on knees, head hanging. *Why? Why?* The question echoed in the vast canyons of his inner desolation.

Benjamín went to the sink in his cell and splashed water on his face. Cupping his hands, he drank in desperate gulps. He straightened and reached for his towel. The number 243 was printed on it in black ink; it was etched on his fork and spoon. Prisoner 243. It was painted on his door.

I'm not a number! he wanted to shout. *I'm Benjamín Nyman Vizcarra, son of General Lucio Nyman Berquist! I don't belong here in this freaking closet!*

He hadn't been in the penitentiary a full twenty-four hours yet, and already he was fighting a rising sense of claustrophobia. He fought it with anger, raw and terrible. It was precisely at that moment that a guard unlocked the cell with a loud clanking of the metal door. A tall young woman stood in the doorway, a girl-woman with eyes bluer than the skies of Morelos.

"You have a visitor!" the man announced with a lascivious smile. "I'll leave the door unlocked, but you can't go down into the courtyard until we ring the morning bell, is that clear?"

The couple waited until the guard had closed the door. Then the girl rushed forward.

The visit lasted less than two minutes. Isabel emerged clutching her throat with one hand and her bag with the other. Her eyes had the wide, raw look of an animal that has narrowly escaped powerful claws and fangs. She hurried down the long corridors. The guard who had just escorted her ran after her and grasped her by an arm.

"Señora! What's wrong?"

She struggled for breath, unable to respond. The chafe marks on her neck spoke for her. When the guard released his hold on her arm, she fled down the stairs.

Benjamín Nyman Vizcarra submitted to his inner demons. He and they grasped the only chair in the cell and used it to batter the walls and door. When the chair fell apart in his hands, he turned his rage on the bed. As he overturned the cot and tried to tear the coarse bedding, three men entered the cell and dragged him into a nearby cell that was larger and empty. Then they turned on him, wielding clubs with the indifferent ferocity of a hurricane making landfall.

MICTLÁN

THE PRISONER STUMBLED to his knees. His immediate response was astonishment at their impudence. Didn't they know who he was? He struggled to his feet and faced them, making no effort to shield himself. "Stop! I'm Captain Benjamín Nyman Vizcarra, an officer of the revolutionary army!" he boomed as if they were his to command. "I'm the son of General Lucio Nyman Berquist!"

"And I'm Calixto Contreras, son of the devil!" one of the guards jeered while striking him again with his club.

Prisoner 243 fought his attackers, swearing at them with volcanic rage. But rage stood by him only for a short time, crouching by his side as the men broke his left arm. When the clubs fractured his left leg and several ribs, he screamed in a voice that startled him—high-pitched and frenetic. The world of reason vanished. It rained blood and filth as he lost control of his bowels. When he felt his skull crack, even rage abandoned him. For a brief moment, Benjamín Nyman Vizcarra became a child who cried out for his mother in the anguished voice of a man. Then he fell into a pit of darkness.

Twice he lost consciousness.

The first time he awoke to his body, he yelped desperately like a dog being crushed under a great wheel. Language devolved, leaving him helpless as an animal being clubbed to death. The world, the very cosmos, shrank to the particularity of pain, pain so intense that it left room for nothing else. The men with the clubs were all-powerful gods of the universe, masters of hell, indifferent to his pain and terror.

A wind blew from somewhere. With savage strength, it slammed wooden shutters open. Before him rose a window, dis-embodied, floating in a transparent wall. He rose and went to it, leaving behind a bloody mass that no longer writhed. He opened the window. *Is this death?* he wondered. Swinging his left leg over the windowsill, he paused long enough to glance one last time at the men and at the red-black lake that splattered the tips of their boots. He heard a crunching sound, the speech of his shoulder as it split, but he felt no pain, only an enormous sense of free-dom—freedom and relief. The shortest of his attackers, a sallow-faced man, kept kicking the body.

"Damn Spaniard! Let's castrate him!"

"That's enough!" Contreras muttered as he struggled to catch his breath.

The sallow-faced man held his club high over his head. He brought it to rest, but he kicked the prisoner one more time.

"Do we haul him to the infirmary?" the third man asked the leader.

Benjamín Nyman did not wait for the answer. It no longer mattered. Swinging his body over the ledge, he calmly climbed out the window into a field that shimmered with light and warmth.

Manuela clung to the arm of her oldest son. Called away from a formal dinner, Rodolfo arrived at the penitentiary dressed in coat and tails. Paying three separate bribes admitted them into the infirmary after visiting hours. Manuela gripped Rodolfo's arm tightly as a guard escorted them along a poorly lit corridor.

They were shown into a long, narrow room with a dozen beds. Eight of them were occupied. Samuel sat by a bed in the farthest corner. The moment he saw his mother, the young priest jumped to his feet.

"What's happened?" She rushed forward.

Samuel intercepted her. The top of her head grazed his chin. "Benjamín has been seriously injured, Mamá. I want you to prepare yourself—"

"Let me see him!"

"I want you to remember that with God's help he'll heal."

"Let me see him!"

The moment Manuela reached Benjamín's bedside, she felt a surge of relief. "This isn't my son! What's going on?" Her eyes narrowed. "Why do they want us to believe—"

"It *is* Benjamín, Mamá. It's just that his face is very swollen," Samuel said gently.

There was a pause, intense as flame held close to the hand, then the spasm of pain.

"My God! What have they done to him?"

Rodolfo and Samuel caught her as her knees buckled under her.

"He's going to be all right, Mamá." Samuel continued in a calm voice, though he felt taut as a violin string. "I sent for Dr. Rodriquez Siqueiros. He himself set the bones and performed the necessary surgery." Samuel refrained from telling her that after the beating, Benjamín had lain on the floor for at least two hours, that it was only Samuel's visit that had prompted Benjamín's removal to the prison infirmary.

"Surgery? *Dios mío! I* caused this!" Manuela gasped. "*I* set all this in motion!"

"No, no! It was nothing that you did. They punished Benjamín for trying to destroy his room."

"*Punished* him! Why, why would they do this to him? Oh, my boy! My poor boy!" In her anguish, she tried to lift her unconscious son into a protective embrace.

"Careful, Mamá!" Rodolfo rushed forward. "He needs to lie flat."

"His ribs are broken, and . . ." Samuel's voice trailed off.

"What else did they break?"

No one answered. Her gaze grappled with the casts on the left leg and left arm and with the bandaged chest and forehead. "What kind of animals are these people?"

Manuela took Benjamín's right hand gently into both of hers and kissed it over and over. "Benjamín! Can you hear me? I'm here now. I'm here! I won't let them hurt you anymore. They'll have to kill me first! Oh, my son, my child!" she sobbed. "Why, why did they do this to you?"

"They said he was in a rage and was uncontrollable."

"When did it happen?" Rodolfo asked in a voice flattened by disbelief.

"This morning."

Manuela stopped kissing Benjamín's hand.

"All those hours! You knew and didn't tell me!" Her eyes accused Samuel as strongly as her words.

"I'm sorry, Mamá, but my first task was to bring in Dr. Siqueiros as quickly as possible." The young priest spoke in his reasonable manner, but his hands shook. "There was nothing you could have done while Benjamín was in surgery. I called Rodolfo as soon as—"

"Of course! Forgive me, Samuelito. Forgive me." Manuela Nyman cupped Samuel's face softly, but her tenderness melted in the heat of dark thought. "My God!" she gasped again. "*I* caused this!"

"No, of course not!" Rodolfo hastened to reassure her.

"I did! I never should have told him about Isabel! Never! All I did was add to his torment! We all know his passionate nature. I should have known he would overreact!" Turning to the bed, Manuela sank to her knees, grasping the edge of her son's blanket in a spasm of despair. "Oh, Benjamín! Forgive me! Please, please forgive me!" Manuela sobbed.

"None of this is your fault. You only told him the truth."
Samuel fought back tears, his usually serene manner subverted.
"Please don't blame yourself, Mamá!"

"*I* did this! I was so intent on exposing that woman—"

"No. It wasn't your fault, Mamá," Samuel kept intoning, as if
praying on a rosary. He could see that she didn't believe him, that
she needed proof, so he offered it on a platter. "According to one
of the guards, it was Isabel's visit that set him off."

Manuela's head jerked up. "*She* was here!"

Samuel felt like a child caught red-handed at a prank gone
wrong and then shifting the blame. "Please don't cry, Mamá.
Pray with me," he entreated as he knelt alongside her, fully aware
of his own desperate need for prayer. "The Lord is merciful—"

Manuela rose up like a newly branded steer. "Merciful! You
call this mercy? Don't talk to me about God! Where was he when
my son needed him? Tell me that! As for the Brentt woman and
her lover, I swear on my mother's grave that I will bring them to
their knees!"

Samuel insisted to himself that he had not meant to blame
Isabel. Or had he?

7

TWIN TEMPLES

Days later Benjamín regained consciousness. His hands flailed. Someone grasped them. The face blurred into the walls, but he knew the hands as if they were his own.

"Am I dead?" he whispered to his twin.

Samuel leaned over him. "No!" His voice was both exultation and dirge. "You've been unconscious for six days. Mamá! He's awake!"

Though Benjamín could not distinguish the features of one from the other, he heard his mother's cries of joy. Drifting back to sleep, he was conscious that she was trying to hold him. He could also hear the tremor in Samuel's voice as he prayed.

"Glory to thee, O God, that you have heard my prayers! Glory to thee, O Lord, that you have shown mercy to these your servants!"

Benjamín did not speak again.

Over the next few days, Benjamín Nyman Vizcarra fluctuated between dreams that returned him to a field of shimmering light and wanderings that drove him into the darkest of regions.

There seemed to be no final destination, only a journey. He traveled in cycles he could neither control nor predict. Samuel and his mother were the only constants. Whenever he cried out, one or both would grasp his hands and speak soothing words, anchoring him somewhere between the hell of his nightmares and a heaven dimly remembered.

Prisoner 243 walked one dream so often it became a well-trod path. Yet it still had the power to unnerve him each time. He was running through a forest, stumbling, staggering, his hands outstretched as he ran through thick undergrowth. He was being chased. When he felt their hands clamp down on him, he was not surprised that their faces were painted, that they wore plumed helmets, that they tied him to a line of prisoners that stretched all the way to the distant horizon, that they dragged them to a place of stone and blood, that he was naked, and that he stood alongside an enormous rack full of human skulls. He gazed straight up at it and remembered the Nahuatl word for it: *Tzompantli.*

He felt a sudden rush of recognition. *I'm in Tenochtitlán!*

Benjamín Nyman was fully aware that he was in Mexico City, downtown in fact. Not the modern downtown with its wide, open Spanish *Zócalo* and colonial architecture, its tram lines and electric street lights, but the one that all Mexicans carry embedded in the darkest recesses of a collective memory—Tenochtitlán of the Mexicas; Tenochtitlán, heart of the Aztec empire; Tenochtitlán of blood and sorrow. He was there, staring up at buildings made of stone, the very stones that Spain would reconfigure into the cathedral, the National Palace, and other buildings of New Spain. He did not question the impossibility of being simultaneously in the sixteenth and twentieth centuries. He felt oddly elated. *I've stood here many times! I know you!*

Benjamín felt a savage tug on the rope around his neck. The line, endless as humanity itself, was moving again, up the steep side of a pyramid. They were climbing the twin pyramids of ancient Tenochtitlán. Twins. *Which one is consecrated to the god of war? I'm the warrior in the family; my twin is the priest,* he wanted to tell them. As he climbed higher, he turned and saw the gleaming Lake Texcoco. Manmade islands rose from its center, and on those islands, a splendid gridwork of canals, temples, and palaces. For a moment, the sheer beauty of Tenochtitlán over-whelmed him, filling him with a sense of awe—and then desper-ate sadness.

My God! It's so beautiful, and so doomed!

He heard a woman sobbing. Or was it a thousand women?

"Stop the killings!" he shouted. "You can't save the city!"

A plumed warrior wearing a jaguar mask approached him, cudgel raised high.

"Stop the sacrifices! There's no point. The Spaniards are going to destroy everything!" Benjamín told him.

The jaguar warrior raised himself on the balls of his feet and brought down his cudgel. Benjamín stumbled to the ground, a sharp pain in his left shoulder. A second blow made him spit up blood.

"Stop! Even the lake will vanish! I swear it! Stop!"

No one was listening. Rose petals, red as blood, spilled from his mouth and carpeted the stone plaza. All the while, the line moved forward, inexorably forward. Corpses, their chests slashed open, tumbled past him down the steep staircase. He was hurried up the narrow treads, still coughing up rose petals, up to the blood-spattered priests. Four men stretched him across a flat stone, pulling his arms over his head. Then a priest held an obsidian knife over his chest. The man's face was masked by thick layers of ochre and green paint; clotted blood clung to his hair and eyebrows. The priest cut a thin line on Benjamín Nyman's chest as if to mark the spot. At the first touch of the blade, the plumes and face paint vanished, melting, melding into the robe of a black-cowled monk. The transformation was so sudden that Benjamín could not tell if he was going to die at the hands of a pagan priest or of a Torquemada. It made no difference. The horror was equal. He stared up into the haggard face of an old man with blue eyes.

"Father!" he gasped. "Father, it's me!"

Lucio Nyman hesitated as their eyes met. Then he raised the dagger and plunged it into the prisoner's chest.

"Damn you!" Benjamín ranted as saw his heart held high in gnarled hands. "And damn the church!"

A damp cloth touched his face. "Shh, shh . . . It's just a dream," Samuel soothed as he blotted the sweat on his face.

"Give that to me," the patient heard his mother say. "I'm here! I'm with you, my little son! Don't be afraid! I won't let them hurt you! They'll have to kill me first!"

Samuel had asked for an extended leave of absence from his parish for two months. He spent most of that time by his brother's bedside or ministering to the other prisoners. His voice, soothing as soft-breaking waves, could be heard in different quarters of the prison, particularly in the infirmary:

> God, whose mercy and compassion never fail,
> Look kindly upon the sufferings of all mankind:
> The needs of the homeless, the anxieties of prisoners,
> The pains of the sick and the injured,
> The sorrows of the bereaved,
> The helplessness of the aged and weak.
> Comfort and strengthen them for the sake of your Son,
> Our Savior Jesus Christ.

The swelling in Benjamín's face disappeared slowly. Dark bands under his eyes and around his broken nose went from black to purple to a sallow shade of yellow as he healed. Manuela visited daily, spending the entire day at her son's side so that she could stroke the hair off his forehead and press cold hands to his cheeks. She was able to bribe prison officials to move him into a larger cell with a private bathroom and to allow her physician daily access to him for his ongoing care. Just as importantly, Manuela paid for protection for her son via two bodyguards carefully chosen from among the prisoners. Food was another matter over which she could exert some control.

"Benjamín will not be subjected to prison food," she told her family.

So lunch and dinner from the Sylvein, the city's finest restaurant, were delivered to Benjamín's cell twice a day every day. For breakfast, she herself brought pastries and coffee from El Globo pastry shop downtown. Nothing but the best food would do. And it was she who spoon-fed him his meals, a task that nearly broke her spirit. He hardly ate, allowing most of the food to dribble down his chest. But worse, far worse, was his gaze—vacant as the rooms of San Justín. Manuela would search for him, wandering past the green irises into the tight blackness of his pupils, searching, calling his name, tearfully begging him to come back to her.

Benjamín had vanished far beyond her reach.

Manuela expanded her nursing to include decorating his cell. Bribing the right officials allowed her to have a mahogany bed delivered to the cell, along with expensive linens and brocade curtains, two armchairs, a bookcase filled with his favorite books—especially the ones on ornithology—a table with two chairs, a desk, carpets, and beautifully framed prints of exotic birds. She lavished him with everything that imagination and money could buy to make a prison cell luxurious, but she could not restore the broken bones that kept him imprisoned in a wheelchair any more than she could breathe life back into his eyes or tighten the slackness of his facial muscles. Much as she searched for him, her son had vanished. A silent stranger stared back, unresponsive to everyone and to everything.

Stubbornly, Manuela continued to transform his cell on every one of her visits. She would enter with an air of expectancy, half believing that he would suddenly look up and smile at her with recognition. But he never did. It seemed to make no difference to him whether she turned his wheelchair to face her or a blank wall. Benjamín's face remained expressionless, his eyes vacant, his spirit as removed from her as the murdered Lucio Nyman.

One afternoon, Manuela put down the spoon with which she had been trying to feed him. She wiped his face with one of the fine linen napkins from the Sylvein. Then, cradling his face with both hands, she kissed him with finality.

"Goodbye, son."

She might as well have added, *we'll meet again in heaven, not in this life*—since she determined then and there never again to set foot in his cell or in the prison.

From that day on, Manuela Vizcarra de Nyman devoted herself with fanatical zeal to running the family's plantation and to mourning Benjamín as if he had died. Samuel, who could no longer delay his return to his parish, also left for Morelos. As a final parting gift and to assure that no one would dare harass her son, Manuela arranged for a third bodyguard to be brought in. She did not interview the man, leaving the hiring to others. Her only instructions were that he was to be the toughest, fiercest man that money could buy. But she forgot that money can also buy trouble.

JESÚS MANGEL

THE BELÉN PRISON—named, ironically, for the city of Bethlehem—was as dark and as old as the penitentiary was new. A hundred men were crammed together in a world of shadow forms and bestiality, a space dominated by the stench of urine, feces, and sweat. Two prisoners fought to the death until one snapped the neck of the other. Several nameless, faceless forms objected with a collective roar. Or perhaps it was a groan, the groan of the helpless and the hopeless.

"I warned him!" a guttural voice stabbed the darkness. "I told him to stay the hell away from me!"

Armed guards opened the cell door. "Mangel! Jesús Mangel! Step forward!"

An enormous man stepped into a damp corridor. He was instantly manacled and led out. Moments later, he stood in the night air. Then he was shoved into an enclosed coach parked behind the prison. Two guards climbed in, flanking him. A third guard took a seat opposite, sitting alongside a civilian, a man in an elegant coat and top hat. A street lamp cast a stingy light, enough for the men to have clear forms but indistinct features. The man in the top hat was obscured the most. He kept a cologne-scented scarf wrapped around his neck and over his nose. The prisoner, a great hulk of a man who seemed to take up most of the coach, grinned.

"You make us live in a pigsty and object when we smell like hogs."

The guard sitting opposite him struck him across the face with a short club. Since the prisoner's hands were manacled behind his back, he could only deflect the expected blow slightly by hunching his powerful shoulders forward. He hardly flinched.

"Pay attention, you bastard! Don't waste the señor's time!" the guard with the club ordered. The prisoner settled into immutability. The gentleman kept his long silk scarf wrapped around his face.

"Do you want to leave Belén?" he asked the prisoner in a slightly muffled, distinctly Castilian accent.

"Maybe."

"I'm not offering you your freedom. I'm told that you've killed enough men for ten life sentences. But I *am* offering you the chance to spend the rest of your miserable life under better conditions. Interested?"

The prisoner nodded slowly. "Yes."

The gentleman reached into an inner pocket. Moments later he lit a cigarette lighter and held it close to the prisoner's face. The brightness of the flame highlighted a face of singular brutality while blurring the others all the more into the darkness of the coach's interior. Mangel blinked once but did not flinch from the flame's heat. The man in the top hat studied him with wary fascination, the way one stares into the eyes of an enormous bear that is uncaged but still chained by his caretakers. Mangel's eyes were small, dark, and recessed under thick brows. A large nose, flattened by years of combat, rose slightly above a wild tangle of beard and moustache. His skin was sallow from lack of exposure to the sun, but the man's musculature seemed unaffected by the years of imprisonment. Only a few thick strands of gray called into question whether the prisoner was middle-aged or a younger man prematurely aged. His bemused attitude contrasted sharply with the stony seriousness of the Spaniard.

"Wait outside the coach," the gentleman ordered the guards.

The three men hesitated, but only long enough for a final bribe. They jumped out and took up positions from which they could still guard the prisoner and yet not offend their patron. Inside the coach, the lighter went out, then on again, this time illuminating a photograph.

"Do you see this face, Mangel? Memorize it. He's a prisoner like you. His family wants the best bodyguard they can get for him. My contacts tell me you're that man, so I'm going to give you the opportunity to prove yourself. But get it straight. You're not working for him or his family. You're working for *me.* Watch him as though your life depended on it—because in a very real way it does. I expect a report every single week: who visits him, how often, and is he showing any sign, any sign at all, of recovering his wits."

"What is he, an idiot?"

"Yes."

"And do I have to wipe his butt and the spittle off his face?"

"No."

Mangel knew better than to ask the Spaniard's name or why he was so interested in an imprisoned idiot. Instead he focused on the photograph.

"Who is he?"

"Benjamín Nyman Vizcarra. He's well-connected."

"Meaning, he's rich." Mangel studied the photograph. "How did a fine bird like him end up caged?"

"By murdering his father."

Mangel leaned back into the leather seat. "Can't trust drooling idiots!" He grinned.

"He wasn't always that way. He was nearly beaten to death by some of the guards."

Mangel laughed uproariously. When his mirth spent itself out, the Spaniard resumed in a calm voice, "Your job—and that of the other two bodyguards—is to see that that never happens again. The family's attorney will pay all necessary bribes to keep the guards at bay. Your job is to protect him from other inmates."

"I want more than better food. I want a woman."

"That depends on how well you do your job."

"Will you be collecting my reports in person?"

"No. I'll send a man who is going to call himself Venancio Mangel and pose as your brother. Give your reports to him."

"You'll get your reports. When do I get my whore?"

The gentleman studied him. The prisoner could see only the eyes peering over the edge of the scarf.

"In a month. Now get it straight. You are not to discuss our conversation with anyone. Do you understand? It's just as easy for me to pay someone to silence you as it is to get you into the penitentiary. One word of this to anyone and you're a dead man."

"How do I know you won't double-cross me after you have what you want?"

"Because I give you my word."

"And how do I know what *that's* worth?"

"You don't. You're free to return to the snake pit of Belén. Or you can believe that some men value their honor more than their lives."

The ghost of an old question flitted across the prisoner's mind—a dilemma a childhood companion used to pose as the great conundrum of life itself. *What would you rather, to be eaten by a panther or a tiger?* Mangel thought about the stench of the overcrowded cells where panther darkness was perpetual. Why not face tigers for a change?

"All right. You'll have your reports."

"Good. One more thing. It's the reason I've chosen you. When the time comes, and only when I give the order, you're to kill Benjamín Nyman."

9

TARAHUMARA

BENJAMÍN NYMAN VIZCARRA hid deep inside his eyes, and there he stayed. Or perhaps he was lost in the netherworld of the Aztecs, wandering aimlessly in the shadowlands of Mictlán. He himself was a shadow, so it made no difference to him whether his wheelchair faced his tastefully furnished room or a blank wall. His eyes registered neither surprise nor anger nor any other emotion whenever his newest bodyguard looted the room.

"You don't mind swapping pillows with me, do you? Mine is a bit lumpy." Mangel would lean toward the seated figure, his face only a few centimeters from his. "No, I didn't think so. And while I'm at it, I'll borrow your bed covers too. I prefer silk to the horse blanket they gave me. But don't worry! You'll get it all back before that fancy big-city lawyer or your doctor make their weekly rounds. We wouldn't want them to get the wrong idea."

Benjamín stared through him. The other two bodyguards shifted uneasily from one foot to the other. They, like everyone else in the penitentiary, understood the hierarchy of power. No inmate was more feared than Jesús Mangel, who seemed to have a special immunity from retribution. In the brief time since he had arrived, his iron fists had sent at least six men to the hospital. Everyone gave him a wide berth. Only one of the bodyguards challenged him from time to time, a feisty mestizo from Oaxaca that everyone called El Manco—"One-Arm"—because he was missing his right hand. El Manco had dark, curly hair, unlike most of the other prisoners, and a thick moustache that divided and plunged to the jawline, completely covering his upper lip. The effect was that it was hard to tell if he was smiling. Most doubted he could. El Manco had the reputation of avoiding fights but of pummeling men ruthlessly if egged on. In the long course of his incarceration he had learned to wield his stump like a short battering ram that packed an astonishing punch.

"You shouldn't talk to him like that," El Manco cautioned.

Mangel straightened and turned to face him. "Why the hell not? You think he even hears me?"

Thrusting his face five centimeters from Benjamín's, Mangel bared his teeth and roared so loudly, so suddenly, that the other two bodyguards jumped back.

"See? The bastard didn't even blink!" Mangel laughed. "They knocked the brains out of his pretty head. You're a son of a bitch, do you know that?" he told his ward. "Your mother is a whore and her mother before her and your great-grandmothers, all four of them, and . . ."

The genealogical rant went on for several minutes, reaching back half a dozen generations. It was interrupted only by the arrival of a guard escorting the delivery boy from the Sylvein. The third bodyguard, a man nicknamed El Vago—"The Slacker"—in reference to his enormous capacity to evade any form of work, glanced anxiously at the box with its glorious food. His hair stood straight up in wild defiance of any comb or grooming gel. Half his teeth were gone, though he was barely in his late twenties, but he never let that interfere with the pleasure of a good meal. El Vago may have been a slacker with an idiotic grin pasted on his smooth face, but he was also astonishingly adept at gaining access to knives and wielding them—not to kill but to intimidate. The contrast between his looks and his violent skills caused the other prisoners to give him a wide berth. Yet even the wiry, unpredictable El Vago, who had never backed down from anyone, feared Mangel like everyone else did.

When the delivery boy set down the boxed meal from the Sylvein, El Vago knew enough to stand back. He abided by the strict hierarchy and followed its routine: wheel Nyman to the table and make a show of putting a napkin under his chin, at least until the guard and the delivery boy were gone. Step aside. Let Mangel sit opposite the catatonic prisoner, yank the napkin off him, and anchor it around his own thick neck. Then watch him eat Nyman's lunch with his fingers, chewing it with slow deliberation, a meal prepared by none other than a former chef of the Tsar of Russia, whoever the hell that was. When Mangel had had his fill, he pushed away the plate and motioned to El Manco. "Help yourself." El Vago could have whatever scraps El Manco left behind.

So he smelled the tantalizing wine sauce on the meat and waited like a hungry dog. Both he and El Manco could have pointed to their ward and asked, what about him? But why bother? They already knew Mangel's answer. *Feed him from your rations of beans and tortillas.*

"Go on! Help yourself!" Mangel motioned expansively to the second man under his hierarchical control.

El Manco approached the table, his stump held to his chest as if he were making a pledge of loyalty. He remembered Manuela Nyman. Something about the way she scooped food off her son's lips and chin with the edge of a spoon, carefully, lovingly, and the way she wiped his face with a linen napkin, had imprinted itself on his memory, or perhaps it had summoned up something from long ago in his own life—something he was not willing to expose to the Mangels of the world; whatever it was, it made him hesitant to abuse the catatonic prisoner. But the scent of the burgundy sauce on the steak broke his resolve. Using his fingers, he grabbed what was left of the steak and bit off a piece.

El Vago watched him with painful intensity. The moment the fragment was back on the plate and El Manco had stepped away, he moved in quickly. Without warning, Mangel struck him on the side of the head and sent him sprawling.

"Hey! Leave some for the idiot! You want to be jobless if he starves to death?"

The days blurred into weeks, and weeks into months. The fall eased into winter and winter into spring. Dr. Siqueiros had removed the casts on Benjamín's left leg and left arm. "You're healed," he told his patient. Yet he knew that wasn't entirely true. Only the bones had healed. "It's time you learned to walk again," he said in a fatherly tone.

The doctor even managed to get Benjamín on his feet on several occasions, with Mangel officiously supporting him.

"He's like a sack of corn, sir," Mangel shook his head regretfully. "I'm afraid it's all quite useless in spite of your great skill."

The doctor sighed. "Set him down," he told Mangel, and spoke directly to his unheeding patient. "Captain, there's nothing more I can do for you. Now you must let your bodyguards help you with the exercises I have prescribed. Do them daily. Do you understand? They'll build up the strength in your legs again."

The physician had the unpleasant sensation that he was talking to himself, that age was creeping up on him, betraying him through his soliloquies.

"See that you do those exercises with him—at least every two days," he amended his recommendation. All three bodyguards nodded. Then he was gone, this time not to return for another month. El Manco and El Vago tried to follow the doctor's orders, moving the patient's legs for him in piston-like motions. Then they too gave up, for how do you resurrect the dead?

On a morning when once again Mangel could not be bothered with his ward, El Manco took up his post in a vacant armchair in Benjamín's cell to protect it from looters (other than Mangel). El Vago mustered just enough energy to wheel their catatonic ward to the open-air corridor that overlooked the central courtyard. Then El Vago slumped onto the floor, pressed his back to the railing, and let the morning sun caress his face with womanly hands. Benjamín's vacant stare cut straight across to the opposite corridor. The inmates there were just being let out of their cells. Most of them ambled down the staircase or peered over the railing, their motions sluggish and purposeless. Benjamín Nyman's mind moved with even greater sluggishness, nothing stirring, nothing receiving or reacting—until a flash of red caught his eye.

A red-breasted . . . His mind groped for the bird's name and floundered.

The next morning was the same, with El Vago slumped in the sun, El Manco guarding the cell, and Mangel snoring in his own nearby cell with its stolen goods, his massive body wrapped in Benjamín's silk coverlet. A flash of red streaked across Benjamín's line of vision. Red and black.

The crested doradito. Pseudocolopteryx sclateri. The thought fluttered its wings. *No. A black-capped lory . . . Lorius lory.*

Benjamín squinted. Branches became brown legs, and the bird a man in a white breechcloth with the unmistakable billowy red shirt of his tribe.

Tarahumara.

The name rose from the depths of memory. Without moving a muscle, the prisoner-ornithologist studied the man's motions, the soft frenzy of legs yearning to run and frustrated at every turn.

"Hey, you! No running!" a guard yelled at the Tarahumara Indian.

Other inmates blocked him too, shoving and taunting him. The Tarahumara hardly seemed aware of them. Eyes fixed straight ahead, he ran in place, back straight, motions silent and smooth, his bare feet hardly touching the tile floor. The morning wore on, giving way to sulky afternoon winds, and still he ran in place. Then the Tarahumara vanished from sight as Mangel yanked the brake free and wheeled Benjamín back to his cell.

"Hey, *idiota*! It's time for you to watch me eat lunch!"

When Mangel had had his fill of the Sylvein's beef stroganoff and red wine, he threw himself onto Benjamín's bed and promptly fell into a deep sleep. El Vago drew up a chair so he could spoon-feed Benjamín some rice, but Benjamín knocked the bowl out of his hands and waved his arm.

"What the hell . . ." El Vago drew back as if he had spotted a poisonous snake.

El Manco, who was comfortably leaning against a wall on one leg, pushed away sharply. "I think he wants to go back to the corridor!" His voice betrayed a sense of astonishment.

El Vago pushed the wheelchair. Moments later, Benjamín grunted. El Manco leaned over Benjamín. "Here? Do you want us to stop here?"

Prisoner 243 did not answer. He was intent on watching the Tarahumara Indian in the opposite corridor. Spotting him, he leaned forward in his chair, his attention fixed on every motion as the man continued to run in place. Every now and then the runner would try to break loose. Benjamín could sense his yearning, the longing to race down the stone treads as if they led to the bottom of a canyon and then to climb back up the stairs without breaking his stride. Guards and inmates kept thwarting the man.

"Let him run," Benjamín spoke barely above a whisper.

El Vago nearly fell off his perch on the railing. "Did he just speak?"

"Let him run," Benjamín repeated in a quiet voice without looking at them, his gaze fixed on the Tarahumara.

The two bodyguards jumped to their feet, their muscles tense with nervous energy, but neither responded. Benjamín turned his head and fixed angry eyes on them. "Tell them! I'll pay their damn bribes!"

El Manco nodded and took off at a brisk walk. A few minutes later, guards began to clear out the upper corridor.

"Out of the way! Let the damn Indian run! You! Start running!"

The Tarahumara became visibly wary.

"Go!"

"Why?"

"Because that man has paid to see you run. Now go, damn you! Take the stairs and the upper corridors."

The Tarahumara gazed at Benjamín across the space that separated their corridors. They locked eyes. Benjamín nodded ever so slightly, but it was enough. The man took flight. He ran the length of the upper corridor, bounded down the stairs and across the courtyard of startled prisoners. Some threw themselves on the ground as they braced for the inevitable shot in the back in the name of the fugitive law. The guards were not too particular about which "fugitive" they shot. But on this day, nothing of the sort happened. The Tarahumara ran up the stairs and along the three upper corridors, then down the stairs again and around the perimeter of the spacious courtyard, on and on, hour after hour into the lengthening shadows of the day. Everyone hung back and watched him, even Mangel when he awoke from his afternoon siesta. He had no idea who had ordered the Indian to run or why, and he didn't care. Taking up his favorite position in the courtyard, as far as possible from his bodyguard duties, he played round after round of poker with other inmates. Yet as the hours passed, he found himself admiring the resilience of the runner, who showed no signs whatever of tiring.

At dinnertime, most of the inmates withdrew into their cells to prepare their nightly meals. When the Sylvein delivered a dinner of filet mignon, Mangel left his game of poker to wolf it down alone, this time leaving nothing for scavengers. All the while, Benjamín Nyman continued to sit in his wheelchair, eyes fixed on the runner, hands clenching and unclenching, legs twitching as if awakening from a long sleep. Moments before the lockdown for the night, El Vago whistled softly. "Look at the bastard! He's been running all day and hasn't stopped once, not even for water!"

It took two guards to stop the runner. As they shoved him back into his cell, he was still shuffling his feet, back straight, headband tied tightly around his black hair. He showed no emotion as he stared across the darkening space into Benjamín's eyes, but Benjamín felt a surge of energy flow through him, jerking him to his feet. He leaned awkwardly over the railing for a few seconds before falling back into the wheelchair.

El Vago wheeled him back to his cell.

El Manco walked alongside. "Does Mangel know?" he whispered to El Vago.

"No."

"Bring him up to table." Mangel motioned with gravy-coated fingers to the spot opposite him.

El Manco and El Vago watched their ward, who seemed no different than ever, but for the clenching and unclenching of his hands under the table.

"I think you should eat something, Captain," El Vago murmured.

"Captain!" Mangel smirked. "Here, I'll feed the little bastard tonight! You! Captain! I want you to know that the meat was particularly good. I left you the dessert. I don't care much for sweets. Here!" He slid the dessert plate across the small table. "It's time you started feeding yourself, little man. . . . Give him a fork."

El Vago obeyed, placing a fork next to the plate. Benjamín stared vacantly.

"Put it in his hand. . . . That's right. Now feed yourself, little man. On second thought, I should at least sample it."

Reaching across the table, he plunged his fingers into the slice of cake with its white frosting. Instantly, Benjamín jammed his fork into the cake, grazing the man's fingers. Startled, Mangel looked into eyes that blazed.

"If you ever touch my food again, or anything that's mine, I'll kill you."

Benjamín Nyman was done wandering through Mictlán.

10

THE SHAMAN

BENJAMÍN KNEW THAT he had to assert himself now or lose the war. His old arrogance came into play. He treated all three of his bodyguards with contempt, especially Mangel. He made it a point to eat all his meals in front of them, chewing slowly, tossing scraps as one would to hungry dogs. On rare occasions, he surprised them by ordering a meal for them from the Sylvein, not out of charity but as a further way to control them, to make them beholden to him. It was all charged to the hacienda. When boxed meals would arrive for the bodyguards, he would motion with a slight jerk of his head that said, *Eat yours out there. We're not closing the social gap between us.*

They were quick to obey and scoffed up the meals. He could hear their laughter as they squatted outside his door. He also saw clearly when Mangel yanked away El Vago's plate.

"Mangel!" Benjamín shouted as he would to a man under his command. Not because he wanted to stop an injustice, or because he cared one fig about the lazy El Vago, but to assert his authority.

The giant approached him, still chewing El Vago's steak.

"I make the decisions here. If I choose to feed all three of you on occasion, that's *my* choice. El Vago works for me as much as you do. Don't interfere with my plans, got that?"

Mangel chewed in sullen silence and nodded. He wanted to break the aristocrat's neck, wanted to and knew he could easily do it. *But what then? The end of a cushy job? The overcrowded cells of Belén? No. Better to put up with the overindulged bastard.*

"It won't happen again, boss—Captain!" Mangel smiled. "I just get carried away sometimes. The Sylvein cooks know how to tempt a man to sin."

Mangel returned to his post outside Benjamín's door to work out a thorny problem: what to put into his weekly reports.

Should I tell the Spaniard that Nyman is talking again, pushing his weight around like the arrogant son of a bitch that he is? Will that be the signal for me to kill him? So? What would be bad about that? That miserable son of a whore of a Spaniard wouldn't need me anymore, that's what . . .

But what if the Spaniard hears about the change in Nyman? What if he actually visits and sees it for himself? Then he'd know I wasn't doing my job and he'd toss me back into the pit . . . Play it safe. Tell the Spaniard that Nyman raves now and then, and that when he talks, he talks like a drunkard. He's still an idiot in a wheelchair. That should please him.

Benjamín had his own problems, one of which was how to keep his mother from finding out about his recovery until he was ready to see her again. The hacienda administrator, a shrewd Spaniard named Valle Inclán, showed up once a month to settle accounts with the Sylvein, the prison laundry, the bodyguards, and the prison guards. Then he would visit "don Benjamín," as he called him, keeping the visit as brief as possible. El Manco was under orders to alert Benjamín the moment Valle Inclán showed up. Benjamín would then slump forward in his wheelchair and let his face grow slack.

Valle Inclán always entered the cell as warily as if he were entering a wolf's den. He would grunt a greeting to the body-guards, deposit a basket with goods from the hacienda, and ask the men the same question: "Any change?"

"No, sir," Mangel would answer with an obsequious shake of regret. "But his appetite is improving. Tell his good mother that he does enjoy the goods she sends him, especially the fig pre-serves!"—which in fact Mangel happened to like far more than Benjamín did. *Maybe the captain will toss them my way again,* he would think hopefully.

Valle Inclán would grunt, touch the tip of his hat ever so slightly, and depart.

Time gained, Benjamín would smile.

A more serious problem ambushed him while he slept. Night after night he found himself trapped in the same dream. It began with water and the dazzling light that skipped along the surface. An extraordinary city rose up from the lake, filling him with yearning. The sheer beauty of Tenochtitlán moved him to tears, stirring in him the desperate desire to live life's plenitude. Texcoco's water gleamed with an ethereal light that spoke more of heaven than earth. But inevitably he found himself tethered to a long line of sacrificial victims. The ropes around his neck and wrists pulled him inexorably up the pyramid's steep face. The treads often felt sticky with blood. And always at the peak he was met by the same priest, thin and ghastly pale—his own father—Abrahamic with knife held high to strike a son.

"No, Father, please!" he would beg, sometimes in his own voice, other times in the voice of the child he once was. "I'll do whatever you want! Tell me what you want!"

But there were no words, no pleas, no threats that could stop Lucio Nyman.

One night, moments before Benjamín underwent his tor-ture, he screamed in anguish, "Forgive me! Forgive me! I never meant to hurt you! I swear it!"

Lucio Nyman never spoke, never acknowledged that he knew him apart from the thousands of others before or after him. They were all one to him, all sacrificial victims to an obsession. The knife always found its mark. Night after night Benjamín knew that there was neither forgiveness nor acknowledgement, no ram to take his place, no God to spare him.

Sometimes he cried out, waking himself. Sometimes he reached compulsively for the revolver on his side table so he could end his miserable life, only to realize that there *was* no gun. No deliverance. Only a perpetual, promethean torture to endure. He was stuck in a wheelchair for the rest of his life, forced to live among the lowest element. His so-called comforts were just tinsel. Worst of all was the chilling realization that in all the world there was no one he loved anymore. Not Isabel. Not his brothers. Not his sister, not even his mother. His mother least of all, gorging herself on the vengeance that had sucked him dry. No, damn her! She'd robbed him of his very capacity to love more thoroughly than the men who had nearly beaten him to death. Nothing mattered. No one mattered . . . except . . . except that for some irrational reason, he wanted to liberate the Tarahumara and see him fly.

Prisoner 243 contrived to gain access to the upper corridor every morning before any of the other inmates were awake. Only he and the Tarahumara had permission to leave their cells a full two hours before the official time. Arranging it had been easy. Benjamín, who continued to play the catatonic prisoner during the attorney's monthly visit, had instructed Mangel what to say.

"Sir, we've noticed that Captain Nyman seems to perk up a little whenever we wheel him outdoors and the air is cool."

"The captain reacts?" The attorney swung around to stare at the man in the wheelchair, who was facing the wall.

"Oh, just the slightest flutter of the eyes, nothing more!" Mangel rushed to divert the man's attention away from Benjamín.

"Yet it *is* something—a bit of hope. Well, not enough to get his dear mother's hopes up! We wouldn't want to do that, but enough to make us keep trying to bring him around ever so slowly. Anyway, we think that the captain would benefit greatly by being allowed out of his cell every morning before the others, so he can enjoy fresh air without being jostled or troubled by the rougher element of this establishment. Since you are authorized by the family to pay the necessary compensation to the warden . . ."

It was arranged.

At first Benjamín and the Tarahumara Indian were closely guarded. It wasn't long, though, before it became apparent to the guards that the morning routine was nothing more than a rich man's whim and a poor man's obsession. Escape was not the object. It was all about running.

For Benjamín, it was also about surreptitiously restoring strength to his legs while perpetuating the illusion that he was still completely wheelchair bound. In his cell, he had his bodyguards work his legs as Dr. Siqueiros had originally instructed, but his legs felt utterly mechanical and separate from him—pistons that moved only when moved by others. On his own, he was able to take no more than a stumbling step before collapsing. On the other hand, he could work successfully on upper-body strength, regaining muscle tone in his arms, back, and chest. But even doing pushups required that one of his bodyguards position his feet and grip them tightly to keep them from splaying out under the weight of his inert legs. Benjamín worked tirelessly, clinging to the hope that at least the exercises would keep his muscles from atrophying.

As for the early morning run, he had to content himself with simply observing the Tarahumara. Yet Benjamín soon began pulling himself out of his chair, leaning heavily against the railing as he watched. He worked up to the point where he could stand unassisted, from a few seconds to a full five minutes before slumping back into his chair. Day by day he grew stronger, remembering to sit down simply to maintain the illusion of his disability. One morning the Tarahumara ran past him, then circled back and murmured, "Come with me."

"No. I'm not ready." Benjamín clutched the railing, his wheelchair ready to catch him.

The Tarahumara disappeared into the dark, predawn chill and ducked into his cell. A few minutes later he reappeared. Without breaking his stride, he pulled up alongside the wheelchair. Running in place, he held out a gourd.

"Drink this."

"What is it?" Benjamín stared up into the dark, angular lines of a face he did not yet know how to read. It was granite-hard, immutable and ageless. Was the man thirty years old or sixty? He seemed at once youthful and old.

"*Iskiate.*"

"Getting me drunk won't change the fact that my legs are dead." Benjamín handed back the gourd.

The Tarahumara continued to run in place. "It's not what you think. Drink it."

In a flash, the man was off again, his bare feet gently skimming across the cold tiles. El Brujo—"The Witch Doctor," as the inmates called the Tarahumara—was rumored to be a full-fledged shaman. Benjamín's interest in him was as a runner. He noted that the man seemed to defy gravity, his feet barely touching the ground, his back straight as a knife, knees slightly bent, feet shuffling in a kind of tiptoeing motion, never punching or pounding. After making another circuit, he returned to Benjamín.

"All of it." And he was off again.

Nyman stared into a murky slime. *What's the shaman put into it? Mouse droppings and frog eggs?* He smelled the brew. It had a faint scent of lime. *Well, what the hell!* Benjamín took a mouthful and spit it out. The thick, custard-like texture startled him, yet it left a pleasant aftertaste of lime in his mouth. *Don't think. Just drink it.*

Twenty minutes or so after he had downed it and the shaman had not yet returned, Benjamín pulled himself out of his chair and peered over the railing into the courtyard below. *Where the devil has he gone?* He was halfway down the corridor before he stopped and shot a startled look at his abandoned wheelchair.

"Brujo! Brujo!" He half shouted, half laughed the name. A hawk shadow flew past him, then circled around him.

"Run!" The Tarahumara spoke softly by his side.

Benjamín hesitated, yet he felt a rush of energy unlike anything he had ever experienced before. He sprang forward, and just as quickly El Brujo stopped him, facing him with both hands on his shoulders.

"No, not like that! Like this!"

He pressed Benjamín to the nearest wall and showed him how to run in place, back straight, knees slightly bent.

"No. Don't land on your heels. Like this."

And now it was Benjamín who felt the urge to fly and found himself withheld from flight. El Brujo taught him to run in place, insisting he do it barefoot for ten minutes, working up to twenty and forty and sixty, slowly but steadily across the weeks. Training in his cell, back against the wall, running, he rediscovered the muscles of his feet and legs and back. He learned how to run without landing on his heels, feeling his way in bare feet, training, training, week after week, until one cool morning El Brujo and the *iskiate* released him, and Benjamín flew down corridors and stairs, no longer concerned with maintaining the illusion of a disability, no longer caring who saw him run. With the Tarahumara alongside him, corridors became plateaus with scraggly sage brush; stairs rose steeply to cliff heights. Prison walls morphed into the walls of the Copper Canyons. The predawn air filled his lungs, awakening not only his body from its sluggishness, but his spirit. From that moment, running became his umbilical cord to the world.

Then one afternoon, because the hacienda administrator was not due back for another three weeks and El Manco was engrossed in watching a fight that was about to erupt in the courtyard, Benjamín was not alerted about the arrival of a guest. Samuel stood in the doorway of the cell, his tall, cassocked form momentarily blocking out the sunlight. Taken off guard, Benjamín was unable to fake a vacant stare.

KUIRA-BÁ

"Benjamín!" Samuel bounded across the room, drawing him into a tight embrace. "I knew it! I knew you were back! God be praised!" Samuel was both tremulous and radiant. "For months I've had recurrent dreams where you're always trying to break free—from your wheelchair, from boxes, from chairs with restraints, even from Aztec warriors! You name it! But last week was no dream. I saw you running for pure joy!"

"Now how the devil did you manage that, padre?" Benjamín crossed his arms and smiled, adopting a skeptical stance while thinking: *So you can still read my thoughts! How long since I could read yours? Have I grown that self-absorbed?*

"You know that state between sleep and full wakefulness? It happened just before dawn, when it was still dark. Yet through half-closed eyelids, just for a few seconds, I saw you running alongside a red bird, or a man in a red shirt, I'm still not sure which."

"It was a man, and I want you to meet him, Samuel!" Benjamín dropped all pretense as he embraced his brother with genuine enthusiasm.

"Gladly! I wanted to come right over but couldn't get away from parish duties until now. By all the saints above! I'll never allow myself to despair again!" the young priest vowed solemnly. Then brightening, he stood back. "So let me see you walk!"

"Nah! That's too easy. I can do better!"

Dropping his arms to his sides, his back straight as the back of a chair, Benjamín ran in place, his feet softly touching the floor.

"That's Irish step-dancing, isn't it?" Samuel asked innocently.

"No, you idiot! It's Tarahumaran, and I'm not dancing. I'm running in place."

Samuel watched with a hint of apprehension.

"Don't worry. The head has mended too, Father Samuel. And I can also walk, see? Satisfied?"

Samuel laughed in pure joy, causing his brother to mirror him.

"So you're as good as new!"

"Now you're overstating the case, padre." The prisoner rolled up his left pant leg to reveal the scar that ran from knee to foot. Bending slightly, he pushing the hair off his brow. "They were considerate enough to give me a scar right at the hairline. These are my badges of honor, my induction. I'm now a true *asesino convicto!*"

Samuel shook his head. "Don't talk that way, Benjamín. You are no murderer."

"Well, I'm here. What does that tell you, Father Samuel?"

"That to err is human, and that we all need God's help and forgiveness."

"Right now it's your help that I need. Please do not tell Mamá about my recovery—not yet. Promise me, Samuel!"

"Not tell her! Do you know the anguish she—"

"She'll swamp me. She'll suffocate me."

Samuel drew back. "Do you ever think of anyone but yourself?" he asked quietly.

Benjamín looked away for a moment. Then he locked eyes with his twin. "Look, I have to learn to live in this place on my own terms. Manuela Vizcarra de Nyman will come here with a team of tailors and order up a dozen suits so I can strut around in attire worthy of our lofty name! Then she'll reorganize my bookshelves and my day, doing all but spoon-feeding me! Don't you see? She'll try turning me into a lap dog—the most pampered of prisoners!"

"You *are* the most pampered of prisoners! How many inmates have a cell like this? Who makes this possible, along with your gourmet meals and personal bodyguards?"

"But it's still a gilded cage! You're free to go where you want, when you want. I can't step out for a walk in the Alameda, or saddle up for a day in the hills, or just step outside to look at the moon! Everything is by their leave, not mine! I have to stay shut up in this room, grand as you think it is! So don't judge me!"

"I'm only saying—"

"That I'm a selfish pig! Well, I am! But I'm begging you to allow me what little freedom I have. Don't tell her just yet."

"It would mean so much to her."

"Give me a couple of months, Samuel! Sixty days! Then I promise to write to her the most eloquent letter ever penned in Castilian, to let her know that I'm back from the dead. Just sixty days, Samuel!"

"No. It's appallingly unfair to our mother."

A thought flew across Benjamín's mind. "Let it go. Let's not quarrel any more. Please sit down and tell me about everyone."

They settled into two comfortable wing chairs by a window.

"Well, Eva, Pancho, and the girls are still in Naples; Rodolfo has gone to Paris for a spell."

"Until the scandal blows over? Until people forget? He'll have forgotten his Spanish if has to wait that long." Then Benjamín asked with studied casualness, "What about the will? I suppose we're fighting Isabel in court?"

"No. She signed everything over to Mamá."

"What? What do you mean, she signed it over?"

"She relinquished her claim to Father's estate."

"What did she keep for herself?"

"Nothing."

Benjamín clenched the nape of his neck, his mind racing, ambushed by the memory of his hands around Isabel's throat. Bolting up from his chair, he began to pace.

"Well, then what the hell did she and Tepaneca gain from all this?"

"Nothing." Samuel spoke softly, eyes on floor.

"But I suppose she's with him?"

"No."

"What do you mean, no?"

"Look, I don't understand her any more than you do! The only thing I can tell you is that she is not with Tepaneca, and she signed everything back to us."

Benjamín slumped into his chair. He felt as if he had just dropped a complex, fully finished puzzle onto the floor, its parts scattered and disconnected. It was all fragments: the blue of her dress, the blue of her eyes, the photographs, Isa's lips, her neck, his hands. His hands around her throat—those puzzle pieces reconnected. *No, I won't kill you now,* he had muttered when he loosened his grip slightly, but not enough to let her speak. *I want you to know that when I get out of here, I'm going to hunt you down, the two of you, and kill you! No one tramples my honor, do you hear me! No one!*

"You're sure she's not with Tepaneca anymore?"

"Yes, I'm sure."

Benjamín threw his head back and laughed. "That's rich! She proved too honest for him, and not honest enough for me!"

The brothers grew silent. They could hear the sounds of a brawl coming from one of several courtyards in the prison.

Guards and inmates were shouting, but the drama just beyond their immediate walls did not seem to touch them. It was background noise, nothing more. "Where is she, Samuel?"

"With her grandfather." Now it was Samuel who paced, face red, hands clenched. "Now you listen to me, Benjamín. I hate secrets and will not be bound by them, do you hear me? So you're going to come clean with Mamá. I won't have you put me under some slavish vow of secrecy! If you don't tell her about your recovery, I will!"

"All right! All right! Calm down." Benjamín waited for his brother to resume his seat. "I know you think I'm an ingrate, but I'm not. I *am* grateful. You hear them? That's daily. I have only to walk through the courtyard downstairs or along the corridor to see the faces of men who are scared out of their wits, or hungry, or brutalized, or half crazy with hopelessness. I see them and those who brutalize them, and I know I am safe only as long as the bribe money keeps coming. God help me the day we miss even one payment! So I do thank our mother from the bottom of my heart. But try to see it from my perspective." The prisoner leaned forward, elbows on knees, hands palm up, fingers taut. "I *need* to feel independent on some level, especially from her—whether that freedom is real or illusory!"

"I have to go now," Samuel rose abruptly. "I'll come back tomorrow. I promise."

"No, don't go yet!" Benjamín dropped to his knees. "Bless me, Father, for I have sinned. Please hear my confession."

Benjamín Nyman, who had not bothered to go to confession in years, did so there and then, forcing his brother's hand—for among his sins, all of which he knew must be kept confidential by the priest—he added one more: "I am keeping the news of my recovery from my mother for two months, Father. Please grant me absolution from my sin of silence."

Father Samuel groaned. "*Te absolvo, in nomine Patris, et Filii, et Spiritus Sancti, Amen.*"

And because Father Samuel was not entirely above the sin of revenge himself, he added, "But you must say one thousand Hail Marys, *now.*"

Most of the prisoners avoided El Brujo. Even Mangel knew not to bully him, not only because Benjamín Nyman favored him, but because he was superstitious enough to fear the dark silence in the shaman's eyes. Mangel could mutter to El Manco, "Did you ever see an uglier bastard?" He would grin and El Manco knew to take it as a half-truth and as a grudging compliment. No one had ever seen El Brujo smile. Some even swore that he never slept. Rumors abounded, including speculations about the strange friendship between the aristocratic Benjamín Nyman and the Tarahumara Indian. None of the prisoners spoke to Nyman with the same openness and sense of equality as the shaman did.

"*Kuira-bá,*" El Brujo would greet Benjamín softly in the morning while the inmates slept.

"*Kuira,*" Benjamín had learned to respond. We are one.

Whether or not he actually believed that, the son of General Nyman did not begrudge the greeting. One day, as if to give some credence to the words, Benjamín invited his bodyguards and El Brujo to sit at his table with him to enjoy meals from the Sylvein. *Kuira-bá.*

He also began to venture daily into the courtyard to see the rest of the aviary, as he called it, to smell its smells, to identify its "birds" by name, to sort songbirds from birds of prey, to listen to the cacophony of fellow inmates—their bantering and joking and taunting—and to note vacant stares and bruised bodies. *Kuira-bá.*

Benjamín Nyman returned from another of his morning runs, his skin glistening from the exertion, blood surging like a strong river through his veins. He was headed to his private bathroom to shower when he happened to glance at the calendar on his desk.

July 7, 1912.

He stopped in the middle of the room, a hand on his brow, his index finger riding the scar line on his scalp. He realized that it was a year to the day since the reading of his father's will. In a sense, this also marked the anniversary of Isabel's betrayal. *How did it all happen, this unraveling of my marriage, of my life?* he wondered. How had he managed to fall so far from grace in so short a time? Was he indeed just another victim of a *belle dame sans merci?* A victim, more than a perpetrator?

His thoughts flashed back to the first time he kissed Isabel and just as quickly to the day when he threatened to murder her. In that abrupt overlapping of images, he thought of the masses of men who were trapped in prisons for their crimes of passion. *How am I any different from them?* The thought hit him straight on, violent as the horns of a charging bull. It was an assertion, not really a question, for the answer rushed at him with the undeniable starkness of collision. For the first time in his life, Benjamín Nyman perceived the illusory nature of his sense of self. He saw with startling clarity the walls that he had constructed around himself, a fortification built on the solid notion of his superiority to other mortals. Yet what was it but a fortress of paper, a kite torn by hurricane winds?

I had every advantage in the world, yet I ended up here! The thought accused him. *How did I become no better than the others? A man of base passions, I who should have known better? What was the precise moment when I started toward this prison? Was it in childhood when I tried to break as many rules as a day held? Or in those years of adolescent hubris at Chapultepec, when I was the star cadet who thought he could outdo, outride, outthink everyone? Was it later, when I betrayed the army for an ideal? Or when I betrayed a brother for love? Yes. That must have been it—when I betrayed my own brother.*

On impulse, Benjamín sat at his desk and reached for a sheet of paper. He thought of home, a walled compound of terraced gardens under generous skies. Home, the hacienda San Serafín—San Serafín where birds from every state in the republic nested in the trees or in gilded cages—inmates of a greener, kinder prison. San Serafín, the paradise he had lost. He had tried to stop Samuel from losing it, too, back when he first announced his intention to enter the priesthood and a life of celibacy. Neither reason nor fists had been able to dissuade his twin.

"Then I must live for both of us," Benjamín had vowed.

He would write a story—a parable—about the inevitable eviction from paradise, and he would write it for Samuel.

I hereby dedicate these sketches to you, Samuel, that you may learn about life's foibles through me.

Benjamín wrote the dedication in English and resolved to do the same in the all the pages to come. He hoped this would safeguard his musings from the prying eyes of Mangel, whom he trusted about as much as a scorpion on his bed curtains. He reached for a second sheet of paper. All the while his thoughts hawk-circled. Hovered. Waited. Then he sighted it—the precise beginning, the overlapping of garden and woman, ideal and reality. He dove, ready at last to write about Isabel, not to rail or lament, but to admit with humor and self-deprecation his kinship with other men, other fools. *Kuira-bá.*

A smile swept across his handsome face. Then the hawk-pen carved two words as it swooped.

Paradise Misplaced

Part 2

PARADISE MISPLACED

Memoir of
Captain Benjamín Nyman Vizcarra

PROLOGUE

I KNEW THE secret as a child before anyone else did—that God planted the Garden of Eden just seventy-five kilometers south of Mexico City, near the town of Cuernavaca. I wasn't sure of the order in which he accomplished all this, but here's the gist of it: He scattered seeds so only the most colorful flowers and the best climbing trees would grow in that semitropical paradise. He filled the stables with the fastest, strongest Arabians, Mother's aviary with more birds than anywhere else in the world; the kitchen he staffed with Bardomiana and her helpers, who knew how to make *tamales de dulce* and all of my other favorite foods. Then he constructed a wall twice as tall as Father and encircled our Eden to keep it safe. On the other side of the wall, God added cane fields, woods, and mountains and gave them only to my family, and then we named the garden San Serafín.

I loved our sugar plantation in Morelos far more than San Justín de los Moros, our house near Mexico City. So I made a vow. I swore that when I grew up and could make my own choices, I would never leave San Serafín. I would spend the rest of my life there, where nothing bad ever happens—except for catechism classes from Father Eustacious. The old priest warned us that paradise can be lost all too easily. All it takes is the tiniest nibble of forbidden fruit.

He neglected to mention that Eve has other names.

✦ *Sketch 1* ✦

ISABEL

No one knew what to make of Isabel Brentt. She was as beautiful as sunrise in Tepoztlán. Her eyes were the blue of Morelos's skies. Her hair was the color of candlelight; whenever she released it from the captivity of high fashion, it fell to her waist in a cascade as thick as the bougainvillea that spilled over the walls of Cuernavaca. When it was swept up in the prevailing Gibson style, she was as genteel looking as a Gainsborough lady. But the astonishing fact is that Isabel Brentt spoke a thoroughly coarse Spanish.

It was not that she mispronounced her words with American abandon. We could have forgiven her that. No, the problem was that she spoke our language with all too much native fluency. She may have looked like the daughter of a great *hacendado,* but daughters of the landed gentry do not speak like scullery maids. Even the servants in my mother's house looked askance at Isabel the moment she spoke to them. Perhaps they thought that the young lady was mocking them by imitating them so skillfully. But the fact is, though she had lived in Mexico most of her life, she knew no other Spanish. How could she? Isabel Brentt had been raised by the most notorious eccentric in all of Cuernavaca.

Her entire family consisted of one old man, her grandfather, a Bohemian painter who wore sandals with his threadbare cashmere suits. Cadwallader Brentt was an American expatriate, a penniless Boston Brahmin who fancied himself a near-Mexican. I liked the old man, in spite of the facts that he was a drunkard and spoke our language as badly as he painted, and he had as much understanding of Mexico as I have of the Belgian Congo or the moon. The gringo artist had given his orphaned grandchild the freedom of a street dog. From the time Isabel could walk, she had run free, dirty, and disheveled with the equally free, dirty, and disheveled children of peons and beggars. Since Brentt regarded schools as prisons of the mind, he did not send the child to one. That she could read at all was deemed a miracle.

"She's a disgrace!" respectable women railed across the years. "What ails the man! Why is he letting her grow up like a wild animal? Shouldn't someone intervene?" The questions flew about the parlors and gardens of Cuernavaca like dragonflies unable to find the open window again. Then when she turned fifteen, at the very point when her uncorseted beauty and natural condition unsettled people the most, Isabel vanished. The old man remained in his garret, and no one had to fret about Isabel Brentt.

Like a phoenix or a curse, she materialized five years later. On a bronzed morning in the spring of 1910, Cadwallader Brentt slipped into his old sandals and a frayed linen suit the color of oatmeal. (He always wore frayed linen suits the color of oatmeal.) He lived in a two-story tenement as ubiquitous in style as weeds on the roadside. It was a poor man's house dressed up in bougainvillea. Fuchsia and purple blossoms helped to disguise the chipped adobe and exposed bricks. The door, which opened directly onto the street, looked as if it had weathered every storm since the Spanish conquest. There was nothing of value in the place but the value Brentt placed on his unsold canvases. He paused to lock the door. Then he set off to the train station on foot. (And here I must admit that I write this part of the account not as an eyewitness but as one who heard it later from two observers.) Out of deference to his granddaughter (one of the observers), he was reasonably sober that morning. Neighbors sweeping their portions of the sidewalk must have paused to stare. They knew the old recluse by sight. They had observed the lank foreigner just often enough across the years to know his stride, the way they knew the strut of pigeons in the park or the slow, lazy circling of vultures. I suspect that the gringo's pace, steady and purposeful, would have caught their attention.

Brentt arrived at the station and waited on the platform. I can picture him pacing and chewing on the tips of his bristly white moustache. How many times did he reach for his pocket watch? When the train pulled in, did he hang back, afraid of the stranger he might encounter? His anxiety must have escalated when the train offered up neither stranger nor granddaughter. Isabel was not among the passengers. He had to have known, like everyone else in Cuernavaca, that there was only one train a day from the city. He should have gone home. Instead, Cadwallader Brentt sat on a bench and reached for the small flask he always kept close at hand. As he drank away his disappointment, a second train from the city—my family's private train—materialized a mere ten minutes later. And who should step out but my brother Rodolfo, who immediately turned to help Isabel onto the platform. I can picture Rodolfo playing the gallant, as he does so expertly, leaving her side only long enough to see that the porters unloaded her trunk. In that brief span Brentt had his first look at the young woman his grandchild had become.

He had to have noted the graceful curves of her corseted, bustled figure, the tilt of her head, and the hat whose ostrich plumes framed a face of perfect proportions and startling blue eyes. I suspect that in those initial moments, the grandfather saw her only with an artist's eye. She was indeed a stranger, hardly the barefooted, ill-clad girl he remembered. Did he fumble to hide the flask as Isabel ran to him, both arms extended?

One thing I'll say for the pair: they are genuinely devoted to each other. Brentt is the only father Isabel has ever known. She adores the man. She must have lavished her affection on him in those first few moments before remembering to introduce my brother to him.

"Cadwally, I'd like you to meet Mr. Rodolfo Nyman. Mr. Nyman, this is my grandfather, Mr. Cadwallader Brentt!"

"Delighted, sir," my brother said in his smooth Oxford English as he extended his hand.

Brentt nodded, taking the hand with marked reluctance. Isabel stepped in quickly, as life with Cadwallader Brentt had trained her to do.

"My train from Veracruz was delayed just long enough that I missed the Cuernavaca train by a mere ten minutes! Fortunately, Mr. Nyman, who was also traveling from Veracruz, learned of my predicament and kindly came to the rescue."

"Thank you." Brentt muttered the words.

"I am grateful for the opportunity to have been of service to Miss Brentt. Would you now allow me the privilege of putting my carriage to your use, sir?"

"No. I can take it from here."

Without another word, Brentt signaled to the porter who was waiting with the trunk. Taking Isabel by the arm, he turned his back on my brother and hurried his granddaughter to the hack he had hired.

"At first I thought it was the age difference between Isabel and me that triggered his disapproval," Rodolfo would tell me much later. "Or a general antipathy toward Mexicans. But you know, I think it's our family name itself. I hear that Mr. Brentt champions the peasants and fancies we are feudal lords!"

But I think the old gringo read my brother's intentions clearly. And indeed Rodolfo contrived from that day on to run into Isabel at every opportunity. Actually, it was easily done. Cuernavaca is a small town, and Isabel stood out like a scarlet tanager.

As for Isabel, I have to wonder: what did she feel that first day of her homecoming as the horse plodded past the homes of the wealthy into the narrower side streets of Cuernavaca? Was her grandfather's house as she idealized it? Or did she see the chipped stucco and exposed bricks of a tenement? The prison bars on the one window that fronted the street? The fact that all the abutting houses looked the same? That there were no sidewalks, only a hill that climbed sharply; that her grandfather's house staggered halfway up the incline and stopped as if to catch its breath? Did all this oppress her, or was she flushed with a sense of victory at her chance meeting with Rodolfo Nyman?

Rumors about Isabel Brentt flew thick and raucous as starlings. Where did she get the money to dress like that? Certainly not from the paintings that Brentt occasionally managed to sell to tourists! I'd seen women of her type and suspected back then what everyone else saw as self-evident: that she was the mistress of a wealthy man, in all probability a man many years her senior. Perhaps she was looking for a new lover—one who could rescue her from her grandfather's penury?

Rodolfo was a perfect candidate, and in all fairness, he was just as conniving. He intended to make Isabel Brentt his mistress. She was young and pretty, this misplaced daughter of the Celts. She had just turned twenty. Rodolfo was nearly forty years old, but he looked younger than his years. I'll be the first to admit that my brother is an imposing figure. Then, as now, he had an air about him that made you feel that he had been born to command an empire, or at the very least a respectable duchy. The truth was that he had little interest in commanding anybody but his servants. He was handsome, urbane, and hopelessly charming. As the firstborn son of General Nyman Berquist, he was also poised to become one of the wealthiest men in Mexico. It is no wonder that women found him fascinating. The fascination was mutual. Rodolfo acquired and discarded mistresses as easily as he boarded ships for Europe or ordered new suits from his tailor in

London. From the moment that he met Isabel, Rodolfo resolved to add her to his list of acquisitions. It should have been easy. After all, Isabel came to him without the encumbrances of family or Mexican convention. But she proved formidable. Somewhere between a waltz and the drinking of stars and moonlight in a terraced garden, he stumbled into uncharted territory. To his astonishment, Rodolfo found himself transposing his intended proposition into a proposal of marriage. Ardent bachelor that he was, he surrendered then and there. He asked a socially inferior, penniless girl to be his wife. She wasn't even Catholic, but a Swedenborgian of all things!

When Mother, an arch defender of the church, returned from Europe to find that her son wanted to marry a heretic, she put him through quite an inquisition. I remember a conversation when she gathered all four of her children in the sitting room of her bedroom. Crossing her arms, she began the inquest.

"So what manner of heretics are these people?"

"I wouldn't call them heretics. They believe in the Bible and above all in Christ."

"Do they venerate the blessed Mother?"

Rodolfo squirmed. "Not quite as we do. They—"

"Then they're heretics."

Here Samuel stepped in. "They're Christians who interpret the Bible—and Christianity—according to the theological works of Emanuel Swedenborg."

"Sweden-who?" Mother's lips were smiling, but her eyes were pins fixing an insect to a board.

"Emanuel Swedenborg was an eighteenth-century scientist and theologian—quite a fascinating man, actually." Samuel spoke in his calm manner. "I once came across a short treatise of his. A lot of what he said made sense."

"I absolutely agree!" Rodolfo fairly glowed. Mother waited. My sister, Eva, and I knew not to mistake a pause for appeasement on her part. Rodolfo seemed to have forgotten that.

"Give us an example," Mother prodded, lips smiling, eyes stalking.

"Well, they have an exalted conception of marriage!" Rodolfo went on eagerly, too eagerly. "They're very serious about it. They believe that marriage continues after death."

"Heaven help me!" she scoffed. "An eternity with Lucio Nyman would send me fleeing straight to hell!"

"No. Only kindred spirits stay together. It makes perfect sense, if you think about it." He spoke in his most reasonable tone.

We all knew that it was not Swedenborg he was defending from ridicule but his beloved. Mother's sarcasm must have rankled him. Eva, who was just as unhappily wed as our mother, joined in the lynching.

"I think that one lifetime with a man is quite enough, thank you!"

Hilarity splashed his studied calm, thoroughly soaking it. He grew silent. I saw his jaw tighten and knew that by baiting him, they were simply making him all the more resolved to marry Isabel. Nothing would stop him now.

Rodolfo later admitted to me that when he proposed to Isabel, she grew very still. I can picture the tremor of her slender, bare shoulders, a gloved hand seeking the pink sash of her white gown.

Oh, she was an actress to rival Sarah Bernhardt! I can picture her striking the pose of tragic vestal virgin carefully searching for words—English words, of course—the only ones Rodolfo allowed between them, English words that flowed from her lips like the poetry of Shelly and Keats, English that defied her inferior social status. I can see him waiting for her to reach up to his cologne-scented face to thank him with a rapturous kiss. Yet Isabel Brentt, granddaughter of a half-starved artist and daughter to no one, remained silent. When the words finally broke free, they stunned him.

"Thank you, Rodolfo, but I cannot accept. I do not intend to marry for a very long time."

He stepped closer. She stepped back, her gaze steady as the North Star.

"I want us to remain friends," she told him firmly.

I can picture my idiot brother smiling as he walked directly into her snare. "Then you must allow me the kiss of friendship."

When his lips found hers in a deft motion, she pulled back decisively. And it was then, in the glaring light of her refusal, that he desired her above all other women.

Rodolfo became obsessed with her. My brother is a passionate, impatient man. Yet he courted Isabel with a patience and perseverance that astonished us all. He did not seem to see any of the obstacles. If her rejection stood rock solid on a beach, he saw himself as unstoppable as the ocean. He would wear her down, grinding her resolve into fine sand. But it would not happen in Cuernavaca. Rodolfo took it into his head that he could only win Isabel Brentt in Mexico City, at the grandest of the nation's centennial celebrations—the Centennial Ball at the National Palace. Aside from the facts that she had no inclination to accept, no money for hotels, no gown worthy of the occasion, and no one to chaperone her, it was a good plan. Rodolfo continued to court her in Cuernavaca and to wait for fate to intervene on his behalf. It did.

In the summer of 1910, as the dictatorship of Porfirio Díaz drew closer to its inexorable end, a former schoolmate of Isabel's, a Miss Emiline Synnestvedt of Bryn Athyn, Pennsylvania, arrived in Cuernavaca with her parents. Emiline was a couple of years younger than Isabel and claimed to have shared two of Isabel's four years at a girls' school near Philadelphia. A tidy story. My best friend Gustavo Romero de la Cruz had been fed a similar line. He had been thoroughly duped. Within a few weeks of meeting his own Isabel, Gustavo was prepared to risk everything for her—to leave his regiment and to be disinherited by his father. Then he discovered that his beloved had spent far more time being educated in a brothel than in the convent schools she touted. We got drunk together and swore off women. At that point Gustavo was beginning to make sense. Then the damn fool drew his pistol and put the tip of the barrel in his mouth. When I wrestled it from him, he almost blew my head off. So, no, I was in no mood for more romantic fiascos. I could sense with something akin to clairvoyance that my own brother was headed for disaster.

Since my regiment was quartered in Cuautla, some fifty kilometers away, I was able to go home to San Serafín on weekend leave with some regularity. Rodolfo, who had his own house in Mexico City, was now spending his days in Cuernavaca to be near the object of his desire and his nights at home in San Serafín. Mother happened to be in Italy with my sister, who was about to deliver her third child, and Father was still in self-imposed exile in San Justín, so Rodolfo had San Serafín all to himself. Now that Isabel had her supposed chaperones, he could invite her to visit and even invite the lot of them to stay overnight for a few days. More to the point: he could let the hacienda court her for him.

I decided to forego the tedium of her admiring remarks. What could she possibly say about my home that I hadn't heard before? Every visitor to the hacienda was always awestruck by the sheer massiveness of the compound, the beauty of the terraced gardens and free-ranging peacocks, the enormous aviary that rose up like a chapel at the bottom of the garden, the elaborate labyrinth that stumped all neophytes, the Spanish colonial house with its high-beamed ceilings and twenty-three bedrooms. No, damn it! I didn't have to stay and listen to sycophantic chatter. So I had Falco saddled. The Americans outmaneuvered me with their maddening punctuality. They arrived with Rodolfo in one of our carriages before I could escape. What could I do but behave in a civil manner?

I let Rodolfo do most of the talking. I merely fell in line and observed Miss Brentt closely. I managed to engage her in conversation in Spanish briefly. It was enough to confirm what I'd heard—that she spoke fluently and like a common peasant. Having confirmed it for myself, I slipped back into English and tried to be hospitable. Miss Brentt said little; Miss Synnestvedt gushed with appreciation of everything. "Oh! This is glorious! What a garden! Are your skies always this blue, Mr. Nyman?"

Isabel listened with a far-off look. A good tactic, I decided. It made Rodolfo double his efforts. After lunch we set off on horseback to tour San Serafín beyond the walls of the compound. We showed the Americans the colorful Mexico they had come to see: stone aqueducts set off against the green cliffs, the barrancas; endless fields of sugar cane still too green to harvest; armies of workers in the white, pajama-like outfits and the sharply peaked sombreros of the Morelos peasants. We passed women carrying baskets on their heads or babies strapped to their backs in *cucupache* fashion, which prompted Miss Synnestvedt to ask Rodolfo, "Do you have slaves, Mr. Nyman?"

"Goodness, no!" my brother responded, laughing, with the perfect British intonation he was so adept at affecting. His studies in Oxford had nearly ruined him as a Mexican. "Our workers are paid for their labor, and they labor under the most modern and hygienic conditions."

Flores Magón wouldn't agree, I felt the urge to tell them, just to wipe Rodolfo's smile of satisfaction off his face. Not that I gave much credence to the ranting of an anarchist. Magón's socialist agenda called for the elimination of all private land holdings. I was a moderate liberal, not a radical. Like most people of my generation, I yearned for political reform, not anarchy, so in 1909 I had pinned my hopes on the presidential candidacy of Francisco Madero. I even attended a few anti-reelectionist club meetings; their aim was both simple and staggeringly difficult: to thwart another "reelection" of our dictator and to foster support for Madero's run for the presidency. As if reading my mind, Mr. Synnestvedt nudged his horse over to me and asked point-blank, "Tell me, Captain, are you satisfied with the results of the presidential election?"

"No, sir. I am not."

"But the people have spoken, and they seem to prefer four more years of benign dictatorship. Why is that?"

"If opponents of the Díaz regime, more than sixty thousand of them, had not been thrown into prison this past spring and summer, the election results would have been far different. Without the usual fraud that accompanies our electoral process, I assure you that Francisco Madero would have won the election by an overwhelming majority."

"It's true then that Mr. Madero was put under house arrest?"

"Yes. This June. That kept him safely out of the way during the primary election on June 21 and during the final election July 8."

I glared into the shimmering fields. Mr. Synnestvedt seemed uncertain what to say. He must have sensed my bitterness. *My God! Does nothing ever change in Mexico?* I wanted to yell sometimes. That summer of 1910 I found myself asking more unsettling questions. How much longer could I continue to serve in the army? Would I defend the government if it finally came to revolution?

"Is it true that Mr. Madero hails from one of the wealthiest families in Mexico?"

"Yes, sir."

"And that he's a Spiritualist?" Synnestvedt asked with a scowl.

I could have explained that many people in our social circle dabbled in Spiritualism. Had I known anything about devout Swedenborgianism—or the New Church, as the religionists in their ranks call it—I would have understood his disdain for such parlor games and séances.

"I am thoroughly grounded in commonsense reality," I answered after a pause. "I allow Madero his eccentricities, vegetarianism and all. It's his political vision that I champion."

He nodded. After a pause he added, "I must admit that I have long been an admirer of President Díaz. He's been of tremendous use to the material progress of your country—for how many years now?"

"Thirty years, sir."

He chuckled and shook his head. "Well, it certainly is time for him to let another, younger man guide the nation. It will happen, you know. He simply cannot live forever!"

On our return home, we paused on a hill for a panoramic view of San Serafín. The sun had washed the walled compound with a magnificent shade of ochre. The tiled dome of the family chapel rose into a sky of crystalline transparency.

"Goodness, Mr. Nyman!" Miss Synnestvedt exclaimed to my brother. "Your home is like a marvelous medieval city! What are all those buildings anyway?"

"We have our own hospital, church, school, and stores, all fully staffed," Rodolfo answered, perhaps still stung by her slave question. "That building there is the mill where we process the raw sugar cane."

"What about those?" She pointed at the obelisks that characterize our Mexican sugar plantations.

"Those are silos for the sugar."

Moments later we drew up to a loading platform.

"You have your own train!" she gasped.

"We also have our own jail," I could not resist adding.

Rodolfo launched the next salvo in his campaign to win Isabel Brentt. Turning to Mrs. Synnestvedt, a shy woman who said little but carefully guarded the social propriety of her young charges, he placed our family Pullman at their disposal. "Mrs. Synnestvedt, would you allow me the honor of escorting you to Mexico and showing you around over the next two weeks?"

"Mexico?"

She turned to her husband.

"He means the capital, my dear."

Laughter over the Mexican propensity to conflate country and capital rippled through the ranks. Rodolfo continued to unfurl his plan.

"Furthermore, as you may have heard, the capstone of our nation's centennial celebrations is the upcoming ball at the National Palace. Would you grant me the privilege of attending it with me, all four of you? I am certain I can acquire the necessary invitations."

"Oh, Mother! Do say yes!" Miss Synnestvedt cried with joy.

So it was that five and a half months after meeting the most notorious ragamuffin of Cuernavaca, Rodolfo was escorting her to many of the centennial celebrations. The whole country was celebrating our one hundredth anniversary of independence from Spain, blissfully unaware that every parade, every ball, every inauguration of a new public structure drew us ever closer to the inevitable revolution.

Sketch 2

VOLCANOES

RODOLFO'S PLAN STARTED off as promisingly as the Habsburg Empire in Mexico. Similarly, it soon snagged on vanity and miscalculation. Rodolfo longed to dress Isabel Brentt in the finest gown that Mexican couturiers could produce, to drape diamonds and sapphires around her slender throat, to present to Mexican society the woman he intended to marry. So he offered to buy Isabel a gown for the Centennial Ball. She was savvy enough to reject his offer with a show of diamond-hard pride.

It was two days before she would allow Rodolfo to join her and her friends in their daily outings. When she finally relented and allowed him to put his carriage and himself at their disposal again, my penitent brother was ecstatic. I saw through the ruse. He, in turn, was learning that his oceanic passion could not reshape rock that quickly. Yet he must have wondered how a penniless girl who seemed to own only five outfits could possibly compete with women from the diplomatic corps and from Mexico's elite. He had forgotten about Emiline Synnestvedt.

On that September evening I met Rodolfo in his newly constructed house in the Colonia Juarez, the city's newest and most

desirable neighborhood. The entire place is as illusory as freedom. The houses are Italianate or French. Everything, from porticos and blue mansard rooflines to the immaculate, tree-shaded
boulevards, tries to trick the mind into believing itself in Europe.
But the craggy, volcanic peaks of Popocatepetl and Ixtaccihuatl
break the illusion. Rodolfo was also under the illusion that I
was going to be Miss Synnestvedt's escort at the ball. I set him
straight as I tugged on my white gloves.

"I'll dance once or twice with her, but don't expect me to
anchor myself to one girl all evening, charming and pretty
though she may be, while Mexico's finest beauties glide past me!"

"Relax, kid." He smiled as he reached to straighten my epaulettes. I pulled back and straightened them myself. I put on my
plumed hat and tapped Father's gold-hilted sword. Rodolfo
studied me.

"You turned into a good-looking cuss after all, Captain
Nyman Vizcarra!"

I stared directly into his face, not quite eye to eye. We are tall
men, all three of us Nyman brothers. Samuel and I had intended
to surpass Rodolfo in height, but maddeningly, we had stopped
growing one inch shy of the mark at six feet three inches—regu-
lation height for all the Nyman men, including our celebrated
father. Mother's side of the family, the Vizcarras, could not
boast a man over five and a half feet tall. Clearly, we are proof
of the dominance of the gene for tallness. I took in my brother's
appearance, aware once again of how much darker he is than
Samuel and I. Rodolfo Nyman is our illegitimate brother, a solid
reminder of father's former profligacy. Eva is our half-sister, the
legitimate product of Father's first marriage. Eva's mother died
when Eva was three years old.

In Rodolfo, as in Eva's mother and the Vizcarras, you find
true *mestizaje,* the marriage of Indian and Spaniard, at its finest.
In purely aesthetic terms, Rodolfo and Eva exemplify the best of
such a union. Combine the bronzed skin of a Mexican Indian

with the more delicate features of Spain or Sweden and the effect is stunning. My venerable twin and I pale by comparison.

Father was a Swedish transplant. At age fifteen he crossed the Atlantic by working in the bowels of a cargo ship. When they put in at Veracruz, he jumped ship. A year later he spoke Spanish with near-native fluency. Father's exploits in his adopted country have always suggested to me more of the shipwrecked pirate than the immigrant. I saw Lucio Nyman Berquist as a Viking who charged onto our shores and managed to pillage his way to wealth and fame—first as a soldier of fortune and then through judicious marriages. His military career was catapulted by the French invasion of Mexico. A few heroics and a close friendship with Porfirio Díaz gave him a hefty boost up the Porfirian ladder of success. By marrying the only daughter of Ezequías Zaragoza Santiago, a sickly young woman who died four years later, he inherited a kingdom of silver mines in Zacatecas. When he married my mother shortly afterward, he was handed one of the finest sugar plantations and exporting concerns in all of Mexico. A fiefdom. With such a fortune, he could afford to retire from military service and enjoy the pleasures of the landed gentry. And he did.

No one was a better host or equestrian in all of Morelos. He seemed to have none of the taciturnity attributed to the Swedes. Far from it. I got to witness a man who incarnated exuberance. I still find myself listening for his laughter punctuating a crisp new morning or lighting up the overarching darkness of night. He taught me to ride, to fly across the open spaces. In the first ten years of my life, Father was the life-giving sun that I orbited in joyous motion. We all did.

Mother was the first to break from his gravitational pull. She had been able to forgive his womanizing before their marriage, but not afterward. I suspect she loved him deeply, El Vikingo, as friends liked to call him. He was strikingly handsome even in late middle life: his blond hair fading to white—no, not fading—

flaming into white light, and his blue eyes glinting. His boldness of manner either grated or fascinated. Mother was living quietly in San Serafín when her father brought him home one rainy night.

I don't think Manuela Vizcarra ever expected to marry. At forty, she was plain and strong minded—*chiquita pero picosa,* we all say of her: small but spicy. She was also determined not to forfeit her inheritance to a man, a precondition her patriarchal father imposed on her. Yet she seems to have pushed aside all such considerations when El Vikingo fixed his eyes on her. She married him and readily adopted both Rodolfo and Eva as if she had given birth to them. I'm sure she was stunned when Samuel and I took root inside her, wrestling each other for the chance to see the light first. I won and have never let Samuel forget it. Forget. Forgive. I would have forgiven Father almost anything, but Mother would not, could not. She wore rumors of his infidelity like a thick veil over her face. In their last year together, that veil was no longer enough. Manuela Vizcarra erected a barricade he was never able to breach. They continued to live under the same roof, but their paths rarely intersected. Eva married just to escape the glacial silence of that house. Rodolfo left it within a month of her marriage. And then came the final rupture: Father's gradual descent into madness.

It began when he suffered a stroke that nearly killed him. It fell to me to finish the job fifteen years later.

～

Benjamín stopped. He could neither joke about his father's death nor confess to it fully. With a swift motion he crossed out the last sentence, determined to maintain a light tone. He wanted to get back to his Edenic narrative with Eve as the seductress of hapless males, but a dark mood roosted on his shoulders. It would not let him get back to his story until the next day, after another two-hour run with El Brujo. Whatever darkness had threatened to silence Benjamín, he and a cup of *iskiate* outran it.

Returning to his desk, he waited, leaning forward, listening for something. Or perhaps he was more like a falcon, wings spread, body poised on the edge of a cliff, waiting for a hot thermal. He waited. When the words came, he leaped and soared on the page.

~

After my father's stroke, Mother was constantly at his bedside. They were together again, so it seemed to us a blessing. But so was Father Casimiro, a parasite that Mother herself brought into our lives so that Father wouldn't die without absolution. With death close, she was determined to forgive Lucio Nyman everything. The trouble was, he didn't die. He morphed. The gaunt figure that staggered out of the sickroom several weeks later was a stranger. Humorless. Joyless. A fanatic with one quest and one alone: his own salvation, with the obsequious Father Casimiro to guide him. Yet I think Father's zeal stunned his spiritual mentor as well.

Father's first step was to rid himself of all attachments. He focused on San Justín. Samuel and I were ten years old when he piled every stick of furniture in the courtyard and set fire to the mound in a zealous frenzy. Even his priceless collection of colonial art was consigned to the flames. "Vanity! It's all vanity!" he ranted.

Ignoring Mother's pleas, he ordered the servants to empty every single room, heaping everything onto the pyre. That was the day she left him. She fled south with her children to her own ancestral home, south to the state of Morelos, where life and salvation were not mutually exclusive. In the end, even Father Casimiro could not take Lucio Nyman's brand of asceticism and moved out, preferring to visit Father whenever he was short on funds. Only old Eufemio chose to stay with Father in San Justín. Stripped of its furnishings and ornaments, the old place reverted once again to the grim fortress it had been in the sixteenth century. With Father trading his finery for the coarse robe and cowl of a monk, the fort was further reduced to a bizarre one-man monastery full of empty rooms and doors that rattled in the wind.

It took courage for my siblings and me to visit him once or twice a year. Mother never set foot in that house again until the reading of his last will and testament. All of which brings me back circuitously to my original topic: his Scandinavian blood and its alleged taciturnity. By the end of his life he had almost lost the power of speech, not because of the stroke but through simple disuse of language. My God! Whatever made me think I could reason with him? A rational fanatic is oxymoronic—and almost as moronic as the fool who thinks he can dislodge that level of religious zeal.

So was Father a marauding Viking or a Spanish inquisitor? To his victims it amounted to the same thing. And what does that make his children? I don't know anymore. I only know that we are as Mexican as our volcanoes, and that we possess all their outward calm and potential destructive power.

Volcanic or not, we Nyman brothers are said to be good-looking. I'll accept the compliment. But if it's dramatic looks you want, look to Rodolfo. He's a Mexican Lord Byron—except for the fact that he doesn't have a clubfoot and doesn't know dactyls from iambs or any other kind of metrical feet. I'm the poet in the family and the unofficial ornithologist. I am also the military man, like my father before me. On the night of the Centennial Ball I donned my dress uniform, vaguely aware that it would be for the last time.

"Samuel should be with us tonight," Rodolfo said wistfully.

Neither of us could accept that Samuel had willingly taken vows of celibacy that year, that he could content himself with serving a parish of illiterate Indians in a small village in the middle of nowhere when wealth and social position would have given him an enviable life. Rodolfo had tried every rhetorical strategy in his arsenal but had failed to dissuade him. I resorted to a less sophisticated method—a downright adolescent one. I picked a fight with Samuel moments before we mounted up for our morning ride.

"Priests are nothing but lechers! Your mentor . . . what's his name?" I snapped my fingers as if trying to recall the name. "Father Leandro . . . Lecheriano . . . he's nothing but a foul old lecher!"

"You don't know the first thing about him." The calmness of his manner rankled me.

"I know that he's a filthy lecher!" I yanked Samuel around before he could mount his horse. "He's a lecher and I want you to admit it! Say it!" I shoved him hard and sent him sprawling backwards into a stall.

"What's got into you?" He tried to rise. I pounced, pinning him to the ground.

"Admit it! He's a lecher!"

"No. He's a good man. Now get off me." He had adopted the firm tone of a schoolmaster who is beginning to lose patience with a rowdy child.

"Maybe you're right. He's not a womanizer. Maybe the problem is you! Maybe you don't like women and want to hide behind the long skirts of the clergy, is that it?"

Now he was mad, madder than I've ever seen him. His eyes blazed like Father's. Startled at first, then triumphant, I released my hold, certain I had finally shamed him into seeing sense. He was my brother after all, and his machismo was coming through. I had struck a chord that resonated in both of us. In a flash he broke free and sent me sprawling. Now the would-be padre had me pinned.

"Never denigrate the church that way again, do you hear me!"

When I saw that my gambit had backfired, confirming him all the more in his decision and turning him into a defender of the faith, all hell broke loose. I besmirched the church with all the profanity that army life had taught me. Locked in combat, we kicked up dirt and hay to the point where we could hardly breathe. Yet neither of us would give in. We were trapped in a surge of rage that we seemed unable to stop. We pummeled each other with our fists until both of us were bloodied.

"You're not going to become a despicable priest, do you hear me!" I panted as I hit again. "I'm not going to let you become another Lucio Nyman, damn you!"

Samuel suddenly stopped fighting. He lay limp and took the pounding like a damn martyr, letting the blood spurt from his mouth and run sideways down his cheeks.

"Don't do it, damn you!" I begged while shaking him. "You won't win Father this way, you idiot! Don't you know that?"

"I'm . . . I'm looking for our *real* father," he gasped.

I looked at my hands. They were as red and as smeared as his cheeks. Yanking him into a sitting position, I shook him one last time. We were clutching each other now, as entwined as we had been in our mother's womb.

"You can't win him over either!" he gasped.

I realized there in the dirt that we had kicked up, in the scent of horse manure, in the tears that broke free, that he was right. Neither of us could please Father: not Samuel with his religiosity, not me with my military career. Now I begged in broken tones, "Don't do this, Samuel. For cripe's sake, you've never even kissed a girl!"

Don't throw away your life, I kept pleading as if speaking to a stone wall. Exhausted, I pressed my aching forehead to his and found myself making a pledge: "Then I must live and love for both of us."

❖ *Sketch 3* ❖

COMETS AND TROGONS

I KNOW TROGONS.

My mother's aviary always held a few of them hostage across the years. I studied them up close from childhood on and in my ornithology books. I knew at age eight that there are at least three genera and thirty-seven species of trogons; that most of them can be found from Argentina to Arizona; that they might seem parrot-like with their straight-backed stance and short legs, but that they are in a class all of their own—from the quetzal with its long, regal tail to the more modest Asian red-headed trogon. Above all, I know that they do not do well in captivity. My mother had warned me that trogons cannot be held; that their need to fly free can make them dangerous, particularly to small boys like me. I sneaked inside the aviary anyway. When I reached for a female quetzal, I felt the bird's sharp bill tear open my index finger clear to the bone.

Isabel Brentt was a trogon. Rodolfo saw only the plumage and was taken in. I knew better. Samuel has often lamented over my suspicious cast of mind, my "automatic skepticism." No doubt that's why I make a better cavalry officer than priest. I expect to be ambushed and do all I can to avoid it or, if the enemy must be engaged, to defeat it. I knew on September 23, the night of the Centennial Ball, that Rodolfo was going to be ambushed. I went with him and his Americans with an almost morbid curiosity to watch a cunning woman set her trap. Rodolfo, who is a full fifteen years older than Samuel and me, seemed a child that evening, a child whose eyes widen with the approach of birthday gifts. He rode in the carriage with a lovesick grin on his face that made me want to kick him.

We stopped at the hotel to pick up Isabel and Emiline Synnestvedt. For all his promises, Rodolfo had been unable to obtain invitations for Mr. and Mrs. Synnestvedt. They, for their part, were only too happy to allow their daughter and Isabel to experience such an extraordinary event as the ball that was drawing diplomats from all around the world. I suppose, too, that we had passed some kind of litmus test as men of honor.

As we continued along Reforma Avenue, Rodolfo bubbled like uncorked champagne, drawing laughter from our guests. It was all I could do to be civil. Then his team of Arabians drew up in front of the National Palace, and I found myself getting caught up in everyone's excitement. The buildings along all four sides of the central square, the *Zócalo,* were ablaze with lights, more than I have ever seen in any one place. As I helped the ladies out, I was conscious of the multilayered reality of the place, the former heart of the Spanish empire in Mexico, and before that of the Aztec. The cathedral on one side of the square had been built by Spain over the foundations of the Aztec twin pyramids. What was the *Zócalo* but a reshuffling of stones into new configurations?

Tenochtitlán gloriously reconfigured, I murmured inwardly.

The palace was dressed for the occasion. The entire arcade of the somber old building was outlined in thousands of electric lights. Scores of valets in red livery greeted us at the Gate of Honor. As we ascended the red-carpeted staircase, we could hear the strings, woodwinds, and horns of two hundred musicians. A dome woven entirely of fresh flowers guided us up into the central courtyard that was bathed not just in the glow of myriad lights but in the splendid tail of a comet. Though I had been watching Halley's Comet for days now, for a few seconds I was stunned into immobility.

"It's so beautiful!" Isabel murmured.

"It augurs great things for you!" Rodolfo smiled, as if offering it up to her alone.

"The Byzantines wouldn't agree," I countered. "They saw that comet over Constantinople the night before it fell to the Turks. Neither would the Saxons, who saw the very same comet just before the Battle of Hastings. It augurs nothing but disaster." I glowered at my brother.

We had reached the ladies' coatroom, and he was more intent on watching his beloved remove her velvet cloak than on worrying about the fall of empires. For a moment, as the cloak left her shoulders, I hoped that it would reveal her in a day dress—a gaudy red one—and that her faux pas would jolt him into the realization that one does not marry the pretty dairymaid. I knew that as much as he was in love, he desperately needed for her gown to pass the test. Damn her! She was resplendent. I don't pay much attention to what women wear, only to the effect. But I remember every detail of that gown and how the blue silk clung to her body. Rodolfo bowed and extended his arm as if to a queen who has granted him a third of the kingdom. Together, they stepped into the last great night of the *Porfiriato*. I suspect that the elaborate centennial celebrations, and especially the ball, will be remembered as crowning symbols of don Porfirio's reign.

Though I desperately wanted to challenge the regime and to embrace the political reforms that Madero promoted, I will be the first to acknowledge that the old man did us proud that night. Diplomats from all around the world paid their respects— not just to the old dictator who kept a stubborn grip on the helm, but to the progressive nation he was in the process of building just one hundred years after independence.

The National Palace was dazzling. Flowers from every part of the country outlined the tall stone arches. Buffet tables as long as Baja California offered up Gulf shrimp; the choicest cuts of beef, lamb, and pork; fruits and vegetables from every state in the nation; French pastries too beautiful to eat without remorse; and the finest of imported wines. Two orchestras tossed Viennese waltzes into the crystalline night air. Above the open-air ballroom hung Halley's Comet. Our doomsayers warned that it augured an apocalypse for Mexico. But who could believe that in the wake of Mexico's enormous material progress? Rodolfo pocketed the comet in the miniature effigy of a diamond for Isabel. For it was there, in the splendor of that night, that he proposed again and that Isabel accepted.

The fool fancied that he had worn her down at last. Without missing a beat, Isabel lifted her smooth face and met the bristly touch of his moustache and the ardor of his lips. When he slipped the ring on her finger, his eyes must have brimmed with poetry. I doubt if he knew or cared whether he was the conqueror or the conquered.

I saw her web clearly, as if outlined by morning dew. Unable to extricate my brother, I made it a point to avoid him that evening. Instead I waltzed my way across the night with every pretty woman who would let me add my name to her *carnet.* Yet I spent most of the evening craning my neck to look at Isabel.

Shortly after Mother returned from Europe Rodolfo made preparations to bring Isabel home for her to meet. The entire household was in a state of frenzy, not so much because of the preparations, which were certainly elaborate, but with the kind of curiosity that shouts and runs unabashedly up and down the halls: *what is she like, this young woman who has roped Rodolfo Nyman?* The air was jubilant in the kitchen, in the stables, and pretty much everywhere in the hacienda—except when Mother walked in to give orders. Here I must pause to describe my mother. I could say she is plain in a pleasing way, small in stature, and thin. I could add that her hair is dark and streaked in silver, and that she carries herself with the bold assurance of her Spanish ancestors who conquered the Mexicas. Yet this does not begin to convey the phenomenon known as Manuela Vizcarra de Nyman.

She is a force of nature, ferocious in her love and defense of home and children. If I am guilty of deceiving her, allowing her to go on thinking of me as I was after the beating, more dead than alive, it is because for now at least I need the space in which to let my new life grow—free from her need to mastermind my life, free from her assertiveness and her class consciousness. How, for example, would I explain El Brujo to her or his presence at my table? She would command me to choose imperious isolation. I would refuse. We would argue. Worse yet, she would seep into my writing, tainting my memories.

Let me be clear. I honor and respect my mother. When she left Father and took us to live in San Serafín, she gave my siblings and me life and sanity. To say that we adored her for rescuing us from Father's fanaticism is an understatement. Yet it's a love that has always carried a hefty price, generous though it is. The absence of love also exacts a price. My siblings and I were never able to free ourselves of our need to regain Father's affection. What is it about human nature that compels us to seek love from even the driest of wells?

But I digress. As the preparations got under way for the dinner party, Mother was just as jittery as Rodolfo. Nothing seemed to please her. The silver wasn't polished brightly enough; the menu the cook suggested would not do. The servants had set out the wrong dishes in the dining room. I had watched her entertain the great and the powerful many times. Porfirio Díaz had sat at our table on numerous occasions over the long years of his dictatorship. My mother had always handled each of these events with efficiency and ease. Something had come over her from the moment Rodolfo announced his marriage plans.

Why are you doing all this? I wanted to ask her. *You don't need to impress a guttersnipe.*

On Mother's orders, we had to postpone the fated meeting of the families until late October to give Eva time to return from Europe. Her return filled San Serafín with a retinue of servants, nannies, and children. Within an hour of her arrival, Eva and Mother had already talked the matter to death—that Rodolfo was acting on impulse; that the girl was unsuitable in every regard; that she was of an inferior social class; that she wasn't even Catholic, but a Swedenborgian, whatever that was; and that she couldn't possibly care for Rodolfo, who was at least twenty years older than her. In short, everyone could see what Rodolfo alone could not—that Isabel Brentt was a fortune hunter.

Why then was Mother making such an inordinate effort with this meeting of the families? Did she hope to intimidate her? Or perhaps to let Isabel Brentt see for herself that she could never hope to fit in our world? Rodolfo was just as difficult to be around; like Mother, he wanted everything to be perfect but for different reasons. Could he not see that it was not Isabel whom he needed to impress tonight? By the time the Brentts arrived, everyone was as agitated as hens in the rain. Only Eva and I saw it for the joke that it was.

I watched the arrival of the Brentts from the darkness of the *portales,* the veranda. I could stand in the cover of the arcade and observe family and guests preen in the glow of chandeliers and candlelight. I remember it was a pleasant evening for late October. Since the doors to the parlor and dining room were wide open, I could easily follow the conversation without being observed. I hardly noticed Cadwallader Brentt. I saw only Isabel. She carved a path of light that blotted out everything else. She was dazzling. I have no idea what she wore that night—something simple and elegant. Pale pink, I think. I do remember that she wore no jewelry. With such eyes, she needed none. Instead, she tied a black ribbon around her neck. I knew that Rodolfo could hardly wait to hang gems around her slender throat, which was pointless. That simple ribbon outdid them all.

I heard Rodolfo's baritone voice tremble ever so slightly as he introduced his fiancée to our mother: "Mamá, it is with the greatest pleasure that I introduce Isabel to you. Isabel, this is my mother, Manuela Vizcarra de Nyman."

"*Mucho gusto, señorita.*" My mother proffered the standard greeting, stiffly, I might add.

"*Mucho gusto.*" The young woman smiled.

So far so good. The trogon had spoken only two words in Spanish.

"And this is my sister, Eva Nyman de Vizcarra . . . I mean, Eva Zaragoza del Renglón . . ."

"Permit me." Eva smiled. I could see that she was enjoying his discomfort immensely. She continued in impeccably elegant Spanish, with extravagant gaiety, "I am the Countess Eva Nyman Zaragoza de Comardo Tejada del Renglón. And I'm delighted to meet you. I'm only sorry my husband can't be here to welcome you. He would have found this a fascinating experience, I assure you."

"*Mucho gusto.*" The trogon smiled again, seeming to sidestep the trap.

"I've been telling Isabel about your home in Naples and how we must plan to visit you during our wedding trip," Rodolfo gushed in English. "I assure you," he turned to Isabel, "that no one has a more splendid view of the Mediterranean, or of Vesuvius for that matter, than Eva and Pancho."

"Why didn't you tell us how pretty she is!" Eva purred in Spanish. She was not about to grant him amnesty.

"Eva, I'd like you to meet Mr. Cadwallader Brentt, Isabel's grandfather. Mr. Brentt, this is my sister, Eva Comardo." He spared himself the elaborate nomenclature of our sister's full name, giving Brentt the abbreviated version.

"Charmed!" She extended her hand for him to kiss. "I've heard so much about you, Mr. Brentt. It's always a privilege to meet a great artist."

The old gentleman laughed and shook his head. He had apparently forgiven us for being landed and wealthy. In fact, he was all affability that night, for Isabel's sake, I suppose. Eva won him over completely. Every time she so much as looked at him, he became noticeably less coherent. Speaking in his broken Spanish, he seemed as vulnerable as a sixteen-year-old boy with his first crush. What is it about feminine beauty that blinds men so easily? I could see that Eva was toying with him. I didn't mind that she had targeted the trogon, but I did feel sorry for the poor old man that evening.

My sister has an uncanny resemblance to my mother, though they are not biologically linked. Both are dark haired, petite, and formidable. Eva is far more beautiful than Mother ever was, yet she seems like a shoot from the same tree. I suppose she was grafted on so early in life that she acquired many of the same gestures. There are differences, of course. Mother has the energy of a gifted businesswoman; my sister is simply a woman gifted in high fashion. No. I do Eva an injustice, Eva who is such a bold fusion of Spain and Mexico. Her eyes are dark as nightfall in the forests of Tabasco. If an artist wanted to render our Mexico in the feminine form, he need look no further than to Eva Comardo. If at times she rages like our volcanoes and weeps as freely as our summer skies, she is also fully as resplendent in the aftermath of her storms. In her restive moments, her eyes reveal the sorrows of our nation. As I reflect on it, I don't think I have ever known a more beautiful woman—and an unhappier one—than Eva. But that night she was in fine form, charmingly playful as she and I set out to save our brother from the fortune hunter.

"So, where are the scamps?" Rodolfo asked in English. In his agitation, he had looked at Mother, who stared back blankly.

Eva stepped in. "Didn't you know? Benjamín can't join us tonight." Turning to Isabel, she continued stubbornly in Spanish. "He's in Cuautla, where he is garrisoned. My brother is a lieutenant—"

"Captain!" Rodolfo corrected, doggedly clinging to English. "Benjamín is a captain."

Eva ignored all hints, sailing on in Spanish. "Captain. Lieutenant. What's the difference if his colonel won't let him be here for our family soiree? And not just any soiree, but the one that is to welcome Isabel and her grandfather!"

"What about Samuel?" Rodolfo searched the room.

And right on cue I left the protected darkness of the arcade with the garden at my back. I stepped into the chandeliered brightness of the parlor, comfortably suited in one of my brother's cassocks. Eva and I had sent word to Samuel about the fateful dinner party, deliberately misinforming him about the date. For our campaign to succeed, we needed his absence far more than his presence.

"Ah, there you are!" Rodolfo embraced me. Then he drew Isabel Brentt toward me. "Darling, you've already met the devil in the shape of Benjamín. It's time you met his twin, Samuel—the angel of the family!"

 *Sketch 4*

PLOTS

RODOLFO LATCHED ON to me with forced cheer. "On the other hand, don't let the cassock fool you," he bantered in his flawless Oxford English. "Samuel is a bit of a scamp too! He just puts on a good show of being our resident saint!"

"How do you do, Miss Brentt?" I greeted her in English, as my kindhearted brother would have. "It's a pleasure to meet you at last."

It was several seconds before Isabel reacted.

"Forgive me! It's just that I've never met two people who were so utterly alike."

"Poor devils!" Rodolfo intercepted again, his words a nervous hail. "Luckily, they're tolerably good-looking!"

"I'm pleased to meet you . . . Father?" Isabel ventured.

"Oh, Samuel! Please!" I even managed to turn pink as a geranium as Samuel would have.

"You have an American accent," she noted—at which point I switched into Spanish, as Eva and I had planned.

"I'll take that as a compliment. But in all honesty, it was easily acquired by going to school in the United States. I understand that you have lived in Cuernavaca most of your life."

"Our Samuel was not discerning enough to insist on an Oxford education as I did!" Rodolfo hurried in with all but a Union Jack in hand. "Well, of course it's just as fine a thing to have an American accent! What I mean to say is that Samuel was not given a choice. In a misguided effort to save their souls, Father packed Samuel and Benjamín off to a Jesuit school in Maryland. Benjamín promptly became a heretic, so Samuel had to tilt the scales in the other direction. But they did learn English tolerably well after only three years."

"Four," I corrected affably—in Spanish.

"Right. Then Benjamín insisted on returning home to pursue a military career. So off he went to Chapultepec, our nation's West Point, while Samuel went on to seminary. Someone had to look after our miserable souls!" Rodolfo laughed.

"You all have such a wonderful ear for accents!" Isabel noted.

"Not really," I insisted modestly. "We had English tutors even before we could spell in Spanish." I carefully set the snare. "I hear that you also speak our language with beautiful fluency."

A faint commotion in the foyer foiled my trap.

"Don Pablo!" Rodolfo exclaimed. Quickly masking his surprise, my brother strode forward to greet don Pablo Escandón and to introduce him to his beloved.

To her credit, Isabel did not seem the least daunted to be socializing with the governor of the state. As don Pablo spoke fluent English and loved to practice it every chance he got, particularly with a beautiful woman, the mood quickly became festive. At dinner, Mother seated Isabel next to don Pablo. I watched her from across the table, marveling again that Cuernavaca's notorious ragamuffin was so thoroughly versed in etiquette. Isabel Brentt was poised and so utterly exquisite that I came perilously close to dropping all animosity. But Eva yanked the white flag from my hands with a simple reprimand.

"Enough English!" She wagged her finger playfully at all of us, even at the governor. "We've left Mamá out long enough!"

"*Ah! Doña Manuela!* Forgive us!" don Pablo apologized to Mother.

Rodolfo set down his fork and knife. "My mother does not mind at all. She understands that we cannot leave our guests out, particularly don Cadwallader!"

"Oh, don't mind me!" The old gentleman smiled, pouring himself his third glass of Merlot. "*Hablar en español! En español!*"

"But don Pablo so enjoys practicing his English—" Rodolfo persisted.

"Yet that hardly seems fair to Mamá!" Eva pouted playfully.

"Of course not!" don Pablo agreed, turning to my mother and continuing in Spanish. "I was just asking the enchanting Miss Brentt if they have set a wedding date."

"No, not yet," Isabel answered well enough, doing no damage to the language of Cervantes, her lovely eyes smiling.

"We should do it soon." Rodolfo took one of her hands, intertwining his fingers with hers. "I've already prevailed on the Synnestvedts to delay their return home, but we can't keep them here much longer, dearest."

Without realizing it, he had just set the trap himself. Everything would have been fine if we could have confined the trogon's responses to two or three words. But now the governor asked if her American friends would be leaving Morelos soon, to which she responded, "*No sé. Pero ya mero se veinen pa' cá.*"

I felt my cheeks glow red for Isabel, for Rodolfo, for all of us. *What* she said was instantly lost on us; *how* she said it became everything—form replacing substance. With its missing syllables and singsong cadence, it was the Spanish of peasants and beggars. Listening to her old grandfather was infinitely easier on the ears. He battered the language like a true gringo. There was nothing native about his Spanish, so he did not offend. But it was different with Isabel. What she said—that they were returning soon—hardly mattered. *How* she said it brought all conversation to a stop. A locomotive crashing through the dining room could hardly have startled the governor more.

Rodolfo flinched. Seated as she was next to him, Isabel could not see his eyes, but I could. They brimmed with shock and pain so deep as to trivialize the merely physical. Don Pablo snatched up his charm and playfulness, locking them up as if to safeguard them from thieves. Lowering his eyes to his plate, he spoke in monosyllables for the rest of the meal. I doubt if Rodolfo could have uttered a single articulate sound. Eva jumped into the gap, shamelessly prompting Isabel to continue in her disastrous Spanish. She even got Isabel to try to explain her religion. I came in for the coup de grace:

"Didn't Immanuel Kant accuse Swedenborg of madness? Could you please set us straight?" I smiled pleasantly. Isa began to fumble, though she was perfectly adept at putting the cantankerous Kant in his place, as I would later discover for myself. But not that evening.

"I'm afraid I don't know much about Kant," she murmured softly, retreating into English for the duration.

I don't know at what exact point Isabel saw the wreckage. We had just settled ourselves in the upstairs parlor for espresso, brandy, and dark chocolate. Old Cadwallader was way ahead of us, merrily downing brandy after brandy. By then he was speaking Spanglish. Before we had finished our first demitasse, Isabel rose as if the drapes were on fire.

"Please excuse us, Rodolfo! We're not going to stay overnight after all. My grandfather is not well. Could we have a coach?"

We men jumped to our feet.

"Of course!" Rodolfo agreed all too quickly. "But traveling this late may not be the best idea."

Isabel wasn't listening. "*Gracias, señora,*" she added, barely looking my mother in the face as she thanked her and excused herself to the rest of the group. "*Buenas noches!*" she murmured as she helped her grandfather out of his chair.

"I'd be happy to escort you home," I offered.

"No, I'll do that!" Rodolfo had the penitent air of an executioner who begs forgiveness from the victim he knows he must soon destroy.

Mother took charge, insisting that they have an armed escort. Rodolfo followed the two Brentts onto the veranda that overlooked the central patio. As he helped Isabel into her wrap, I hurried down the stairs to order that their unopened trunks and the carriage be brought around. I don't know if they spoke at all. For my part, I knew with a sense of relief that Rodolfo was safe now. It was over, whether or not Isabel Brentt realized it yet. Then the fates stepped in.

Poor old Cadwallader lost his footing, tumbling down the whole length of the stairs. It was a spectacular fall. He was knocked unconscious. What could Rodolfo and I do but scoop him off the flagstone floor, carry him back up the stairs, and deposit him in the nearest spare bed? We sent for the hacienda doctor, who arrived moments later. The prognosis: a concussion, a severely broken leg, and cracked ribs. I'm sure Mother would have preferred for us to carry the old man to the hacienda hospital, but the good doctor was adamant that we not risk further injury by moving the patient a second time. He put the old gentleman in traction, with orders that he not be moved until the leg mended.

The upshot is that just when the Brentts were about to ride out of our lives, they ended up living with us. And that changed everything.

I woke up in the room I'd shared with Samuel all my life. Out of habit, I had slept in my own bed. I was vaguely aware that I should mind even the smallest details if I was to continue to impersonate my brother. But did I still need to?

We did it! We saved Rodolfo from the Swedenborgian danger, the triumphant thought somersaulted. *We opened his eyes, or more to the point, his ears.*

I sprang out of bed and bathed. Moments later I stood in front of the big wardrobe opposite the beds. Again out of habit,

I reached for one of the army suit coats that Mother kept there for me. Most of the wardrobe was taken up by Samuel's priestly robes—albs of the finest white linen, tunics, sashes (disconcertingly called girdles), and whatnot. Then there were the chasubles—the vestments worn at mass, the *pièce de résistance.* In a fit of delirious maternal pride, Mother had ordered a full set to be kept at San Serafín so that Samuel could wear the appropriate liturgical color whenever he visited and offered mass in the family chapel, which was generally once a month. Green to be used after Pentecost; black for masses for the dead; purple for Advent; white for feasts of our Lord, our Lady, and I forget what else; pink for some particular Sunday; and red for Whitsuntide.

They were magnificent. If not for the vow of chastity, I would have been sorely tempted to ditch careers just to be able to strut around in such finery. Each was magnificently embroidered with silver or gold threading and emblazoned with flowers and crosses. I had actually gone so far as to try on the works one day: amice, alb, girdle, maniple—an ornamented strip of cloth I'd seen him wear above his left wrist—stole, tunic, and of course the chasuble. I chose the red one and remembered Samuel explaining that the chasuble is derived from the *poenula,* a cape worn by Roman patricians in the fourth century. I patted my stomach and smirked into the mirror. What I saw unnerved me. I disrobed quickly and returned every item to its place. I may be Mexico's greatest religious skeptic, but it is not in my nature to deliberately dishonor something that others consider sacred.

However, I'd never had any qualms about borrowing Samuel's cassocks—his street clothes so to speak. These make limited claims to sanctity. So I reached for the first one, a long black tunic with more buttons down the front than a general's double-breasted coat. My brother, our misguided angel, only wears them on his home visits. The jackass thinks them too fine to wear around his parishioners, the sorriest lot of Indians in all of Morelos. Throwing the cassock on the bed for a moment, I put on my own uniform one last time and stared at myself in the wardrobe's full-length mirror.

"*El Capitán* Benjamín Nyman Vizcarra of the Ninth Cavalry Regiment!" I saluted.

I continued to stare, motionless, as if posing for the photograph that would capture the federal general I might have become, like my father before me. Then I took off the jacket, giving it a quick burial in the wardrobe. Rummaging among my civilian clothes, I suddenly stopped.

Don't crow victory yet. The trogon is still here, trapped in the aviary.

I reached again into the right side of the wardrobe. Later, when I stepped into the jacaranda-scented predawn, it was as a man of God who for prayers offered up Bécquer's verses to the clear October air. I had planned to have a horse saddled for my morning ride. However, when I passed the sickroom, I remembered the old man and hesitated. Just then the door opened. Isabel stepped out. She was accompanied by my mother. Both were still in evening dress and looked worn out. It was clear that they had been up all night.

"Mamá! Señorita!" I kissed my mother, and out of a mindless sense of deference, I spoke to Isabel in English. "How is your grandfather?"

"He's . . . he's still unconscious." She gasped the words.

"You must rest, Miss Brentt," my mother told her gently in Spanish.

Isabel began to object. Mother grew stern.

"If you do not rest, neither will I."

"I can sit with your grandfather," I offered.

"No, thank you, Father. That's very kind of you, but I—"

"Please, Miss Brentt! You must get some rest—both of you.

My mother means what she says. She won't rest unless you do."

"All right," she sighed. "But just for a few hours, Father Promise me that you'll send for me if there is any change!"

"I promise."

An hour later Eva stepped up beside me. We both stared at the old man.

"How is he?" she asked softly.

"Still unconscious. He hasn't moved a muscle."

"Where's the doctor?"

"Called away to deliver a baby—or more precisely, to assist the midwife."

"And how is *she*?" Eva asked, arching her brows.

"Wishing she had never met the baby's father?" I teased. "Oh, you mean the trogon!"

"The trogon?" Eva frowned. Then reaching for my right hand, she turned it palm up and touched the scar that runs along the second digit of my index finger, the one given to me by the female trogon as a child—the one physical trait that distinguishes me from Samuel.

"Trogon! I like it!" She laughed. And I realized with annoyance that I had given her a loaded weapon to use against a woman I had just seen in tears.

"Where's Romeo?" I was eager to change the conversation.

"He's gone to Mexico." (Now that I think about it, it is strange how we Mexicans make no verbal distinction between the capital and the country.)

"Isn't his timing off?"

"He's gone to fetch a specialist for Mr. Brentt."

"Oh. Of course."

"But that doesn't mean anything." Eva waved her hands emphatically. "After last night, everything is different. Rodolfo is merely extending the same courtesy he would give any guest under our roof."

I was still thinking of Isabel's eyes. Even swollen and red-rimmed, they were extraordinary. I vaguely heard Eva ask me something.

"What?"

"When are *you* leaving us?" Eva repeated her question. "When are you expected back in your garrison?"

"Oh, that. I resigned my commission."

"You've left the army? Can you simply walk out when you've had enough?"

"No. My enlistment was up. I simply chose not to reenlist."

"Why not? I thought you liked the army."

I had not meant to tell anyone just yet, but as Eva and I were already conspirators, I told her the simple truth. "I cannot remain in the Federal Army when I am no longer willing to defend the government."

"The government? Don Porfirio is the government. So what is the problem?"

"He's the problem! How many more years must we put up with the man imposing himself on the nation?"

"He's my godfather, for pity's sake!"

"What has that to do with it?"

"Everything! You can't turn against him!"

"Watch me."

"You're being ridiculous, Benjamín Nyman! Don Porfirio has *made* Mexico what it is today, and everyone knows it."

"A nation where elections are as fraudulent as six aces in a deck of cards!"

"He won by an overwhelming—"

"He won by *jailing* Francisco Madero and all the anti-reelectionists that his police could round up! Tens of thousands of them, Eva!"

She jumped to her feet. Poor old Cadwallader may as well have been a desiccated mummy from Guanajuato for all our care of him at that moment.

"I suppose you'll be telling me next that you agree with those vile anti-reelection sorts!"

"As a matter of fact, I do," I said, rising from my chair. "Don Porfirio may have imprisoned as many as a hundred thousand critics of his regime, but he cannot imprison a nation's hunger for freedom."

Eva's eyes flashed with the kind of rage I've seen in our father. "Freedom! You have no sense of history! Have you forgotten the accounts of what Mexico was like before don Porfirio came along? It was nothing but a country of bandits! No, don't deny it! Did you learn nothing from Mamá's stories about how no one could travel safely in the highways until he established law and order?"

"Law and order at the price of freedom!"

"Of what use is freedom if bandits take over and slit your throat? Who needs freedom when you have everything! We travel here and throughout Europe as we please! We buy what we want, have all that we need. What freedom do you lack?"

"I'm twenty-five years old, Eva, and for my entire life, the same president has run the country year after year after year. I want the freedom to cast my vote and have it count, damn it!"

"Well I'd rather have law and order any day over freedom, thank you very much. And I'll take the trains and all the progress he's brought us! Don Porfirio is respected the world over. You went to the Centennial Ball! While I was stuck in Naples, you were lucky enough to witness Mexico's finest hour! You saw it yourself: our haute couture is every bit as fine as anything in Europe!"

I stared blankly. "Couture?"

Mistaking bafflement for defeat, she wagged her finger at me in triumph. "Our dressmakers can rival the best in Europe— well, except for Parisian couturieres! But we can certainly hold our own, and it makes me proud to be Mexican!"

I held up both hands. "You're right. Why didn't I think of that?"

The mummy from Guanajuato moaned just then. Eva and I both jumped.

"Should I call Mamá?"

"No. Let her sleep."

We peered down at the old man, both of us chastened for a few seconds. What is it about sleep that softens the face? His silver hair, which normally looked long and unkempt, now framed his face against the pillows, giving the old boy a certain dignity. It silenced us, but only momentarily. Resuming our seats on opposite sides of the bed, Eva stared across him and into my eyes. "What are you going to do?"

"Sit by his side until I'm relieved."

"No. I mean, now that you've given up your military career. Oh, don't do it, Benjamín! You look so handsome in your uniform!"

I laughed out loud. Reaching across the old man, I captured one of her hands and kissed it. "Thank you, dear sister. But what makes you think a revolutionary can't be a sharp dresser too?"

She yanked her hand free. "There will be no revolution, Benjamín! They've all been locked up as they deserve!"

"They missed one," I muttered. And this time I wasn't smiling.

"*Viva la revolución!*" The mummy startled us a second time.

He spoke without opening his eyes, and he slurred his words like the good American that he is. But I took his words as a clarion call.

✦ *Sketch 5* ✦

LESSONS

As soon as Brentt regained full consciousness and began to demand whiskey instead of coffee with his breakfast tray, we were able to ditch our sympathy. In less than two days the Brentts became once again personas non gratas—as unwelcome as flies in the kitchen. San Serafín is large by any standards. With Eva and her retinue of personal maids, children, and nannies, and now the Americans, the place felt as crowded as Xochimilco on market day. I had nowhere to go and did not feel ready yet to explain to my mother, as ardently *porfirista* as I was anti-reelectionist, why I had left the army. So I had no choice for the moment but to remain trapped inside my brother. I just had to make sure that Samuel didn't come sauntering in for his promised visit, rosary beads dancing on his belt. I contrived to delay him by one week.

Meanwhile I waited . . . waited for I knew not what. A clarion call louder and more explicit than Cadwallader Brentt's? A definitive call to arms against the regime? Until it came, I played priest. I knew how to bless people and meals in Latin as well as or better than Samuel. I didn't just mimic my twin. I *became* him. It was a skill I had mastered since our earliest boyhood. I remember the two of us standing in front of the wardrobe mirror when we were about nine years old. We were dressed identically in white shirts and blue pants; our hair was combed and parted on the right, our eyes hazel and sleek. The tutors complained that mine were lit by the devil. It's reasonable to suppose that such a light gave my eyes a distinctly diabolical cast. Samuel and I stared into the mirror, Samuel wearing his usual expression of saint in training, his eyes guileless as a doe's.

"Watch this!" I grinned.

I closed my eyes. Then slowly I opened them. The mirror reflected back two boys whose eyes wore an identical look of utter innocence. During those moments, we were exact duplicates. Indistinguishable. As Samuel grew frightened, his eyes widened. I willed mine to do likewise.

"Stop it!" he cried, shoving me with both hands. But he could not stop staring into the mirror.

"I can become you anytime I want," I told him. "But no matter how much you try, or how long you live, you'll never be able to be me."

It was true. Samuel had to live with that. I became so good at it that I could fool everyone, even Mother. However, I did have an Achilles' heel—or digit phalanges. I can thank the damned trogon who bit me all those years ago for that. Yet so long as I kept my fingers loosely curled, thumb resting over the index finger, no one could tell Samuel and me apart if I didn't want them to. Just now, I wanted to see how long it would take Mother to unmask me. I in turn needed to unmask Isabel Brentt, to make certain that she had fully withdrawn her talons from my other gullible brother.

As I soon discovered, Rodolfo had not recovered from the dinner debacle. On the fourth day of Brentt's convalescence, I overheard him talking with Isabel on the upper veranda. I was seated in the arcade directly under them when one of the servants asked if she could enter Señor Brentt's room to retrieve the breakfast tray. Isabel gave the go-ahead, replying in Spanish, *"Pásale. No hay naiden."*

"When will you learn!" Rodolfo exploded. "It isn't *naiden*, Isabel! It's *nadie! Nadie!* And while we're at it, instead of *pos*, if you could humor us with *pues*, that would be one less assault on our ears! And do you need to singsong everything you say as if you were an Indian fresh off the mountain?"

He stomped down the stairs. Our eyes met briefly. Neither of us spoke. Moments later he was on his way to the city. Lowering my newspaper, I waited for the trogon's response. For several moments there was a deep stillness. Isabel descended the stairs into the garden, slowly. When she noticed me, her eyes welled up. She ran across the central courtyard and into the back garden. Setting aside the paper, I willed myself into Samuel and followed her.

The back garden with its high walls and exuberant growth was a veritable sanctuary of trellised paths. Much of Morelos was a dust bowl after the rainy season. Our garden, which was watered daily, was a riot of blossoms, of swaying jacarandas and towering cedars. It even had a labyrinth of tall boxwoods, quite intricate, that Mother designed years ago for Samuel and me. At first I couldn't tell if Isabel had disappeared under the bougainvillea trellises or into the labyrinth. The air was charged with the songs and squawks of myriad species of birds—from the crude grackle and the ubiquitous sparrows to the vainglorious peacocks that strutted on the lawns and the dozens of exotic birds that filled the aviary and assorted cages—cockatoos, lories, parrots, cuckoos, hoatzins, hummingbirds like the rare Peruvian spatuletail, and the glory of all trogons, the resplendent quetzal. I strained to filter from the cacophony one voice. Then I heard it, sorrow escaping from the heart of the labyrinth.

I should have turned back. That was the decisive moment. Like the fool that I am, I hurried into the labyrinth, imagining that because I knew its twists and turns, I understood it. I found her at the very center. She sat on the edge of the fountain with her back to me. When my feet scuffed the gravel, she turned, and I, God help me, fell into the azure depths of those eyes.

"I'm so sorry," I managed, suddenly feeling as awkward as a thirteen-year-old boy.

She had not yet confined her hair for the day. It cascaded down her back and over her breasts in soft waves. I had stumbled across an angel, and all I could do was fumble with mere words.

"Please, don't let Rodolfo upset you," I entreated in English as I seated myself near her.

Feeling self-conscious, she turned slightly, giving me her profile.

"It's just that—I had no idea—" she murmured, her voice husky with tears. "I never imagined—I *embarrass* him!" Her lower lip trembled as the thought surfaced, scaly and monstrous. Isabel turned a tear-streaked faced toward me.

"Please tell me, Father. Is my Spanish—is my Spanish like Cockney English?"

I understood the import of her question and hesitated. Yet, how do you lie to an angel? "Yes," I said as gently as the word would allow. I quickly added, "No, probably not as bad as all that. You do not mispronounce that many words. It's more a matter of your intonation. You have that gentle *cantadito* of the people of Morelos."

"Of the peasants," she murmured. "I'm told I singsong my words."

She was listening intently, her marvelous eyes fixed firmly—bravely—on mine. I could tell that she had not truly understood the consequences of her upbringing until that morning. As the truth rippled in ever-widening circles, she brought both hands to her lips, as if to trap the reality behind her slender fingers.

"Governor Escandón! Your mother! What must they all think of me!" Her shoulders slumped forward as she began to cry again, spilling sorrow into the cheery fountain.

I was beside myself that I should be the one causing her such pain. "No! They all think you're beautiful and gracious—"

"No . . ."

Her shoulders shook with despair. If I had not been in Samuel's cassock, if I did not love my mother, if the sky were not blue and all men fools, I would have shouted that Rodolfo is a son of a bitch! Instead I found myself leaning toward her and betraying every single one of my earlier resolutions.

"It's all so trivial, Isabel! What one group considers a refined tone or proper diction! And it's all so easily fixed!"

"No." She shook her head.

"Yes! It's all mimicry, Isabel! There's nothing to it! I can teach you in an hour how to speak the most refined Spanish!"

And that's how I became Isabel Brentt's tutor.

I confess that it did not take me a mere hour to undo the damage of a lifetime, but Isabel did learn quickly. Fortunately, we had plenty of time to ourselves.

Eva declared that she needed to return to Mexico for a dress fitting, leaving her children and assorted nannies with us for a few days.

"Don't worry!" Eva smiled as she boarded the family train. "I won't abandon you to the trogon. I'll be back for the fireworks."

"What fireworks?"

"You haven't heard? Before this fiasco, Rodolfo planned a dinner party to officially announce the engagement! He invited everybody we know. He told Mother and me that he can't in good conscience back down now. What would everyone say? Besides that, he doesn't want to hurt Isabel. Isn't that the stupidest thing you ever heard?" She laughed darkly.

Leaning toward me, she whispered conspiratorially, "We have to finish what we started, you and I! See you Thursday or Friday!"

Rodolfo left the hacienda also, presumably absorbed in business affairs that could not bring him back to Cuernavaca until the weekend. That gave us five days in which to work our miracle. Isabel and I met each day in the labyrinth—early in the morning, before anyone else was up, and in the languid afternoons when Mother retreated to her room for an hour or two and most of the house napped.

I began with a prayer book that I found in the library but soon substituted Bécquer, Calderón de la Barca, and all my other favorite poets. As her lovely lips formed the words I had loved since boyhood, I found myself wanting to kiss them. Every time the thought surfaced, I pushed it back down, drowning it, reminding myself that I loved that idiot brother of mine, and that what I was doing in the magical recesses of the labyrinth was to give him the best damn wedding gift he could possibly receive.

"We only have two more days," I told her early on Thursday morning. "You, my dear Isabel, are going to stun them all at that dinner party!"

"Oh, Samuel! Do you really think so?"

It was she who stunned me. Sitting very straight on the edge of the fountain, her eyes bluer than the water-lacquered cobalt tiles, she recited from memory Bécquer's Rima 53, which I had given her to learn the day before. Every student recites it in grammar school, rendering it almost trivial. But on her lips, the words became dazzling as the day the poet penned them:

> *Volverán las oscuras golondrinas*
> *en tu balcón sus nidos a colgar?*
> *Y otra vez con el ala a sus cristales,*
> *Jugando llamarán . . .*

> Will ever the dark swallows
> Hang their nests in your balcony?
> And once again with wing at its glass
> Playfully call . . .

Her voice was music. I should have listened more closely to the lyrics. Bécquer's dark swallows augur the end of a passionate relationship. Yet I could only think of the twenty-first *Rima*.

What is poetry? You say while piercing
Into my pupil your blue pupil.
What is poetry? And you ask me?
Poetry . . . is you.

And then the poetry of my longing chanted its own refrain: *He doesn't deserve you. He doesn't deserve you.*

❖ *Sketch 6* ❖

TERESA GAMA

EXPEDIENCY. HOW MANY crimes do we commit under its black banner? I remember the first and only execution I ever ordered. I wear it like a brand on my thick hide. The actual order came from the commandant, Colonel Angel Negromonte. It fell to me to carry it out. A small picket brought out the condemned man. I still remember his name: Margarito Chitla. I can't recall his crime, only that he waited stoically while I gave the order, and that he crumpled to the ground with barely a groan. Because his arms were still twitching, I had to give him the coup de grace. My hands shook uncontrollably when I reholstered my revolver. Later, I learned that Chitla's guilt was not at all certain. I got dead drunk that night. Rigoberto Suárez, one of my fellow officers, tried to make me feel better: "Don't fret about it, Benjamín. Sometimes it's expedient that an innocent man die in order to prevent worse evils!"

His words resurrected a line from one of the Gospels that the good padre Eustacious had struggled to teach me as a child. Squinting in an effort to bring Suárez's face in focus, I muttered, "Isn't that what Caiaphas said about Christ?"

"Who the hell is that?"

I assumed Suárez was asking about Caiaphas. I shrugged and drank myself into an absolute stupor. Looking back on it now, it seems to me that expediency must be the most common and most abused of all justifications. I have no doubt that it is often used with the very best of intentions. Like Rigoberto Suárez, Eva availed herself of a similar justification. My sister is a good woman. She only meant to help our brother out of his predicament. Yet the day that she returned, she acted with all the carelessness of a muddy dog shaking itself dry next to women in white gowns. Then again, a dog has no malicious intent.

Eva arrived Thursday evening. On Friday, the day before the fateful engagement party, she invited Isabel to have lunch in Cuernavaca at the Bella Vista. I knew nothing about this. Isabel and I had completed another of our secret lessons in the labyrinth. I was off on my morning ride when they set out. Both Eva and Isabel fed me the details much later, each one with her own distinctive perspective—perspectives so opposite that one might well ask if they weren't talking about two totally different days.

As they rode through the gates of San Serafín, Isabel suspected nothing. Eva spoke to her in English all the way into town, undoubtedly to put her at ease. They arrived at the hotel without incident—one of those large colonial buildings that fronts the central park of a hundred towns, massive stone monuments to Spanish imperialism. Here I must pause to credit Rosa King, the English entrepreneur who purchased and anglicized it, turning the old place into a haven of linen tablecloths and big, comfortable chairs. The Bella Vista was a fortuitous marriage of English gentility and Mexican vigor. Mrs. King also offered patrons a well-trained staff. I can picture her army of liveried waiters fluttering about as my beautiful sister led the way to a table in the airy arcade. Mrs. King, flushed with joy that her fledgling venture was attracting Mexican high society, greeted them personally.

"Countess! What a pleasure to see you again, and so soon after your last visit!"

I can picture Eva, the very model of haute couture in her Parisian finery, taking regal possession as she does everywhere she goes.

"Mrs. King, allow me the honor of introducing you to Miss Isabel Brentt!" Eva gushed in her splendid English.

"So you are the lovely Miss Brentt who is causing such a stir!"

"Am I?"

"The hotel is full of guests who will be attending your engagement party. They are all anxious to meet you. It's a pleasure to welcome you to the Bella Vista!"

English words swooped gracefully about the room like swallows in the park across the street. After Mrs. King withdrew to attend to other guests, Eva's plan continued to unfold with a precision any officer in the field of battle would envy.

"Ah! Here they are!" My sister smiled in delight as a woman and three children alighted from a coach that had just pulled up in front of the great porticos of the hotel. The children were dressed in their Sunday best. According to Eva, the two girls wore white dresses with garish bows perched on their dark hair; the little boy wore the standard knickers and navy blue Chinchilla reefer. Knowing Teresa, I'm sure they arrived carefully groomed and with shoes polished like silver.

As for Teresa Gama . . . how do I describe her? A small, slender woman in her midthirties? One whose beauty was once bright as a hibiscus and just as short-lived? A long-suffering woman who loved too generously? Or do I describe her in Eva's terms: "Not even middle class; a seamstress who reached far beyond her station"?

Teresa Gama smoothed the folds of her black skirt and whispered instructions to her children before approaching the table. As Eva described her to me, she wore a tailored suit of coarse taffeta and a plumed hat "too grotesque for words." I can see the whole scene as if I had been one of the officious waiters hovering over them. Extending a gloved hand to Teresa, which she took with an awkward curtsy, Eva switched to Spanish. There was no other choice. "*Qué gusto verte de nuevo, Teresa.*" What a pleasure to see you again. My sister spoke familiarly as one would with a friend—or a servant.

Teresa replied politely, "*Señora Condesa!* Thank you so much for going to so much trouble for us. It's very kind of you."

Teresa thanked her for sending a carriage for them. Throughout, as Isa later observed to me, Teresa spoke with proper diction and respectful formality. Eva turned a radiant face to Isabel. Still speaking in Spanish, she proceeded with introductions.

"Isabel! It is my great pleasure to introduce Teresa and her children. Teresa, this is Miss Isabel Brentt."

Eva spoke as offhandedly as if introducing a servant. Isa rushed to fill the breach. "*Mucho gusto, señora.*" She spoke respectfully.

"The pleasure is mine, Miss Brentt."

I can picture Eva fawning over the children, exclaiming how much they had grown and confusing the names of the two little girls. She embraced them all, especially the little boy, in a show of maternal largesse. Then she cut it short. According to Isa's version, Eva rose just seconds after they had been seated and announced with an imperious gesture, "And now, you must excuse me. I have a dress fitting for tomorrow's festivities. But I do so want for the two of you to get to know each other. As Isabel speaks Spanish so marvelously, I know that I am leaving you in good hands, Teresa!"

Teresa and Isabel both looked startled, but what was there to do but acquiesce as Eva gathered up her purse and gloves.

"Don't wait for me. Go ahead into the dining room and order. Put it on my account, of course! I'd like to promise that I'll join you in time for coffee and dessert. But you know all too well how unreliable dressmakers are! Well, most of them." She directed that last comment to Teresa. Then she left them.

They sat in awkward silence. Then Isabel asked with respectful formality, *"No quiere pasar 'pa 'dentro?"* She stopped and corrected her diction. "Would you care to go inside, señora?"

Teresa smiled and nodded. Gathering the children, they left
the arcade and entered the dining room. Before they had finished
the soup entrée, they were all at ease with one another and chatting comfortably in Spanish.

"Do you live here in Cuernavaca, señora?" Isabel ventured.

"No. In Cuautla."

"Well, that's not too far. So I hope we'll see more of you."

"Thank you! I hope so too." Teresa smiled.

"You have beautiful children, señora. How old are they?"

"Teresita is the oldest. She's nine. Laurita is seven. And this
little angel is almost four. We call him El Borreguito."

"I can see why!" Isabel laughed in delight. "He *is* a little
lamb! You have lovely children!"

Just as they were beginning to enjoy each other's company,
two women passed their table and paused to speak with Isabel.
They might as well have doused the tablecloth with gasoline and
dropped a lit match.

"Excuse me, but are you the Señorita Isabel Brentt that everyone is so excited about? The fiancée of don Rodolfo Nyman?"

When Eva deigned to return to the Bella Vista, Isabel sat
alone at the table.

"Where's Teresa?" my sister asked in English, smooth as the
leather of the chairs.

"She left a few minutes ago. She seemed very upset," Isa
replied, likewise in English.

"What about?"

"I don't know . . . We were enjoying our meal and our conversation. Then two ladies congratulated me for my engagement—"

"Ah! Then there's no mystery here! Of course she would be
upset if this is the first that she's heard of it. I'll have a Napoleon

with my coffee," she told a waiter. Then returning to Isabel, she added cheerfully, "Rosa King is a veritable miracle-maker! She's brought to Cuernavaca a much-needed touch of England. I don't know how she does it! I swear that I have not had better pastries even in the cafés along the Champs-Elysées!"

"What should Rodolfo have told Señora Gama?"

"The truth. Oh, men are so inconsiderate! Even the best of them! I simply think that Rodolfo should have told her himself. He owes her that much!" Eva stirred her coffee, making brisk, outraged circles.

"What should he have told her?"

Eva stopped stirring. "*Madre santísima!* You don't know! Now listen, my dear, you mustn't be hard on my misguided brother. Rodolfo has a way of getting himself entangled—"

Isabel's hands flew to her lips. "Are they his children?" she gasped.

"Well, yes."

"He's married and no one told me!" Isabel pushed back her chair so forcefully that it tipped over.

Waiters flew to the rescue.

"Of course he's not married!" Eva responded in a low voice. "My brother wouldn't marry such a woman! She's a dressmaker! Please bring the señorita a pot of tea."

A waiter held the chair for Isabel. Another hurried to get the tea. Isabel remained standing, her face as rigid as her body.

"Sit down, my dear," Eva cooed, for I suspect even she was growing uncomfortable about the looks darting about the room. "Do sit down."

"I want to leave. Now."

Without waiting for a response, Isabel walked to the waiting carriage. The lovely countess found herself obeying an "inferior."

On the trip back to San Serafín, Eva hurried to explain and of course to *justify* all.

"This must be such a shock to you, my dear," she began in her lightly accented English. "Please don't think harshly of Rodolfo—or of me. I thought you knew. And it is important for you to know. You have every right to. I tell you this as a woman. Teresa was his mistress for a number of years, but he dropped her. There were others before her and after her, but none of course after you came into the picture! Believe me! Rodolfo is devoted to you! So never worry about Teresa. She is the greatest mistake of his life, and he has paid for it dearly."

The carriage wound its way past the deep barrancas that separate San Serafín from Cuernavaca. Isabel said nothing. She stared straight ahead, remaining dry-eyed as Eva continued to enlighten her.

"You must not think ill of Rodolfo. My brother is reckless at times, but he is a man who never shirks responsibility. He still provides for Teresa Gama. He bought her a house, he sends produce from the hacienda at least once a month, and he pays for the children's education. What more can a man do?"

The fields rose up to greet them, the cane tall and undulating in the afternoon sun. Some of the *peones* straightened and doffed their hats as the carriage rolled past them.

"Never think of Teresa Gama as a rival. You are prettier and younger! She doesn't carry her years well. It's no wonder he grew tired of her. But of course, that's hardly the fault of the children. Illegitimate or not, they're part of the family. You can see now why it was imperative that you meet them. They're really quite darling . . ."

The carriage pulled up to the front door. As luck would have it, all of the Nyman siblings converged on the same spot at the same time—*all* of us. My twin, the good padre, had arrived earlier than expected. He stood in the central arcade chatting with Rodolfo as I blundered in. Isabel, who walked with firm steps ahead of Eva, stopped abruptly at the sight of the two of us dressed in identical cassocks. For a moment she seemed unable to comprehend the dual image.

"*Ay, muchachos!*" Eva scolded us as if were children. "When will you boys stop your pranks! Don't mind them, Isabel. For as long as any of us can remember, they have been switching roles and thinking they can fool us. Well, they can't fool me! The one on the right is Samuel; the one with the guilty look is Benjamín, who thinks he's so clever!"

Isabel turned in my direction. Our eyes met briefly. Even now I cringe at the memory, absurd as that is. We were no more conniving with her than she with us. Yet I can't shake the notion, even now, that she was genuinely grieved by my betrayal of her trust. I stood cringing like a boy caught with a club in one hand and a broken window at his back. Rodolfo, who seemed poised to step into his role of the gallant greeting his beloved, missed his cue. Perhaps the unscripted transition in her manner, in her eyes, threw him off. Eva simply looked bemused that we had been caught at childish pranks. Isabel said nothing, but her eyes shimmered. She paused to take the measure of us, like a hawk that can take in the whole landscape in one majestic arc of its flight. Turning her back on us—even on Samuel, who had innocently started forward to introduce himself—she ascended the stairs slowly and with dignity. With that one magnificent gesture, she had me.

～

Prisoner 243 slept. In his dream, no one stopped him when he walked down a series of hallways and through the courtyard right to the very entrance of the prison. None of the guards questioned him, not even Calixto Contreras or the other two who had nearly beaten him to death. Contreras stared, his eyes narrow slits of dull light, but he did not stop him. Benjamín Nyman walked with a calm, steady gait out the front entrance. He was a free man rejoining a city teeming with life—but it was that other city, the one of his nightmares, and he was a captive again, ever a captive.

Once again he found himself forced to climb the steep face of the twin pyramid of Tenochtitlán. It was an overcast day. Lake and sky, watery expanses of slate gray, blurred into each other. Even the *chinampas*—manmade islands where farmers grew vegetables in patterns colorful as flower beds—melted into the molten grayness of the day. Only the great pyramid stood out sharply. For the first time Benjamín focused on the people tethered to him. He could see their faces with heightened clarity, Indian men and women, long suffering and silent. "I know you!" he told them excitedly, as if the fact could mean anything to them. "I just don't remember your names." That mattered even less as they continued to heft grief on their stooped shoulders. When they reached the temple on the pinnacle of the pyramid, four men dragged a woman to a large slab of stone. The ritual proceeded with horrific monotony.

When it was his turn, Benjamín did not fight it.

"Do it, Father!" he told the priest with the clotted blood in his hair. "Just get on with it!"

This time the priest was neither old nor gaunt but a younger version of Lucio Nyman. Then Benjamín realized it wasn't his father at all.

"Samuel!" he gasped.

Despite the ochre paint, the features were unmistakable, unmistakable until he noticed the eyes and knew with a sickening certainty that he was staring at himself, and that the victim on the sacrificial stone was a beautiful woman with blue eyes.

"Please, Ben!" she cried out. "Please listen!"

He plunged the knife deep into her chest, reaching with bare fingers for her palpitating heart.

"You didn't let me speak!" the heart moaned.

"Isa!" Benjamín sat bolt upright in his bed, face and chest dripping with perspiration, heart pounding like an Aztec drum. *Isa, Isa . . .* He remembered the day she visited him in the prison.

I let the damn photographs testify against you and condemn you, but I didn't let you speak a word! Not a single word!

Half an hour later he was running barefoot into the morning, deliberately outdistancing El Brujo, deliberately throwing himself into the sickly light of the corridors and courtyard, intent on silence and silencing his guilt, guilt riding on his shoulders, doubt shadowing them both, all running, running until Benjamín's lungs expanded and his body opened itself to a new day, a day made bearable by two hours of unhampered motion, but never quite shaking doubt, doubt gaining on him, passing him, and circling back to taunt him.

What if you have it wrong?

Sketch 7

THE RHETORIC OF SILENCE

I HAD BEEN caught masquerading as Samuel. Isa said nothing; her silence chastised us as she walked up the stairs with firm, unhurried footsteps. The four of us Nymans stood like deer, heads turned in the same direction, ears on the alert. We were released from our idiotic immobility only when we heard Isabel's door shut. Then Eva sailed toward one of the sitting rooms, Rodolfo on her heels. I gave a last glance at Isa's door before following, and of course Samuel came with us. As soon as my brother crossed the threshold, I spun and lit into him, venting the anger I felt toward myself. "What the hell are you doing here? You weren't supposed to get back until tomorrow, you moron!" My brother, the good priest, stared silently at my cassock—his cassock—and waited patiently for me to explain my latest theft of his identity. I slumped into an armchair and glared a hole into the opposite wall. Rodolfo turned to Eva and asked her point-blank, "Did you tell her? Does she know?"

Eva slipped off her kid gloves. Removing her hatpin and hat, she flopped into one of the large armchairs. "I did better than that. I had her meet Teresa and the children."

"My God, Eva!" Rodolfo dropped into the chair opposite her. His hand trembled as he rubbed his cheek and chin.

"You did what?" I leaped in, my face growing hot.

"It was the only way; the best way. Now don't all look at me that way! You did say to me that you would call the whole thing off if you could." She wagged a finger at Rodolfo. "Correct me if I am wrong."

"Without *hurting* her! Yes! And certainly without humiliating Teresa!"

"No!" Eva shot back, her black irises spewing anger like Father's eyes. "*You* did that yourself! I merely told them the truth that you were too cowardly to tell either of them! Or to be more precise, it was the good ladies of Cuernavaca who told them the truth that everyone knows. I merely brought them together."

"By deceiving Isabel!" I pounced as if doing the death leap in a rodeo. But in leaping off my horse at full gallop onto the unsaddled mare, I missed spectacularly.

"*You* talk to me about deception?" She arched her brows.

I backed off. Rodolfo continued to massage his chin.

"How did Teresa take it?" His voice was shaking like a mediocre tenor overreaching his ability.

"I don't know. She was gone by the time I got back to them. I told them I had a dress fitting—as if that were remotely possible in Cuernavaca of all places—and they both believed me!" She sniggered. When none of us laughed, she shrugged impatiently. "You men! You deceive women and then get so self-righteous when the truth comes out!"

"You're right," Rodolfo murmured in a hoarse voice.

"Cheer up!" She leaned toward him across the coffee table. "I've made it possible for Isabel to break off the engagement herself. Surely that should free your conscience. As for Teresa, she needs to learn once and for all that the past is dead. That she—"

"She didn't know about Isabel."

"Of course she knew! Rodolfo, *everyone* knows everyone's business in Cuernavaca and in miserable towns like Cuautla!

Your engagement to an American, and not just any American but to Isabel Brentt of all people, has been *the* topic of conversation and gossip for weeks!"

"I tell you, Teresa knew nothing about my engagement."

"Of course she did!"

"No, I tell you! I just saw her last week—"

I turned on him. "Why the hell does an engaged man need to be visiting a former mistress?"

"That's none of your damn business!" Rodolfo bristled.

"But Benjamín does raise a valid concern," Samuel interjected in his ever-reasonable way, perhaps sensing that asking for an explanation of my deception would only make things worse.

"You stay out of this!" Rodolfo snarled.

Isabel was brilliant. She turned absence into a weapon. By locking herself in her room for the next twenty-four hours, she utterly unnerved Rodolfo and me. I would have slit my own throat if she had asked me—anything but to have her think that I had deliberately set out to mock her. All right. That was my original intention—a little fun at her expense. But God or the devil transformed it into something higher—a genuine desire to help her.

I wrote to her. No, that sounds too easy. I went into brutal single-handed combat for her. While Samuel went into the chapel to pray for this brood of scorpions, I locked myself in our room and spent the rest of that miserable day battling against a language that refused to surrender to my shame, regret, and escalating desperation.

I filled reams of paper, marshaling battalions of words that always broke rank and turned tail or that crumpled as if shattered by artillery. I could not seem to get past the opening paragraph, which always ran something like this:

Dear Isabel,

All of us are beneath contempt. I am ashamed of the whole miserable lot of us. But most of all I so deeply regret my deception. I don't know how to begin to excuse it, for it cannot be excused. I can only try to explain it in the hope that a heart as generous as yours will forgive one who deserves nothing but *contempt.*

And there it stayed, my apology impaled by the contempt she had every right to feel toward me.

I ignored the summons to the dinner table. Since Isabel remained locked in her room and I in mine, the rest of the family was free to celebrate the dissolution of the engagement. Mother, Rodolfo, and Eva, that is. Samuel had never even met her. I can picture him listening in perplexed, dismayed silence as they strategized whether to send out a barrage of telegrams calling off the engagement party or to host it anyway under some clever guise that would help us all save face.

When Samuel returned to our room, he had to wade through a sea of crumpled balls of paper. I sat at the desk, sleeves rolled up, ink stains on my fingers, left hand cradling my head. He knew better than to talk to me until I tossed the pen aside. He sat on his bed, watching me. When I finally turned toward him, he asked, "What is she like, this Miss Brentt? Should we be relieved that the engagement is off?"

"No, no!" I dropped down alongside him. "They're all wrong about her! She's perfect! Better than perfect, but Rodolfo is too stupid to see it! He doesn't deserve her, damn him! The fact is, she's too good for any of us!" I hung my head.

Samuel rested his elbows on his knees and turned to look at me. It was obvious that he was wrestling with divergent opinions.

"Yet if she's as coarse as Mother and Eva say—"

"That's where they're wrong!" I jumped up and started to pace. "I've taken care of that. I tutored her—*you* tutored her. We met every day—"

"Every day? How did you explain my daily presence to Mother, if I may ask?"

"Your church is undergoing some major repairs—the altar and most of the sacristy. So you found it necessary to cancel services for a week."

"Really? And did you perform vespers in the chapel?"

"Now why the devil would I do that?"

"Because that's what I do when I stay here. So, padre, Mother has to have known you were up to your old tricks."

"Damn! You really think she knew?" My vanity as an actor was ruffled. "I wonder why the old lady never let on?"

"Perhaps she thought it was all part of the plot to save our brother," my twin sighed.

"Let me tell you about plots. They're odd things. Believe me, they have a way of turning on their creators. I still can't begin to tell you how I went from mockery to eager servitude. I swear to you, Samuel, I never meant to carry the charade so far. It's just that it was such a pleasure to work with her! To teach her the simple but all-important gift of genteel speech . . ."

As long as I live I'll never forget our first lesson. She was seated on a bench in the labyrinth, her hair radiant in the morning light, her stance utterly attentive. I had handed her one of Samuel's prayer books. Her eyes grappled with the words for a moment. Then she shook her head and explained to me in English, as if afraid to affront my ears, that she had never been taught to read or write in Spanish.

As I think back on it now, I am struck by how quickly my attitude toward her morphed. For her sake, I willed myself into a master teacher able to cut to the essence.

"It's really quite simple, Isabel. Let me show you what I mean. Unlike English, we only have five basic vowels in Spanish. When we combine them, we still sound them out in a consistent manner. No sneakiness as with English's *read* in the present tense and *read* in the past tense! In terms of phonetics, Spanish is simpler than English and so much more honest!"

She laughed. I grew expansive.

"The Spanish *j* sounds like your English *h*—*rojo, ojo, flojo.* Sound them out."

She laughed like a child and learned with adult speed. I waxed metaphoric.

"The whole scheme is straightforward, except for our *h* which is like a ghost—haunting some words, yet to all intents and purposes invisible through its silence."

Her pleasure forged me into a master grammarian and rhetorician on the spot.

"She was astonishing," I confided to Samuel. "Such a fast learner, and not a whit of false pride! How can I say it? She was humble, yet I constantly felt humbled in her presence. Mother and Eva simply don't know her!"

"Do you?"

Rodolfo would have turned the question into an accusation. Not Samuel. Even now at the height of the family crisis, he continued to be the calm voice of reason, taking no sides, judging no one, ever working to direct passion into reasoned discourse.

"Yes."

"Tell me about her."

I stopped pacing and stared into the distance. I ran my fingers through my hair.

"How do I begin to tell you about Isa?"

⁓

The lockdown for the night had begun. Cell doors slammed shut throughout the penitentiary. Guards yelled orders. Seated at his desk, his thoughts far from prison life, Benjamín Nyman seemed deaf to the clamor. As he paused in his writing, it occurred to him that that evening with Samuel was the precise moment when he first began to use the diminutive form of Isabel's name—Isa.

Ee-sah. The very sound was poetry to his ears. Ee-sah. Was it from that moment on that it had become a natural extension of his breathing, he wondered? A steady inhalation and exhalation of her name that he carried with him, even here in prison?

How had he explained to his brother such a force as Isa? Often, especially when they were children, he and Samuel had been able to exchange thoughts without speech.

Is that what happened? the prisoner asked his twin across distance and thick walls. *Did I let you sense what she had come to mean to me? No. I remember now. There was too much clamor in my mind, too much noise. My feelings evaded capture, darting about like starlings startled into aimless flight. I remember slumping down on the bed alongside you and hanging my head. You waited patiently, Samuel, for the flocks of emotions to get their bearings. Then the words knew their course.*

~

"Isabel Brentt isn't just beautiful, Samuel. She's unlike anyone you and I have ever met! Isa has an amazing disregard for convention when convention serves no positive use. A naturalness of speech and manner that reveals a goodness—a genuine goodness—the kind you only dream of finding in others and never expect to encounter." My shoulders drooped. I felt the sudden urge for confession and absolution, but not from him. "What I can't forgive is that I abused her trust, and what I can't bear is that she now thinks that I was mocking her all along. How do I ask her forgiveness?"

"Keep it simple. Truth speaks in simple words."

Later, while Samuel slept in his bed not one meter distant from mine, I rose and groped in the dark for my unfinished letter. Not wanting to wake him, I stepped out into the night. Gazing up at the sky, I wished it were still lit up by Halley's Comet. I could have found the words in comet light. Instead, I had to settle for the banker's lamp on Father's old desk in the study. Following my brother's advice, I wrote the truth. Simply.

> I love you. I love you desperately and long for two things only: to earn your forgiveness and the privilege of devoting my life to your service. I would lay down my very life for you, Isa.
>   Benjamín

The next morning I heard Rodolfo knock softly on her door. "Please, Isabel. We must talk."

She remained silent as the *Virgen de los Remedios* in the family chapel. I wanted to knock on that door too, or to knock Rodolfo's head into it until his thick skull broke every panel. I waited. When he was gone, I sealed my note into an envelope and slipped it under her door. I waited like a dog eager for even the faintest hint of his master's presence. A whisper. A cough. Anything! Her silence in the riotous cacophony of the morning was unendurable. I headed downstairs. Actually, I was ravenous. To my annoyance, my thoughts were mindlessly turning from my sublime misery to my miserable stomach. I had just reached the arcade under Isabel's end of the house when she suddenly left her room. She was intercepted by Rodolfo. I stood silent and straight as a sentry, listening to every word that they flung at each other in English.

"Please talk to me, Isabel! Please let me explain," the second most contrite man in Mexico pleaded.

"Let me pass."

"Isabel, I can't tell you how sorry I am! I should have told you about Teresa. I meant to when the time was right."

"How can the time ever be right to admit that you fathered *three* children out of wedlock and abandoned their mother?"

"I have never abandoned them. I'll always take care of their needs. I send their mother monthly supplies from the hacienda."

"Wonderful! Do you really think that's the only thing that your children need—a little raw sugar cane? A bolt of cotton?"

"No, of course not," he murmured, his voice husky and drenched in the molasses of regret. "I pay for their education and will always—"

"That's not enough."

"Tell me what to do. How do I make this up to you?" he asked, even though the rational side of his idiot brain must have been yelling at him to grab the opportunity Eva had created and be done with the Brentts.

"Give this to the right woman, to the mother of your children. Take it, Rodolfo. It rightfully belongs to her."

"No."

"Yes!" She cracked the word like a whip.

I tensed. Was he trying to clasp her to him? Was she trying to pull away? Or were they still keeping a proper adversarial distance?

"Give it to Teresa Gama, Rodolfo!"

"I can't."

"Why not?"

"She and I live in very different worlds."

"Meaning, she's socially inferior to you."

"Yes."

"As I am."

"No. Of course not."

"Take it!"

"Isabel! Everything is in motion! Let's just leave it as it is! Forget yesterday. The guests will be arriving in a couple of hours. It's too late to notify them. Some are traveling great distances—"

With a sudden motion, she threw the ring down into the patio fountain. Her aim was commendable. I heard the ring splash in the tile-tinted water.

"Give your guests my regrets that I cannot join them. Tend to them by all means. After all, none of this is their fault. Rest assured that my grandfather and I will leave this house the very *second* that the doctor tells me that it is safe for him to travel."

This time Rodolfo made no effort to stop her.

"I know this is hard on both you and the girl," Mother told Rodolfo.

We had all gathered in her large bedroom suite after breakfast. For as far back as I can remember, we've always congregated on the sofas and chairs clustered around her fireplace. The room with its high-beamed ceiling has absorbed thousands of our conversations. If the whole hacienda were to vanish tomorrow, I could bear it if this one room survived. For all of us, it has always been the very heart of home.

"I never meant to hurt her or Teresa!" Rodolfo moaned.

"I know, son. But you can't marry a servant or the butcher's daughter just because she's pretty or because you feel sorry for her."

I bristled. "That's nonsense, Mamá. With all due respect, Isabel cannot be classified as such."

"Given that she talks like one, yes, I can classify her as such." Mother spoke firmly, giving me one of her looks that would silence the cockiest rooster from ever greeting the morning sun again. "Now listen carefully, all of you. Our guests do not need to be told the truth at this point. As Señorita Brentt herself has suggested, we will extend her regrets, saying she is feeling ill. The festivities go on as planned. In a few weeks we can inform our closest friends that the engagement is off. News will travel fast enough, and you will be free," she said to Rodolfo, "free to make a *better* choice next time around."

Carriages of all sizes began to roll through the gates of San Serafín by ten o'clock that morning. The twenty-something guest rooms in the west wing of the compound quickly filled up with our closest friends. Ladies' maids and grooms were housed in the smaller rooms above the guest quarters. Others lodged in Rosa King's Bella Vista. Our stables overflowed with carriages and the finest horses in Mexico. The marvel is that we did not feel overrun or overwhelmed. On the contrary! San Serafín expanded generously. We began the festivities with a barbecue in the back lawn that overlooked Mother's three-story aviary.

Ten grills were fired up. I can smell the steaks now, basted in thick brown adobo marinades, smoke rising to the sky like offerings to the gods! And afterward, the *charreadas*, those magnificent rodeos that thrilled guests and *peones* alike, the horsemanship that unified the social classes and brought us all to our feet

shouting and applauding, laughing, thrilling. When I rode Falco
into the ring, I set my misery down among the hay bales. Breaking into a gallop, I sensed my body becoming one with Falco, my
magnificent Falco, as if he and I were a centaur. We flew like the
wind alongside a wild, unsaddled mare that could not quite out-
run us, and then I leaped from Falco onto the mare's back—all
the while without slowing our breakneck pace, all to the crowd's
roar of approval! *Dios Santo!* What would I give to be there again!

That afternoon the hacienda fell into a stupor when the
guests and even the dragonflies stopped to nap. Rodolfo's pièce
de résistance was scheduled for ten o'clock that evening: dinner
and a ball followed by a display of fireworks. It began at eight
o'clock with drinks and hors d'oeuvres in the back garden illu-
minated with hundreds of lanterns. Young couples ventured
eagerly into the labyrinth while their elders talked of politics or
reminisced about the centennial celebrations, already according them legendary status. A mariachi band played on the ter-
race. I wandered the grounds like a dog that had lost its master. I
expected to see Rodolfo looking just as hangdog, but the bastard
was actually enjoying himself as he played host extraordinaire.
He thumped the governor on the back and laughed uproariously
at his stories. I wanted to pound him into red salsa.

Later, we were summoned into the cavernous room that as
a child I nicknamed *la catedral de San Serafín*—an enormous
room with high, vaulted ceilings and bodega-style cupolas. We
used the "cathedral" only for formal occasions that rivaled presidential dinners or balls. It had an unusual table: an enormous
horseshoe that gathered even large crowds around the host in
the center; the effect, especially when lit by candles and all the
magic of linens and dinner finery, was of a luminous intimacy.
The French doors—all eight of them—opened directly onto
the back garden. That night a delicious breeze wafted from the
fragrant flowerbeds through the open doors. Enormous urns of

roses, gardenias, and other floral wonders delineated the dance floor with its twenty-piece orchestra. The mood turned European. Mexican *corridos* gave way to Viennese waltzes. Bottles of champagne and the finest French wines sparkled with the family cutlery and seventeenth-century stemware. The servants sported white gloves and new uniforms. Rodolfo had spared no expense. This was his moment of glory. Yet as he took the seat of honor, with Isabel's seat remaining conspicuously vacant, as he explained to yet another guest that his fiancée was indisposed, and as the refrain—"Oh! What a shame!"—played monotonously as a Wagnerian leitmotif, I actually felt a pang for him. Eva must have sensed the same. Leaving her seat, she approached Rodolfo, intent on taking the empty place herself.

To our astonishment, Isabel entered *la catedral* just then.

Sketch 8

APPEARANCES

Isabel entered the room alone—a vision of radiance in pale green silk. The gown had some kind of a filmy silver overlay that made her shimmer like dew on the grass. She walked steadfastly toward Rodolfo, who had not noticed her yet. When he looked up, he jumped to his feet, almost overturning his chair. Eva, who was about to take Isabel's seat, gasped. Rodolfo rushed to his fiancée.

"Isabel!"

I couldn't decide if he was pleased or dismayed by her apparent forgiveness. I'm certain that he was well aware of the many eyes watching them. Offering her his arm, he escorted her to the table. A number of guests clapped in greeting. Others looked up, inspected the mysterious young bride they had come to see, and then joined in the clapping. Isabel smiled and responded with a gracious nod of her head.

Rodolfo played his role. This was opening night. I watched them both from my side of the horseshoe. The glow of the chandeliers gave Isabel's blonde hair an otherworldliness. An aura. No. It wasn't just her hair. It was her very demeanor. It must have been clear to any observer that she had been crying; her eyes were red-rimmed and a few pearl-like droplets still clung to the eyelashes. Had she spoken, her voice would have been husky. Isabel Brentt never looked more beautiful.

Had she read my note? I anguished like a lovesick fifteen-year-old boy. I tried to read the answer on her face. Once, I managed to catch her eye, but she looked away.

What does she think of me? Why is she here? I kept wondering. *She can't be thinking of forgiving Rodolfo!*

The orchestra struck up the Emperor Waltz. Wine bottles were uncorked. A shrimp bisque was served, and the spectacle was launched. I could hear Rodolfo's Oxford English resonating off the high beams. The governor, who was seated next to Isabel, was in equally fine form, his English flowing as smoothly as the cabernet sauvignon. Don Pablo had apparently decided to forgive her guttersnipe Spanish, to think of her simply as an American who spoke Spanish poorly. Sitting to her left, he frequently leaned toward her in a stance of attentiveness. She spoke so softly that I could not make out her words. I could hear guests speaking sympathetically about Cadwallader's accident. Perhaps they attributed her tears to that.

Right after the second course, Rodolfo rose and asked Isabel to dance. I think she was about to refuse him. As various guests were once again applauding, she nodded. Rodolfo led her to the dance floor. The eyes of Morelos society were upon them. I have to admit even now that they looked the perfect couple—Rodolfo taller than ever in black-tie formal wear; Isabel, tall and majestic as a queen with a tragic air about her. At the conclusion of the waltz, he reached into a pocket and produced the ring. Did it sparkle because of its gaudy size or because of its bath in the fountain? Again, I had the distinct impression that she was refusing it. He, in turn, was murmuring intently into her ear. The guests were cheering and clapping at the privilege of witnessing firsthand the miracle of love, as if it were a wonder newly imported from abroad. She hesitated—I suppose to make him sweat. Then she whispered something in his ear and let him slide the ring onto her finger. A waltz by our own Juventino Rosas followed. The banquet proceeded, rivaling all the pomp of the recent Centennial Ball.

Whenever the orchestra musicians took a break, a mariachi band stepped up and serenaded the couple. Trumpets and violins flirted; a tenor sang lyrics as familiar to us as *café de olla*, the only coffee brewed in San Serafín. Mother looked on silently. Eva's lips twitched as she tried to make light talk. Rodolfo looked considerably chastened. He had dropped his role of ecstatic young groom. I could read tension in his face and in the stiffness of his shoulders. I had no doubt that Isabel had struck a temporary truce, nothing more. The engagement was still off. I was suddenly as light-hearted as the tenor. I smiled inwardly throughout don Pablo's toast. Everyone drank to the couple's health. Then Isabel rose.

"I'd like to offer—"

Rodolfo rose hastily. Extending his glass of champagne, he beat her to the draw:

"To the most beautiful, the most generous woman!"

Everyone drank to that. Rodolfo draped an arm around her shoulders and nonchalantly tried to press her back into her chair. Isabel pulled away and held up her glass.

"I would like to offer a toast to Señora Vizcarra de Nyman. Señora, I wish to thank you from the bottom of my heart for your generous hospitality and for all the kindness that you have shown my grandfather. We are both in your debt. *A la señora!*"

"*A doña Manuela!*"

I puffed up with pride. Isabel had spoken in flawless Spanish. No one in that illustrious gathering could have done better. Mother, Eva, and Rodolfo were nonplussed. And it didn't stop there. Isabel set her glass down but continued to hold the floor.

"In honor of the occasion, I would like to offer a poem that I wrote. It's inspired by the señora's lovely gardens and aviary."

She had everyone's attention—even the servants'. No one moved. Not a spoon or dessert fork stirred. My heart was soaring, hitting notes a full octave higher than an Irish tenor. I felt her triumph to be my own. She gazed off in the distance and recited with beautiful clarity in the language of Cervantes:

> They rustle their feathers with the first golden touch
> Of the morning—the humble doves nesting free
> In the arms of the jacarandas, the lordly peacocks
> Strutting away their days in finery centuries-bought.
> And within the gilded cage the others, by convention
> Imprisoned, victims to their plumage or rarity,
> Contentedly trade flight for a perch of orange peels.
> Only one jars the peaceful cage, her wings
> In wild protest flapping. Her body against
> The barred door crashes, until one fitful night it opens
> To the moon, and the trogon vanishes into the night.

"Lovely!" I heard a woman murmur moments before the applause erupted.

Isabel looked at me just then. Her eyes seemed colder than an alpine lake.

The dinner was a brilliant success. It was followed by fireworks and dancing well into the night. By the time the guests left the next morning, all with thanks, blessings, and warm embraces, Rodolfo had begun to believe the fantasy. I could see it. Buoyed by the ring that was back on her finger and by her stunning performance, he beamed with joy. Then Isabel set him straight. The moment they had walked the last of the guests to the front courtyard, even before the carriage wheels had cleared the gate, she shrugged free of his arms. He hurried after her. She paused at the foot of the garden stairs. And because Spanish architecture trades privacy for intimacy, all of us heard the exchange when she handed back the ring.

"Take it, Rodolfo."

"No. Isabel—"

"Take it, or you'll have to fish it out of the fountain a second time."

"No. It's yours, whatever happens."

Her face flushed red as a rufous hummingbird. The ring clattered on the flagstone floor. "I don't need to be bought off! I am *not* one of your mistresses, now or ever!"

"No, of course not! But then, why did you put on such a show for the guests?"

She reeled around. We listened spellbound, all of us from different parts of the four arcades: Mother, Eva, and I—and half the servants, I'm sure.

"I spared you in front of your guests for one reason only— because of your kindness to my grandfather, because your mother opened her home to us while he convalesces, for which I am genuinely grateful. But the charade is over. I've done my part. I don't owe you anything more."

"I know that. I'm the one who is in your debt." He stepped toward her, his voice betraying his sense of awe. "Isabel, you were splendid! Perfect!"

There was a pause. Then she spoke with exquisite sadness. "I wanted you to love me even when I wasn't splendid or perfect. *That* would have been love."

The next few days were a blur. Rodolfo and I were in purgatory. No matter how hard we tried, there was no expiation for our sins. Isabel punished us with her silence and her utter disdain. She spent her time either at her grandfather's bedside, where she took her meals, or locked in her room. Without words, she made it abundantly clear to us that the miserable roosters that woke us daily were worthier of her attention than either of us. Rodolfo wandered about the house with a stunned expression.

"I can't believe I've lost her . . ." he murmured to Mother, to me, to the walls, to anything that might absorb some of his pain.

Even now I'm amazed at the rigor of her rejection. He ached to drop to one knee and swear his devotion to her and then to spend the rest of his life proving it. Why did she play out her anger as long as she did? The battle was won. She had achieved a stunning victory at the party. She only needed to make him suffer for a day or two and then claim her prize. Didn't she risk overplaying her hand? Was she really surprised that a man of Rodolfo's age and position had had a mistress and had fathered illegitimate children? During their carriage ride from Cuernavaca, had Eva also disclosed Rodolfo's problematic relationship with Father? Is that what was giving Isabel second thoughts about the marriage? Did she suddenly fear that he might not inherit his portion of my father's estate? Given her grandfather's penury, wasn't it reasonable for Isa to reconsider her options? Whatever the case, I fared no better than Rodolfo. However, I did manage to intercept her one evening as she left her grandfather's room.

"Please, Isabel."

"Miss Brentt!" she corrected me without slowing her pace or looking at me.

"Miss Brentt. There is something I must ask you. Did you read my letter?"

"No. I threw it away."

"Without reading it?" I asked, aghast.

"Good night, Captain." She stopped outside her door and finally turned to face me. "It is *captain,* isn't it?"

"Yes."

"And what will you be tomorrow?"

I don't know which was worse, the sarcasm in her voice or the justice of her remark. I nodded penitently.

"I can't begin to tell you how sorry I am."

"Then don't."

She opened her door. I added quickly,

"If you won't speak to me, won't you at least read my letter?"

When she turned to face me, her manner was dignified and as distant as Greenland or the Canary Islands. But by all the saints! At least she was talking to me! "Captain Nyman, I have no intention of rummaging through a wastebasket to retrieve your letter. Good night."

Rodolfo left for Mexico City that Tuesday, a mere three days after his triumphant engagement party. When the doctor told him that the old man would need to remain immobile for at least five or six more weeks, Rodolfo took heart. There was still time to win her back! I had no such hopes for myself. By the end of the week I knew I had to leave San Serafín. I announced my departure. Eva, in turn, betrayed me by telling Mother that I intended to answer Madero's call to arms. Mother was outraged.

"No son of mine is going to betray don Porfirio! Not while I have breath in my body!" she told me with the fierceness of a Yaqui warrior.

"I'm sorry, Mamá. Truly sorry. I admire the man. On a personal level, I even like him. But there comes a time—"

"No! There's never a time when it is right to betray a friend! Never, Benjamín! Don Porfirio is a friend, not only to our family, but to our nation. And what about your allegiance to your regiment? Do your men mean nothing to you?"

"Of course they matter," I answered quietly.

"Listen to me, Benjamín Nyman Vizcarra. If you run off like some adolescent boy to join Madero and his ruffians, you are betraying your family and the very army that you pledged yourself to honor. Oh, son! Don't do it! Could you really fight against the men of your own regiment? Against officers who are friends of yours?"

"If I have to."

"But you *don't* have to!"

"Mamá, there are far bigger issues here than my personal feelings!"

I argued as best I could, but every one of her counterarguments thrust the spear point deeper into my chest. Abandoning my regiment was proving far harder than I had imagined it would. The faces of my men and of my fellow officers haunted my dreams. Yet they were no match for the new feelings awakening in me. I decided that if I couldn't have Isabel Brentt, then the only thing I wanted was to break free and shake the whole establishment upside down! I yearned to help create a new nation or to die in the attempt.

Just before I left Mother's room, when we were both worn out, she grasped my hands. "Promise me one thing, my son," she asked with sudden hope. "Promise me you'll go to the chapel right now and pray for guidance. Promise me!"

"Mamá . . . I'm not Samuel."

"That's why you need to pray! Ask for guidance, son, and God will give it."

"Mamá," I said as gently as I could. "I don't know how to pray anymore. You pray for me."

She pushed me angrily. "No! Some things you must do for yourself! Now you go straight to the altar, light a candle, and ask the Virgin to intercede for you."

"It would be waste of my time and of hers."

"Don't you get clever with me! Not about this!"

In the end I promised I would try to pray. However, I walked right past the chapel with its yellow-tiled dome and headed instead into the back garden. It was quiet, lit dimly by the bedrooms that cast their light from afar. Instinctively, I headed for the aviary where the birds had roosted for the night. Pressing my face to the bars, I tried to say the Lord's Prayer. Halfway into it I stopped, feeling as much a fraud as if I were disguised in one of Samuel's chasubles and about to give mass.

"Are you really joining Madero?"

I started. For a moment I thought the voice was coming from inside the aviary.

"Miss Brentt?" I asked in astonishment.

"Are you a revolutionary then?"

"Yes," I answered, squinting into the gloom. She was standing on the opposite side of the cage.

"When do you leave?"

"Soon." I moved toward her. She drew away just as quickly, both of us traveling on the circumference of a circle that refused to unite us. I stopped, as if she were a rare bird that I was afraid of scaring off.

"If were a man, I would go too," she murmured.

"Then you approve of Francisco Madero?"

"With all my heart."

"I had no idea! Is your grandfather a *maderista* too?"

She laughed softly, her voice more melodious to my ears than all the bird songs that I had come to know and love. "No! My grandfather lives only for his art."

And his alcohol, I might have added, but I wasn't crazy enough to break the magic spell. Her next question reined me in sharply.

"Which ones are trogons?"

My heart pounded in my ears. *She couldn't possibly know about my nickname for her!* I tried to reassure myself. Yet my face must have turned almost as red as a *Rupicola peruviana.*

I squinted into the darkness. "There! Up on the highest perch."

"Which one? I see two birds up there."

"The one with the long, majestic tail feathers. The quetzal."

"Oh, yes! I see it now. . . . Quetzals are trogons?" she asked after a pause.

"Yes. They're the most beautiful of the thirty-seven species of trogons."

I hoped she would step closer, but she seemed intent on keeping the aviary between us.

"Are there other trogons in there?"

"No. That's the only one. The others died. They don't do well in captivity."

"Then you should release it."

"Yes, of course. Unfortunately, it's not mine!" I hastened to add, wishing for all the world that it were so I could free it as a pledge to her. "It's called the resplendent quetzal. In Nahuatl, *quetzal* means 'beautiful' or 'precious.' The Aztecs and the

Mayans valued their plumage far more than gold. It was sacred to them."

"Trogons must be vicious."

"No more than any bird that rightfully defends itself or its young."

"The females are drab, of course."

"No trogon is drab. They are all magnificent, especially the females."

"I don't know much about birds, Captain, but I do know that the males always outdo the females in beauty."

"Not the greater painted snipe," I countered quickly. "That particular species exhibits strong dimorphism."

"Dimorphism?" Did she seem amused? Was there a smile in her voice? I grew expansive.

"There's a sexual role reversal with the male and female snipes. The male incubates the eggs and cares for the chicks. My point is that the female greater painted snipe is decidedly more beautiful than the male."

Couldn't she tell how much I longed to see her? She was like the quetzal, nearly invisible in the velvet shadows, a presence strong as the mountains that blurred into the indigo night.

"In the case of humans," I added, "the females are superior to the males in every single regard."

"Good night, Captain. And good luck."

She was dismissing me, but I noted that she had spoken the words with a gentleness at par with the night. I heard her return up the path. I wanted to run after her. But to what end? This was not the time. I needed to be absolutely free. My immediate obligation was to the revolution.

Or maybe I just knew better than to try to catch a trogon.

✧ *Sketch 9* ✧

WILD PIGEONS

HERE IN THE penitentiary even dreaming becomes a form of punishment, a thing weighted down by regrets you didn't even know you had. Or the old ones get melted down and recast. I stopped dreaming about the wretched Aztec temple, for which I'm grateful. Yet my guilt and despair did not vanish. They simply spoke to me in new images.

In my new recurring dream I am a passenger pigeon—*Ectopistes migratorius.* I am sleek and larger than my cousins the mourning doves and built for speed. My wings slice through time and space. They carry me high above the earth at speeds that transform quietude into storm. I am but one member of the largest flock the skies have ever held, a flock so enormous that we blacken the sun. Hunters stare open-mouthed. What do they know as they block their ears from the clamor of our wings, hundreds of millions strong? What do they know of flight like ours? Of motion perfectly synchronized? Of distances swallowed in seconds? Of migratory paths etched in our collective memory thousands of years ago? Of life lived in its intended harmony?

Yet it is these dull brutes, the commercial trappers, who trick us into their nets, pin our wings to our sides, club us into immobility, destroy our young in their nests . . . From far above, I see the stool pigeon, her eyelids sewn shut, her legs tied to a string, her wings fluttering like a beacon that draws us into the trap. We circle in one synchronized arc. Then I see that her eyes are free. They are blue and her hair bright as the sun. I try to warn the others, but I can not stop them, or myself. We land on a soft bed of pine needles, only to feel the crushing weight of the trappers' nets. They descend on us with their clubs, and I do not know if I am bird or man. Does it matter? The result is the same. I hear my skull crack and know I am robbed of the limitless sky. All that I might have been, the life that I might have lived, is as impossible to restore as it is to halt the inexorable extinction of the passenger pigeons of North America.

This dream of victimization and slaughter speaks to the defeatist in me, but I have another side, dark and volatile.

I remember an officer in my regiment, Emilio Maldonado, who used to beat his horse. The mare was submission itself. One day she crumpled under his whip and savage boots. I started to dismount, ready to kill Maldonado once and for all, except that the horse beat me to it. With a burst of energy that no one expected, the mare reared up on her hind legs. Moments later, Maldonado's brains were oozing out of his skull.

I am that horse.

Rodolfo has never understood that. When he returned to San Serafín a few days after his sham of an engagement party, he set out to goad me. Actually, it was perfectly clear to me even then why he was doing it. He had to vent his frustration. As Samuel and Eva were not in San Serafín just then, I happened to be the most readily available scapegoat. The cause of Rodolfo's anguish was plain enough. To italicize the contempt she felt toward my hapless brother, Isabel had locked herself in her room the moment she heard he was back. Her voluntary exile implied that she was prepared to starve to death if need be rather than speak to him.

That evening Rodolfo took his seat at the far end of the dinner table, placing himself opposite Mother. I headed for the middle of that long expanse. Rodolfo and I stared briefly at the empty place set for Isabel. Leaning back into the chair that Father used to occupy, he asked me with studied indifference and with the very same tilt of the head, "What's this I hear that you've resigned your commission?"

Mother was ladling soup from the tureen.

"He's only on leave, Rodolfo. Here, pass this to your brother."

She and I both had to stretch torso and arms to their physical limits so that I could take the steaming bowl and pass it down the table. I should have wondered where the servants had gone. What I really wanted to ask at that moment was, *why the devil do we continue to use the monster table when the three of us could eat more comfortably in the breakfast room?*

"From what Eva tells me, Captain Benjamín Nyman Vizcarra is on a rather extended leave," he persisted.

"What is he talking about?" Mother turned to me.

"I've resigned my commission. I'm done with the army."

For a few seconds, her soup spoon hovered like a hummingbird before a hibiscus blossom. Then Mother took a sip. "You should have told me sooner." She spoke with marked delicacy, and I knew I was in for it.

"I've been waiting for the right moment."

"Which by the blessed saints has finally arrived!" Rodolfo quipped, leaning back with exaggerated pleasantness. He patted that dapper moustache of his and smiled warning clouds. He looked the very image of Father, especially when the sun vanished from his eyes. "You have the right to quit, I suppose. But betraying your country is about as low a crime as I can think of."

And so the fight exploded. We didn't just argue about my intention to answer Madero's call to arms. We bellowed and slammed our fists on the table, rattling coffee cups and wine glasses.

"You're a goddamned traitor!" he yelled at me across the expanse of white linen and candlelight.

"Don't take the Lord's name in vain!" Mother aimed a finger at him.

"Who are you calling a traitor, goddamn you!" I jumped to my feet, scraping my chair noisily against the tile floor. Mother leaped up.

"Mind your tongue!" she snarled at both of us.

We ignored her. She might as well have been one of our unsmiling ancestors staring down at us from a gilt frame.

"If you *ever* call me a traitor again—"

"What? You think that because you wear epaulettes you're man enough to take me on?"

Rodolfo had jumped to his feet too. We were both ready to pummel each other right there on top of Mother's antique bone china. She beat us to the draw. As we glared across the chasm of irreconcilable politics, ready to tear each other apart, a coffee cup suddenly flew at Rodolfo, hitting him on the side of the head. A second one flew and struck me just above my right eye. Stunned, we turned to Mother, who was on her feet and was taking careful aim with a third cup. That one Rodolfo managed to dodge, but just barely.

"Enough!" she yelled. For good measure, Mother threw a saucer at Rodolfo, hitting him in the chest, and another at me. Both plates shattered on the unforgiving tiles. "Do I have to break every last one of them to restore peace in my own house? Is that the price?"

She scooped up the soup tureen that had been in the family for over two centuries. More to the point, it still held steaming soup. I intercepted her, reaching for it as she held it high above her right shoulder. "No, Mamá! We're done arguing!"

"I'm sorry, Mamá," Rodolfo muttered while rubbing his brow.

I anchored the tureen in a safe harbor—in front of my place setting, just out of her reach.

"Actually, I'm not hungry." I spoke lightly, as if breaking crockery on our heads were perfectly normal etiquette. "I need to set out early tomorrow, so I'll say good night." I bent to kiss her. She pulled back.

"Listen to me, Benjamín Nyman Vizcarra. I want to see you tomorrow before you ride out. Wake me, no matter how early it is. Don't you dare leave without saying goodbye."

"Of course not, Mamá. Good night."

I was packed by 5:30 the next morning. Packing was easy. I was only allowing myself one complete change of clothes; a sweater, since I know it can get cold at night in the deserts of Chihuahua; a wool blanket; two pairs of socks; my army boots; a wide-brimmed slouch hat; and of course my guns—a Winchester .30-30 and my pride, a 9-mm Luger that I won from a Bavarian in a poker game. I also packed a notebook and a small edition of Calderón de la Barca's metaphysical masterpiece, *Life Is a Dream*. As I think back on it, perhaps it wasn't so illogical to take that little drama with me to war, for wasn't it all a dream, that other life of mine?

Rodolfo stepped into my room. Thrusting both hands into his pockets, he rocked on his heels and quipped, "That's some aim Mother has! They might be able to use her up north!" Drawing closer, he studied the purple bruise above my brow. "She really nailed you."

I smiled. "And I know there's a goose egg under all that hair of yours."

"Yep! Right here!" He bent at the waist and showed me the spot.

He was all affability. I was just as eager to put our fight behind us. After all, there was no way of telling when I would be returning home or even *if* I would ever come home again. We shook hands and exchanged hearty embraces, thumping each other on the back. Then we stepped onto the upper veranda.

"I hate to have to wake Mamá."

"You'd better, if you cherish your life!"

We laughed. Then our eyes wandered to Isabel's door. We both knew it was useless to hope that it would open just then. Yet I could not bring myself to leave without a final glimpse of her. As if reading my thoughts, Rodolfo murmured, "I'll tell her you said goodbye—if she lets me say more than two words to her."

I nodded. We headed for Mother's room. Then he stopped me.

"Wait. There's something I'd like you to see before you leave."

"I really need to get going."

He lowered his voice. "I killed a snake in my bathroom."

Knowing Mother's fear of snakes, I also lowered my voice. "What kind of snake?"

"I don't know. A snake. You tell me. You're the naturalist."

I left my duffle bag on the veranda and propped the rifle against a chair. Rodolfo led the way into his bedroom. It was larger than the room that I shared with Samuel and overlooked the cane fields in the south.

"It's under the tub." Rodolfo pointed from the bedroom door.

I was only curious about snakes, not crazy about them. Yet I was not about to betray even the slightest hint of uneasiness. Flicking on the light, I stooped slightly. Nothing. I got down on my knees and peered under the club-footed tub. There was no bloody heap on the white tiles, nothing writhing. Then I checked under the sink, *in* the sink, in the wastebasket, behind the window curtains, everywhere.

"I hate to tell you, but I don't think you succeeded in killing it."

I stepped back into the bedroom, expecting to see him leaning against the door frame. The room was empty. Like the fool that I am, I got down on my knees and continued checking for the snake—under the bed, the bureau, the desk, the bookshelves, and both armchairs. I suspected nothing until I opened Rodolfo's wardrobe. A row of empty clothes hangers quivered as I slammed the door shut. I darted to the door and jangled the doorknob.

"Open up!" I called to him. "I'm locked in!"

"I know," he answered calmly from the other side.

I left the door and threw open the one window that faces the upper veranda. Like all the windows in the house, it was heavily barred. I was ready to curse Moors, Spaniards, and anyone else who ever dreamed up such infernal windows. I watched the bastard drop comfortably into a rawhide chair and prop his feet on an ottoman. I grabbed for him between the bars, but he was just out of my reach. In my frenzy, I even tried to thrust my head between the bars. Anything bigger than a cat would have found it challenging. Rodolfo's chair creaked as he settled in. Then he had the audacity to light up one of his cigars.

"All right. You've had your joke," I forced a laugh. "Now I need to say goodbye to Mother."

"A man with hepatitis needs lots of rest. Since it's highly contagious, we'll have to keep you in isolation while you convalesce. Mother will understand."

"Very funny. Now open the bloody door!"

"In about six months."

"You can't keep me here against my will!"

"Yes, I can."

The calmness of his tone chilled me.

"You can't watch me twenty-four hours a day!"

"True. But the servants and the armed guards that I pay can do it quite well."

"Some are loyal to me!"

"They're loyal to the man who pays them. That's me."

"I'll be missed! My friends will ask for me!"

He leaned back into the cushions and blew smoke rings. "No doubt they'll keep you in their prayers while you convalesce. Or I could simply explain to them our sad family history of insanity. It goes back several generations—we'll pin it on Father's side. Some of the Nyman are too religious for their own good; they simply crack under the strain. Others rant about becoming revolutionaries."

"Very clever! Now open the door before I wake the whole freaking house!"

I rattled the lock ferociously, thinking I could bully it open. It proved as solid and as unmovable as the walls of San Serafín. I ran to the outer windows. The two bedroom windows and the bathroom one were carved into the south wall of the property. They overlooked the fields. Since they were only two stories up from the ground, I judged that I could jump without killing myself. But like the veranda window, they wore the prison bars my ancestors had left for Rodolfo's use, damn them! I was trapped.

Then I remembered the obvious. Reaching into my holster, I drew out the Luger and sang out a warning. "Step aside! I'm going to shoot the lock off the door!"

I could smell his damned cigar. I listened closely, but he didn't move. "Rodolfo! I'll only warn you one more time! Step away from the door! I'm going to shoot!"

"That's going to be tough without ammunition."

It was only then that I looked down and realized that I was not even holding my own gun. I stared in sluggish disbelief. When I checked the cylinder, I found it as empty as my brother's wardrobe.

"I borrowed your Luger while you were asleep. Sorry that mine's so useless. Fortunately, you won't be needing it while you convalesce."

I flung the gun, madly hoping it would fly between the bars and slam him on the side of the head. It merely bounced against the bars with a crisp metallic ring. Grabbing the heavy desk chair,

I struck the door repeatedly. I yelled. I called him every obscenity army life had taught me and grew inventive. I threatened to kill him; I threatened to kill myself. It was the chair that finally gave up the ghost, falling apart in my hands. Exhausted, I sank to the floor and waited for my heart to stop pounding. Mother stood on the other side of the window.

"I appreciate what you're trying to do," she muttered to Rodolfo. She probably meant to whisper, but whispering is simply not among her many talents. "I just don't see how we can keep him locked up like a prisoner."

"We can and we shall," he answered in a clear voice that would have stood him well in a podium or a pulpit.

"But . . . how do we feed him? The moment we open the door, he'll bolt."

"Through the window."

"Mamá!" I held out both arms beseechingly. "Don't let him get away with this!"

"We can't just keep him prisoner, Rodolfo."

"Why not?"

"Mother's right!"

"You can pamper him all you want, Mamá. Have Bardomiana make all his favorite foods; make ample use of the wine cellar. Keep him well stocked with books, pens, and paper. You can write a book or two of poetry," he added cheerfully to me.

"I'll write your epitaph, *imbécil!*"

"But he would need exercise." Mother stroked her chin. I realized with mounting panic that she was actually considering the whole insane scheme.

"He can shove my bed to the far side of the room. That will give him plenty of room to run, to do jumping jacks, army push-ups, and whatever else he can concoct. That's why I gave up my room. It's bigger than—"

"Ah! Such largesse!" I laughed, if you can call a strangled sound a laugh.

"Trust me, Mamá. This will work. Instead of worrying about him disgracing the family and getting himself killed in the bargain, you can sit here on the veranda any time you choose and visit with him. He'll be *safe*."

"You're right."

"No! Mamá. Don't listen to him! I'll go out of my mind here!" I held out my arms to her again through the bars. "Please, Mamá!"

She took my right hand and brought the back of it to her cheek. Then she kissed it tenderly.

"Forgive me, my son. But this is where you must stay."

"Mother. I'm a man. For the love of God, don't treat me like a child."

She held my hand a moment longer. Then she walked away, her footsteps appallingly resolute.

I pulled back. I was reeling. "My own mother . . ." I muttered.

"Don't be hard on her—or me. It's for your own good, Benjamín."

"I'll tell you what's good for you!" I leaped at the window, making a last vain attempt to grab Rodolfo and strangle him. My hands flailed, but my rage tore into him like a peregrine falcon ripping a mouse open. "Stay the hell away from me! In the meantime, go castrate yourself so you don't father any more bastards like yourself!"

In a flash, he leaped out of the chair and reached for me, slamming my face against the bars. "If you ever talk that way about my children again, I'll kill you, right here in front of Mother if I have to!"

Isabel stepped out of her room just then. She paused, then hurried down the stairs. Rodolfo ran after her—giving me a second reason to hate him.

❖ *Sketch 10* ❖

PRISONER OF SAN SERAFÍN

I KNOW THERE are prisons of the mind. However, never underestimate the simple power of a physical prison, particularly the kind with stone walls a meter thick, bars in the windows, and locks forged in hell. My mother, God bless her, was my jailor and more formidable than all the guards of the Federal Penitentiary put together. She was the only one who had the key to Rodolfo's room. It was an oversized relic from the sixteenth century, an inimitable piece of iron that was cast back when Hernán Cortés was busy building his palace in Cuernavaca. The key dangled off the key chain that she attached to her belt and carried with her always. As I tortured myself at night trying to pick the lock with the distended tip of a coat hanger, I cursed the Aztec or Spanish son of a bitch who had fashioned such entrapment. In the end, my lock picking proved as futile as my efforts to talk Mother into giving me back my freedom.

She remained as immune to my careful arguments as to my ranting. Nothing deterred her from her self-appointed task: to save me from my wayward revolutionary impulses and from death in some scorpion-infested battlefield up north. I threatened to hate her for the rest of my life. She sat on the veranda outside my window, knitting needles clicking and clacking without missing a stitch.

"You are no mother of mine!" I declared with bitterness as real as the bars that separated us.

"I happen to know otherwise," she responded, calmly folding her needlework and putting it back in her knitting basket. "I was there when you came bawling into the world. You bawled then and you haven't stopped. Good night, son."

That was my first imprisonment. As prisons go, it was palatial. I suppose that's also true of this, my second incarceration. Mother is quite adept at making prisons almost pleasant. My "cell" in San Serafín had all the comforts of home, literally: oriental carpets on the tile floor, brocade curtains on the bed, comfortable armchairs, a desk wide as Lake Chapala, and a bookcase that housed my collections of prose, poetry, and ornithology. The "cell" came with a private bathroom where I could soak my restlessness in a deep bathtub with gardenia-scented soap. Rodolfo's room was so ample that I could exercise, running around to the point of exhaustion. Bardomiana, our old cook, inquired daily what I'd like to eat. She fortified me with her incomparable tortilla soup and birrias, the stewed lamb in chile sauce that I've loved since childhood. Added to that, she could cook chicken and beef in a thousand stunning varieties; even her rice and vegetable recipes were as varied as chile itself, and her desserts . . . how do I capture in mere words those astonishing textures, scents, and flavors? How do I begin? I had loved all of Bardomiana's cooking since I teethed as a toddler.

The only catch to my culinary feasts was that I could only be fed whatever could be passed between the bars of my window. The door was not to be opened until I died or the government crushed the revolution. So I had to eat many of my meals in clay mugs, which actually did nothing but enhance the flavor. In short, I was in a magnificent gilded cage, pampered and well fed.

But I could only see a fragment of the sky; I could only dream of riding my horse across open fields, and I could only wonder what was happening in the north of Mexico. Mother ordered that no one was to talk to me about the revolution.

In the early days of my captivity, I lamented liked Segismundo in his tower prison that birds and brute beasts had more freedom than I. "*Y teniendo yo más alma / tengo menos libertad?*" And having more soul, do I have less freedom? I also fretted that the revolution was happening without me, that I was missing the greatest adventure of my life. In truth, I care little about politics or social agendas. Like others, I simply wanted to shake off dictatorship—when in fact I was fighting a dictatorship right in San Serafín. Mother and I faced off almost daily. She would perch outside my prison window like a mother robin with gifts that I would spurn.

"Come now! Don't be obstinate, Benjamín!" she would croon good-naturedly as she offered me a miniature meat pie, passing it between the bars. "You and I both know that no one can outdo Bardomiana's gorditas. Eat them while they're hot."

I threw myself at her, with only the bars protecting her from my rage. God knows that I would not have touched a hair on her head. But I would have gladly pushed her aside and ridden out of her life.

"I'm not one of your damn birds!"

"Of course you're not."

"Then treat me like a man! Give me back my freedom!"

"I can't do that."

"Why the hell not?"

"Because I can't let you destroy yourself. You'll thank me someday when you're an old man and can reflect on how I saved you from yourself, from the errors of youth and pride. I love you, Benjamín, more than I—"

"You call that love—making me a prisoner?"

"Yes!" she answered with sudden ferocity. "Yes, I call it love, to be willing to endure your resentment when all I long to do is to embrace you! Yes, I call it love to do whatever it takes to keep you from making the most serious mistakes of your life!"

"They're *my* mistakes, Mother! Mine to make! Who are you to script my life for me? To decide for me how I am to live or not live my life?"

"I brought you into this world."

"Oh! So you're my creator now! Should I light votive candles and drop to my knees? What does my mighty creator want of me?"

"Only that you live a full and happy life."

"As scripted by you! But what if I don't want that life? What if I have my own ideas?"

Tears true as my rage misted her eyes and cheeks.

"Why can't you see that all of this is for your own sake, my child? I may be saving your very life—"

"By taking it away," I finished the sentence.

"How do I take away the life that I save?" she asked in exasperation.

"By strangling it with your own hands, by choking its freedom. Mother," I entreated more softly, "if you love me, please, please give me back my freedom!"

She drew closer. Her hand flew between two bars to my face, gently alighting on my left cheek. "If they killed you, my life would be over. I won't risk losing you."

I pulled back. "You have already."

We argued many times. It was a circular argument that always brought us to the same impasse. She would ensure my future happiness by denying me the freedom to jeopardize that happiness. She was God preventing evil, God forcing all creatures into line against their will.

I began to hate her, the mother I had loved in freedom. I was tormented. As Cadwallader Brentt's bones mended at the pace of a snail circumnavigating the globe, a worse torment became my constant companion. Jealousy. Isabel had made peace with Rodolfo. She had actually forgiven him and was wearing his well-washed ring again. Both kept their distance from me—Rodolfo because he had not yet forgiven what he considered my attack on his children, or, more likely, because he sensed my murderous resentment toward him. Isabel avoided me because Mother had made it clear that she would not tolerate impropriety in her own house, that it was not proper for an engaged woman to visit me unchaperoned.

"Why not?" I challenged Mother. "What possible impropriety can there be! What harm can I do anyone from my prison?"

"That's not the point."

What *was* the point? What was Mother afraid of—that I would fall as much under Isabel's spell as Rodolfo had? That I would fill the loneliness of my hours with dreams of her? Had she seen me watching Isabel? Did yearning fly like a scarlet-feathered bird, too bright to go unnoticed?

Isabel's room was directly opposite mine. I placed my armchair in front of the window so that I could see her the moment she stepped onto the dew-misted veranda. She would drink in the morning air, glance up at the sky, or down into the patio, or briefly across the crystalline span that separated us. It would happen with a hummingbird's quickness, a flash that sent my pulse racing. Then she would disappear down the stairs to get her grandfather's breakfast tray. During the week when Rodolfo was in Mexico City, she spent most of the day with the old man. The moment she stepped back onto the veranda, I would pretend to be reading. When she took a stroll in the garden, I imagined myself at her side, reciting poetry and mentoring her.

And I realized with a start that more than anything in the world, more than my determination to answer Madero's call to arms, I desperately yearned for Isabel Brentt to need me again. I yearned . . .

~

And here he stopped.

Need me! Who the hell needs me now? Prisoner 243 wondered as the sounds of a brawl in the courtyard reached him, raucous yet unimportant under the pummeling of the next question. *Of what use is my worthless life?*

The suspicion took root in him that his life was quite worthless; that rank and privilege were fragile, illusory things, and that nothing mattered so long as he could drink a gourd of El Brujo's *iskiate* and run with the morning wind. That was enough.

"Whatever is in this, I'll keep paying for the ingredients. You just go on making it!" Benjamín murmured as he handed back the gourd—a small vessel with a handle, all hand-hewn from a single piece of gnarled wood.

El Brujo carried it everywhere. After drinking the last of the *iskiate,* the shaman tucked the gourd under his belt and set off into the chill predawn. Halfway into the first lap, El Brujo let Benjamín catch up to him.

"I'm going home," the Tarahumara whispered. "Come with me."

Benjamín was too startled to speak. When they took the stairs to the second floor and were momentarily out of the direct sight of the guards, he whispered to the shaman, "How?"

"By climbing the cliff wall."

Arriving at the upper landing, they emerged again into the full view of the guards. The prisoners ran side by side along two of the three upper corridors that overlooked the courtyard they had just crossed.

"Sound out your laps!" El Brujo instructed as he sprinted toward a wall at the end of the corridor of his own cell block.

When he reached it, a wall that seemed no different than any of the others, the Tarahumara leaped up and slapped it with the flat of his hand. "One!" he sang out in the silence.

Startled, the sentries stopped talking. One of them unslung the rifle from his shoulder. Benjamín felt the hair stand up on the nape of his neck, but he imitated the shaman just the same, slapping his hand to the wall. "Two!"

"No. Count off your own laps," El Brujo muttered.

What the devil for? Benjamín bristled inwardly. What he really wanted to ask was, *Why are you trying to get us shot?* When they were under the temporary protection of the interior staircase again, El Brujo seemed to anticipate his skeptical question.

"To make toeholds."

"What toeholds?"

"So we can climb the cliff face."

Then the shaman was off again, his feet nearly silent as he ran barefoot. "Two!" El Brujo sang out as he slapped the wall. "Two!" his companion imitated, uneasily noting its height and merciless verticality. Back in the temporary cover of the stairwell, El Brujo came to a full stop. "Give me your hand!"

Benjamín extended his hand and felt a blunt object touch his palm. "What the hell?"

In slow stages, lap by lap, seventy-four of them that morning, El Brujo unveiled his plan. It was absurdly simple: to make two toeholds on one particular wall that had been cracked by the June 7 earthquake and its aftershocks and had not yet been repaired; to make tiny gouges in its pockmarked face, gouges in the same two spots by strapping a soup spoon to the inside of their right forearm, binding it tightly as if it were a splint for a broken limb, concealed under their long sleeves; to hit the wall hard in exactly those two spots, muffling the sound of metal striking plaster and brick by calling out the number of laps at the precise moment of contact; to go on making those miniscule dents for as long as it took—be it weeks or months. And then when the time was right, on some moonless, predawn run, to leap onto the wall and up onto the flat roof, and from there to propel down an outer wall of the prison with the rope that they would make for that purpose.

They knew that they would only have a minute, maybe two, before the guards started to miss them. With luck, the sentries might waste several minutes searching for them right there in the cell block, not yet willing to sound the alarm that would point to their own inefficiency. This would buy the prisoners precious time, enough to vanish into the city that was all around them and from there into the mountains.

This part of the plan, blending into the city, actually sounded feasible to Benjamín. Luckily, the penitentiary was in the seamy eastern side of town that he had come to know when sudden poverty had forced him and Isa to live there. He knew that they could more easily escape detection and apprehension in crowded streets, where thousands of people lived in shanties or slept on the ground, than in the well-groomed boulevards and parks of the city's western side. Since prisoners did not have to wear uniforms, that too would work in their favor, helping them to not stand out.

"I'll guide you out of the city," Benjamín whispered to El Brujo on a morning when the exhilaration of the run made it all seem plausible. "You guide me through your mountains and canyons."

And that, the shaman assured him, was the easy part—walking hundreds of kilometers through the sierras and into the Sierra Tarahumara, where no one would ever be able to track them.

Absurdly simple. Benjamín nodded. So simple it might just work. On bad days, however, when doubt jumped on his back and wore him down, he saw the futility of the whole venture and the inevitable retaliation.

"How much longer can we go on gouging the wall right under their noses? This is insane! If they don't shoot us in the back, they'll beat us to within an inch of our sorry lives! Forget it! I'm not risking it!"

"Come with me!"

"No, damn it!"

They had just reemerged onto the second floor. El Brujo suddenly bent forward in a spasm of pain.

"Brujo! What's wrong?"

The shaman clenched his teeth and clutched his chest. When he straightened, he limped to his cell. Benjamín stood in the corridor, unsure what to do next.

"Where's the witch doctor?" one of the guards yelled to him.

"I don't think he feels well."

"Then get back in your cell! Move it!"

A change came over El Brujo. When he refused to run the next day or to eat, Benjamín grew worried. Later in the day he visited him in his cramped cell. The sterility of the tiny space with its one cot and lack of bedding brought home the reality of prison life, the harshness from which his family's money spared him daily.

"Brujo—"

Crouching by the cot, he gazed into the Tarahumara's face. The blankness of the eyes, the sudden absence of will, tore into him.

"Brujo, you're going to see your wife and children soon! We can do this!"

When the shaman still didn't respond, Benjamín searched the clay pots in the room until he smelled the homemade *tesgüino*. Scooping some into the gourd, he crouched again by the man.

"Brujo! Get drunk with me!"

The brew dribbled down El Brujo's chin, his eyes stark sketches of a broken spirit. Benjamín was beside himself. "Brujo! Think of the canyons! Drink up!"

The liquor went untasted. Benjamín's head drooped.

"I don't have to." El Brujo spoke quietly. "I was just there."

❖ *Sketch 11* ❖

CHRISTMAS

BENJAMÍN CONTINUED TO doodle on the margins of his growing manuscript. He remembered the Christmas of 1910, more than a year and a half before, when he was a prisoner in his mother's house and Isabel filled his every waking thought. Reliving it, he sketched mating pairs of birds in the blank spaces between the words: mute swans—cob and pen affectionately rubbing heads; white ibises locked in tender embrace; ringed turtledoves whose sensuous, laughter-like joy he could almost hear.

～

Christmas was festive as ever in San Serafín and particularly miserable for me. I had to imagine most of it or see it in fragments from my "cell." I knew that the multicolored geraniums that normally framed the entire upper veranda had been replaced with poinsettias in ranks and uniform color; that servants had set up the crèche in the garden—not just the stable with the Holy Family, but Bethlehem in miniature, with people who were just like them: men and women who sold water in clay pots, bartered food and wares in shops and roadside stands, traveled on donkeys, dutifully paid taxes, and wisely stepped aside to let troops pass. I knew that the family chapel would be fragrant with flowers and draped in the colors of the Advent; that Samuel would be in fine form, offering the first of his Christmas masses here in our childhood home; that Bardomiana would be frying up the cinnamon and sugar *buñuelos* that she prepared every single Christmas. Right on cue, the dear old woman sent a plateful to me along with the hot chocolate that she had made by crushing cocoa beans and cinnamon sticks and whipping the milk into frothy foam with her *molinillo,* the wood-carved whisk that did sentry duty in her kitchen.

Early on Christmas Eve the children of the men and women who worked in the hacienda were invited into the courtyard. The patio, strung with paper lanterns and whimsical piñatas, resounded with their chatter. I knew the routine: the servants were lighting brightly decorated candles and splitting the children into two groups of singers—the holy couple and the uncooperative innkeepers. I listened as they sang responsively the traditional Posada songs, their birdlike voices chirping the story of Mary and Joseph's search for an inn. Then at last a compassionate soul threw open a door and sang joyously from within the house: *"En-tren san-tos pe-re-gri-nos, pe-re-gri-nos!"*—assuring Mary of a safe haven so that she could give birth to the Savior. It was unutterably sweet, even to my sour state of mind. When the singing was done, there was a brief, reverent hush—as if we were intent on holding on to a memory, old as time itself, that was quickly fading into the cool night air. When children and adults blew out their candles, the patio erupted into the raucous flutterings of an aviary. Eager faces looked up at the candy-laden piñatas.

With my fragmented view from the window, I could just see one of the piñatas, a whimsical bull with bright pink horns. When they lowered the rope so that the first blindfolded child could have a whack at it, the bull vanished from my sight. I continued to hear and to imagine what I could not see. But then, wasn't that what my life had been reduced to—then and even more so now? To crane my neck to see what is just beyond the borders of my frame? Eva and her effete Spanish count were also voyeurs of sorts, observing the revolution from the safety and comfort of their villa in Naples. My brothers, who in their own ways were just as removed from reality, came home for Christmas. In the spirit of the season, the family extended its largesse to the prisoner with a visit. They and Isabel gathered at my window on the veranda before going down to dinner. Isa was wearing the blue gown that she had worn at the Centennial Ball.

"You'll forgive me for not dressing for dinner," I glowered at Rodolfo, who in coat and tails always looked taller and handsomer than usual. He smiled.

Mamá reached into my cage. "Come here, son."

I hesitated before approaching the outstretched arms that penetrated between the bars. When she tried to caress my cheeks, I pulled away. I know I hurt her. I wanted to.

"Merry Christmas, son!" she murmured huskily.

"I'll come up right after dinner and sit with you," Samuel promised.

They all wished me the most apologetic "Merry Christmas" ever and retreated down the stairs without speaking, as if their silence were a balm they could offer me. As they retreated, Isa turned and gave me the only comfort I wanted—her smile.

To his infinite credit, Samuel expressed his disapproval of my imprisonment; he argued with Mother that she should treat me like a man and give me back my freedom. To his infinite discredit, he remained the voice of reason that does not act. By respecting Mother's authority, he acquiesced to what he did not condone. After dinner, they returned to my window. I would have slammed the shutters in their faces, but then I would not have been able to see Isabel. This was one of the rare times when Mother allowed her near me. Rodolfo stood guard with his arm around her slender waist.

"How is your grandfather, Miss Brentt?" I asked.

"He grows a little stronger every day. Thank you, Captain."

By all the saints! What nightingale has a more melodious voice? What instrument sings more brightly? Long after she withdrew to her room, I could hear echoes of those magical tones. I sat by the window hours into the night, trying to capture its essence in poetry, all ardent and ineffectual.

The festivities in the hacienda continued the following day. Mother was generous with our people—*la patrona generosa*. She always has been. However, given the tenor of the times, I think she doubled her efforts to remind our workers, with food, drink and entertainment, that they had good lives growing and harvesting our sugar and processing it in our mill. On Christmas Day, San Serafín hosted a series of *charreadas*. The *peones* loved these rodeos where they could compete against each other and impress the women with their equestrian feats. I should have been there, riding Falco, my Arabian, the noblest breed of horses in all of God's world. Falco had the balance that I would wish on all men: speed and spiritedness combined with gentleness and intelligence. I named him after the genus *falco*, those glorious diurnal birds of prey that soar in the great open spaces.

Standing at the window that overlooks the fields, I could hear the rodeo in progress. Falco must have heard it too. And though the grooms exercised him daily, did he paw the ground in his stall? Did he kick the sideboards with our shared impatience? *We should be there!* I railed inwardly. *Why am I locked away, punished in my room like some sullen schoolboy? Or like a criminal!* And yet, if I had had my freedom, I would have been far from the cheering crowds, fighting instead alongside men who wanted to revolutionize our stagnant political system.

Samuel understood how I felt about my imprisonment. Mother went a step further. She had guessed how I felt about Isabel. I'm certain of it. After the holiday, she became increasingly vigilant, never allowing her to draw near my window to deliver food or books or the chilled fruit drinks that Bardomiana made for me. I was off limits. Then one night as I tossed in bed, a sound, soft and distinct as the flutter of wings, drew my attention to the door. An envelope had been slipped under it. By the time I threw aside the bedcovers and hurried to the window, Isabel had rushed back to her side of the house. I remember hesitating as my hand reached for the nearest light switch. *No! Keep the light off! Don't draw Mother's attention!*

I went into the bathroom and shut the door tightly before turning on the light. Sitting on the edge of the claw-footed tub, I read Isabel's note over and over again. Even now I can record most of it from memory.

Dear Benjamin,

I can't begin to tell you how sorry I am that you have been made a prisoner in your own house. I know that Rodolfo and your mother mean well. Yet I strongly believe that no one should be denied the freedom to make choices, whether good ones or bad ones. What else makes us human but our ability to think rationally and to act freely?

I just wanted you to know that if there is any reasonable, nonviolent way in which I can help you obtain your freedom, I would be happy to assist you.

Isabel

PS. I thought you'd like to know that Madero's call to arms on November 20 has been heeded. Sadly, the word is that the revolution got off to a bad start in Puebla. All the rebels were killed. No one knows yet how many died. However, I heard Rodolfo and Samuel discussing that the northern states are ablaze with small rebellions. A revolutionary named Orozco has besieged and captured Ciudad Guerrero. Take heart!

Heart! I needed to rein it in as it galloped off in a burst of joy. The revolution could proceed without me. What did it matter? What was that to the passion I felt for Isa?—Ee-sah. My God! The very sound of her name still has the power to beguile me. Whether I whisper or shout it, I carry it with every breath of air.

Ee-sah . . . I answered her letter a dozen times before the words could tumble into a semblance of coherence. Later, when Jesusita, the twelve-year-old servant girl from the kitchen, delivered my morning coffee, I gave her a sealed envelope.

"Give this to Señorita Brentt." I smiled. "But don't let anyone, anyone at all, know about it. Slip it under her bedroom door when you know she's in there, or give it to her directly. Just remember, no one must see you do it."

Her eyes widened as she glanced over her shoulder toward Mother's bedroom. It stood at the end of my side of the veranda, to her right.

"I'll reward you with one peso in gold for every letter that you deliver. And when you grow up, the saints will reward you with fortune in love." I winked.

She smiled and slipped the letter into the pocket of her apron.

Late that night, when every bird in mother's aviary perched in immobility, when man and beast slipped into the netherworld of sleep, when desire crept into my bed with tenderness and eroticism, I suddenly sensed Isa's presence. I can't explain how or why. I simply knew that if I went to the window, I would see her materialize out of the dark night. I was naked, so I pulled the top sheet free and draped it around my waist. Moving with soft stealth, I approached the window.

She was there! Neither of us spoke. I reached for one of her hands and reverently brought it to my lips. When she did not pull back, I drew her toward me and into my kiss, kissing her with all the longing and passion of my soul. In spite of the bars, my arms were able to enfold her, to feel the smallness of her waist, the smoothness of her skin. We were defying them all—Rodolfo, who slept but a few doors away, and my mother, who has the hearing of the fiercest guard dog. We spoke in whispers that fluctuated between laughter and confession. My God! Even now, even now the memory leaves me breathless!

～

Benjamín pushed away from his desk, clutching his head with both hands.

Damn it! Have I learned nothing? Am I so dense that I would now go back to believing a boy's illusions about love? I am not that boy! I killed him one night in San Justín—with pride as my fists! I would not suffer the old man's scorn and mockery! I would not beg anymore! There is no love—only honor or dishonor! Honor, it's all that matters, all that is worth defending! By all the saints! Have I learned nothing since then? Why do I go on reliving the past in these pages, the duplicitous past! I'm like Prometheus tied to the rock. Whatever relief or pleasure I find in the telling, my flesh will be torn and my liver eaten again and again.

He paced in his cell. "Get out!" he yelled when El Vago stuck his head around the open door.

The bodyguard ducked away. Benjamín slammed the door. The utter pointlessness of it all jumped on his back, riding him as he paced.

I'm a damn Sisyphus dragging the rock of memory up a mountain! I don't want to remember any more!

He bent forward in a spasm of pain.

Yet you wouldn't let go of the rock. Not this one, the thought whispered alongside him, as if coming from someone else. *Cling to it and remember her!*

Benjamín straightened. In the stillness of his cell, he remembered the contours of her body pressed to his, all the nights and the mornings that he made love to her as he and his wife became one. And he knew then that if such a memory were a rock the size of the moon, he would go on pushing it up the face of the mountain, again and again, for the sheer joy of ecstasy remembered and relived.

He retrieved his pen.

~

There is an intoxication that comes from the touch of lovers' hands, their lips and their whispers. When the cover of darkness began to yield to the predawn light, Isa and I finally yielded to the sobriety that would save us. I watched her hurry back to her room on bare feet, her hair flowing behind her, cloud-fingers lit by orange-yellow sunbeams. She turned and smiled at me. Oh, Isa! What would I give to see that sweet, childlike smile of yours again! Tell me, can such radiance be dissimulated? Can a tarnished soul emit such light? I ached to call you back. But above all, I remember that I wanted you safe behind your door before the house stirred. I sighed with relief when it shut softly. Our secret was safe! No one had seen us!

Then I heard Mother's door close ever so softly.

 *Sketch 12*

FLIGHT

I LAY ON my bed, my thoughts throwing fireworks onto the high wooden beams. *She loves me!* The realization blasted artillery shells into the walls of my prison. Isabel Brentt loves me! I remembered a stanza from an old Spanish *villancico:*

> *Vuestros son mis ojos, Isabel;*
> *Vuestros son mis ojos*
> *Y mi corazón tambien.*

> Yours are my eyes, Isabel;
> Yours are my eyes
> And my heart too.

I fell asleep to its delicious cadence. When I awoke, I stepped into a day that stretched longer and slower than any day on earth. Rodolfo whisked Isabel away for hours. I wouldn't have been any less distressed if he had thrust me, tied and gagged, into a bog. *Is he kissing her? Is she pulling away or playing along with him, to allay suspicion? Last night did happen, didn't it? It wasn't some damnable dream, was it?* The possibility panicked me, though I laughed out loud and chased away the thought with vigorous jumping jacks. *Damn! What's keeping them? Where could he have taken her? Does she regret last night?*

They returned around two, just before lunch. It turns out that Mother had been with them the whole time—ever the vigilant chaperone. I could hear her giving orders downstairs. I stepped away from the window, straining to catch a glimpse of Isa without attracting Rodolfo's attention. Moments later she stood outside her grandfather's door with Rodolfo. I could see by his attire and by the leather skirt that she wore, a skirt Mother had loaned her from Eva's wardrobe, that they had all been riding. I watched Rodolfo cup her face with both hands as he bent to kiss her.

"I must see to my grandfather!" I heard her murmur. "I've neglected him all day."

"You've neglected me as well."

I was in hell.

I waited for Isabel long after the house had wrapped itself in a dark blanket. Nothing stirred but my yearning. Well into the night, I finally went to bed. *Perhaps she thinks it's too dangerous to come to me while Rodolfo is here. He'll leave tomorrow morning. Then we'll both feel freer.* With freedom in my thoughts, I fell asleep and had one of the most vivid dreams of my life.

I dreamed that I had let myself into Mother's aviary. I could see the dark silhouettes of birds on their perches, smell the moist earth of Morelos, feel the cool smoothness of the cage bars, taste the sticky sweetness of oranges split open by eager beaks. In the darkness, I could not distinguish one bird from another, only that they seemed to be roosting in pairs. I made out a solitary form on the highest limb of the aviary's tree—the resplendent quetzal—the last of the trogons in the aviary. I held out my arm. Nothing stirred. I waited, arm bent slightly at the elbow and parallel to the ground. Then I heard the trogon spread its wings, wings black as obsidian with soft metallic-green coverts; it glided toward me, its breast feathers red as blood, its impos-

sibly long tail delicately fluttering in emerald splendor. For a
moment, the quetzal hovered like a hummingbird close to my
face, its sharp beak almost touching the tip of my nose. Then it
landed on my forearm. Its first and second toes pointed back-
ward in unique trogon fashion. I stroked its breast in one gentle
motion.

Instantly, the trogon sank its feet into my flesh as if razors
were strapped to them. Startled, I felt myself sucked into a tight
darkness. I became a man trapped in his mother's womb. My
knees were drawn up to my chin. My arms were tightly pinned to
my sides. I thrashed and kicked. My body curled up tighter. Feet
became clawed; arms feathered. And I was a bird rolled up inside
an egg, beak battering the wall, limbs moist and quivering to be
released—released by wings created to vault the jungle's highest
treetops. I worked my beak in a frenzy. A hole in the egg showed
me a green forest. I pecked away from inside my prison, but I
could not make the hole any bigger than the eye that strained to
see the world.

My God! I'm *the trogon!*

What have I ever been to her but one of her exotic birds?

"Benjamín! Wake up! Wake up!"

I sat up startled, a thin film of sweat on my face. A dark form
stood at the foot of the bed.

"Shh!" she whispered. "Get up. Don't turn on the light."

"Mamá? What's wrong?"

"Shh! You'll wake Rodolfo!" she hissed as she closed the
wooden shutters on all the windows in my room. Only then did
she turn on the light. I squinted. When I could focus, I saw her
watching me intently.

"What's wrong?" I asked a second time.

"I'm setting you free." She spoke the words with a softness
and a firmness at odds with each other. "Go join your revolution
if you must."

I started toward her, to hug her. She drew back.

"I'm still against your going. But Samuel is right. You're a man now. So get dressed and pack quickly. I've had Falco saddled. He'll be waiting by the front gate. Here is money for your trip. Rodolfo has your guns, so you'll have to make do with my revolver."

I embraced her, whether she wanted to be hugged or not. She seemed to hesitate. Then I felt her arms enfold me with fierce tenderness.

"Thank you, Mamá!"

When I released her, I could see that she was fighting back tears.

"You are my favorite, Benjamín. If you let yourself get killed, my life is over. Now go! I won't see you out. Just go quickly!"

She shut off the light and left before I could kiss her again.

Moments later I stood by the front gate, one foot in the stirrup. Falco's ears were pointed sharply upward and his nostrils flared, as if he knew we were war bound. Or perhaps he was simply responding to the incongruity of being saddled in the middle of the night. Yet I could not make myself mount him. If there are precise moments that determine the course of a person's life, moments we can pinpoint decisively, this was one.

"I'll be back," I muttered to the groom as I threw the reins to him.

I ran back across patios, rooms, and stairs, up to Isa's room. I let myself in without knocking. I could see in the moonlight that she was in bed. I approached soundlessly. Sitting on the edge of the bed, I pressed a finger to her lips.

"It's me!" I whispered as she pulled back. "I've come to say goodbye. My mother has released me. I couldn't leave without seeing you one more time."

She flung her arms around my neck and kissed me. And I felt the marvelous contour of her breasts against my chest—no iron bars pressed between us. In seconds I was stretched on top of her, my arms enfolding her, my mouth devouring her.

"Isa, will you wait for me?"

"You know I will," she answered, panting as if she were running.

Even as I kissed her again, my fear stumbled across Rodolfo.

"Come with me, Isa! Tonight!"

"Tonight?"

I could feel her body trembling.

"Yes, tonight! Marry me!"

"How?"

"Samuel! Samuel can marry us. Be my wife!"

She giggled, girlishly happy. "What shall I bring?"

"Nothing. Leave your trunk." I kissed her again and again. "Give me the joy of buying everything for you from now on!"

I waited outside her door while she dressed. Actually, I withdrew into the shadows just beyond her end of the veranda. When she stepped out, she was dressed in riding clothes. For luggage she simply carried a medium-sized bundle in her arms. I realized later that it was a pillowcase stuffed with a few possessions. I carried it for her and hurried her along. My nerves were on edge by now. I expected Rodolfo to throw open the door, my own Luger loaded and pressed to my head. Time was running out. As if to test my fortitude, Isa stepped into her grandfather's room, and what could I do but follow? He was snoring loudly. She shook him.

"Cadwally! Wake up!" she murmured into the silver darkness. "Wake up, dear."

I heard the bed sag ever so slightly as she sat near him and cradled one of his hands.

"Isabel? What's wrong?"

"Shsh! Benjamín and I are running away. We're eloping! And more than anything, I want your blessing."

Even with only the moon for lighting, I knew the old man was frightened.

"Mr. Brentt, I swear to you by the family that I love, that I shall marry your granddaughter this very night, and that I shall honor and cherish her all the days of my life."

I mounted Falco with Isa securely seated in front of me. My arms encircled her as I took the reins from the groom. I nodded and he opened the gate. No one tried to stop us. Mother had obviously alerted the guards that they were to let me pass. They stepped aside. Men who walked grimly with rifles slung over their shoulders smiled knowingly. One released a laugh into the silence. I smiled and tapped a finger to my lips. Silence, boys! One of the men saluted me. Then the great gate swung open, releasing Isa and me into a night that was the very essence of poetry.

More than the moon, it was the girl in my arms who lit the way. With my lips pressed to her hair, a canopy replete with stars, and a surefooted horse, I felt myself happier than I had ever been in my entire life. I would willingly double my prison term if I could go back and relive that one night again! Where was her treachery then? Isa had nothing to gain by running away with me. Nothing! She would have been infinitely better off as the wife of Rodolfo Nyman, who at least had property of his own and stability. What did I have? An army commission I had thrown away and the vague dream of fighting in the revolution! Why do I persist—

～

Benjamín felt the old demon spring onto his back and shook it off.

Just finish the thing, Benjamín told himself. *Don't think beyond that!*

He crossed out the unfinished question and forced himself forward, determined to see his Edenic story to the end, fall and all.

～

We reached the tiny village of San Gabrielín well before dawn. Though I had never been to Samuel's house, I nudged Falco straight to it. There was no mistaking it. In the whole miserable village there were only two buildings worthy of habitation—one for God, the other for the son of Manuela Vizcarra de Nyman. Mother had poured a small fortune into repairing both.

"We're here!" I dismounted, then helped Isa down. My heart was racing.

This is it! We're getting married, whether they like it or not!

I savored the taste of triumph. We had outwitted them all. Yet looking back, shouldn't we have been apprehensive about our impulsiveness? I was about to take on the responsibility of a wife, I who had nothing but bravura. Rodolfo would have given her a life of ease. By choosing me over him, she was about to tie herself to a man with no better prospects than to be a revolutionist. It was insane, but we were insanely happy.

A light breeze blew from the west. I drew her to me and kissed her in the dappled, swaying moonlight. Full of joyous anticipation, I held her close even as I rapped on Samuel's door.

He refused to marry us.

Sketch 13

THE LEAP

"I'm sorry." My brother was all frown lines and regret. "I can't. Isabel is not Catholic."

"Then make her one!"

"It isn't that simple. There are classes she would need to—"

"We don't have *time* for that rot!"

Isabel stopped me with a light touch of her hand on my arm.

"Father, can two Christians marry each other?" she asked the good priest.

What must Samuel have thought as he gazed into those earnest eyes of hers? "Yes, of course."

"I'm a Christian. I believe in our Lord Jesus Christ with all my heart."

"Will you promise to raise your children in the Catholic Church?"

"I promise to raise them to know and to love the Lord Jesus Christ."

"There!" I jumped up. "Are you satisfied now? That's more than *I* would ever promise!"

Samuel was in agony. "I'm sorry! I *wish* with all my heart that I could help you."

I was ready to throttle him.

"You wouldn't hesitate to marry me to whatever Catholic woman I brought before you!" I railed. "Even a whore would do so long as she had been baptized Roman Catholic, is that it?"

Samuel paced. Seminary had not prepared him for such dilemmas. He was still new at the game. Perhaps he was searching his memory for a loophole in the rules. Or maybe he was considering that if he didn't marry us, Isabel's reputation would be ruined, and that such a calamity would rest as much on his shoulders as on hers. Or maybe he could not refute the power of the truth that she spoke so simply.

"Marriage is a serious step," he insisted to both of us. "Are you ready to be joined to each other with bonds that cannot be broken by anything but death?"

"A good marriage is eternal, Father. It does not end with death."

Samuel and I were both startled. I now realize that Isa was speaking from the Swedenborgian conviction that marriage constitutes the very heart of heaven, that angels are men and women who love with all the spirituality of heaven and the physicality of earth. I had only to gaze at her to want to believe it. Samuel, on the other hand, was probably struggling theologically. I didn't want him getting mired in that quicksand.

"So you see how very serious we are about this marriage!" I hastened him along. "We are as committed as two people can be!"

"You realize that we would be breaking the law—civil and ecclesiastical. Isabel, I must warn you for your own protection that this ceremony is not legally binding without a civil marriage. *That* is supposed to be the first step."

I clapped him on the shoulder. "We'll go straight to the nearest justice of the peace as soon as we're clear of Cuernavaca. I promise!"

Samuel ignored me. All his attention was on the young woman whom he was trying to save.

"Understand, Isabel, that you will be the object of scandal if you do not see this through to its legal conclusion. We're proceeding in the wrong order!"

"But, Father, doesn't the Lord teach us to act first from spirit and then to proceed from there?" she answered with that open, childlike smile of hers, so guileless and trusting that even now—

⁓

Benjamín Nyman remembered the day she visited him in the penitentiary: how she hurried toward him with that same glorious smile of hers; how he drove it from her face, from her eyes; how he attacked and threatened to murder her when he got out; how he silenced her protests with hands murderously wrapped around her throat without letting her speak in her defense. Not a single word.

She's innocent! The truth spoke plainly. *My God! What have I done? What have I done?*

The weight of his guilt crumpled him. Hanging his head, he sobbed his remorse aloud, his shoulders heaving, his voice rising and falling in great swells.

Oh, Isa, forgive me! Please forgive me! Father, Father, forgive me! Waves of despair slammed into him again and again throughout the night.

When the guard opened the cell door in the morning, the prisoner, still fully dressed, was sleeping on top of his bed coverings. When Benjamín didn't turn up for their run, El Brujo came looking for him. He held out the usual gourd of *iskiate*. Benjamín waved him away. That day he neither ran nor ate nor stirred from his bed. Mangel wanted to call the physician.

"No! Just leave me alone! Stay the hell away!"

Later that afternoon El Brujo entered on quiet feet. "*Norawa.*" He proffered the Tarahumara word for friend. "I've brought you some *tesgüino*. It will soothe the pain for a while."

The *tesgüino* did more than that. It got the sufferer so thoroughly drunk that he was able to sleep a straight twenty-three hours that day. A couple of days later a gourd of *iskiate* spurred

Benjamín once again into the chill air for two hours of running and gouging the pockmarked wall just enough for a toehold. Day after day, exertion reshaped his remorse into something unexpected. Or perhaps it was both remorse and exertion together that acted like chisels on a block of formless marble, gradually releasing the form of a man newly cut from rock. They sanded down the crude edges, deftly redefining the contours of body and soul. Regret polished his sadness into empathy for his fellow inmates. Running breathed new life into him. Benjamín Nyman returned to his writing, feeling at times something akin to joy.

⁓

The wedding was simple and glorious for its simplicity. Samuel rousted up some of his parishioners and the Spanish couple who ran the only grocery store in town. When he explained to the grocers that circumstances had forced us to elope, they were more than willing to be our *padrinos*—the requisite godparents. The señora took Isabel into her house. When they emerged a few minutes later, Isabel was still in her riding habit, but she was wearing a white mantilla that the señora had lent her. The veil was long and fell in graceful folds down her back. I offered her my arm and fell in step behind Samuel. The sleepy wedding guests followed us. When we reached the door of the church, I broke off several sprigs of *flor de noche* for my bride. What more appropriate flower than one that blooms only after nightfall? She accepted it and paid me amply with a smile that is light itself. And there, on January 10, 1911, in a church with strangers for godparents and the humblest of Indians for guests, I married Isabel Brentt, the single greatest gift of my life.

If a stray bullet had struck me dead there and then, my life would have felt complete. Miraculous. Yet even greater miracles lay ahead. Not just the passion of a man and a woman coming together at last, exuberantly exploring the topography of each other's bodies, but the joy of sharing even the simplest of pleasures. Waking up in each other's arms; rediscovering the quiet drama of sunrises and sunsets; drinking the poetry of a lover's touch and shared secrets; enjoying meals where you hardly notice what you eat, being far more intent on each other's every word, every glance. *Dios Santo!* I can't believe in you on my own. I can't rise above my slavish skepticism. But Isa makes you seem plausible. I knew it then and even now.

So I'll write my Edenic fable, but without the Voltairian cynicism that I had intended. The gullible Candide may have achieved an empty victory at the end, but mine was real and the prize priceless! Whatever blunders I have committed and continue to commit, this much I know. I was loved by an angel. I held her in my arms. And I drove her away, creature of the abyss that I am! Yet I return to the memory of our wedding with nothing but wonder and gratitude.

Something else comes back to me: a flash of intuition that I had while observing Samuel performing the familiar sacrament of marriage. For the first time in my life I sensed majesty in the liturgical Latin and in every aspect of the ritual. Watching my twin, that near-perfect mirror of myself, I became two men at the same time: what Isabel would call a natural man—one who only sees the world around him and cares nothing for the next—and a spiritual man. Moved by the intensity of my brother's devotion, I realized with a start that not only did he believe he was in the presence of God, but that perhaps we all were. I saw in Samuel's demeanor, in his total absorption, the meagerness of my spirit and the amplitude of his. Through him I sensed all that I could be and yearned to be for Isabel's sake. When Samuel blessed us, I channeled that yearning into the kiss that proclaimed us husband and wife, no longer two but one.

For you, Isa, I'll be that better man, I vowed silently then, and I do so again from this cell, Isa. If you and God give me one more chance, I can be that man!

Return with me in memory to that church, Isa! Can you see the gilt and the frescoes, the richly-clothed statues and the candle glow? Can you see the faces of the humble campesinos who left the comfort of their dreams to see ours begin? Arm in arm, we walked down the aisle. On the church steps no one threw rice at us. I suspect it had already become too precious a commodity to waste, especially on two runaways. However, those who had witnessed the ceremony clustered around us with smiles and the laughter of shared joy. We exchanged hearty embraces with humble peasants and the two grocers, hugging each as if we were closest friends.

In my state of mind, I felt nothing but love for them. And they—God bless every last one of them—lit up the night for us with their candles and goodwill. What is it about weddings that has this effect on people who would normally ignore one another? Did they respond to us out of love for their priest? Or did they feel drawn to the ageless drama of a young couple eloping? They would have wakened the village if we had allowed it, and they would have pooled their food to give us as much of a wedding feast as they could afford. They were kindness itself, our people of Morelos. Expediency demanded that we forego all festivities. I thanked them sincerely and made money gifts, which they refused.

"No, please! It would give my wife and me—" Your eyes met mine, and I repeated myself for the sheer joy of hearing that one word. "It would give my *wife* and me great pleasure if you would do us the honor of accepting these gifts. We would have invited you as our guests to a wedding feast if we did not have to escape like thieves in the night! So please, do us the honor of accepting this small token of our appreciation."

They accepted almost reluctantly the gold coins that I pressed into their hands. The men clutched their straw hats to their chest in a gesture of respect. The women called upon the Virgin to bless us with many healthy children. Again, the magnificent power of language! Their blessings on the church steps gave reality to our nascent marriage. Their words made it real. You and I were married! Married!

All right, I'll go back to a proper first-person narrative, since that is how I began my tale! Let me tell you the rest of the story, my love. True, it abounds with conflict, but it need not end sadly. We have choice even within the strictures of prison walls. We have a choice, Isa.

The guests returned to their homes. We followed Samuel back to his house. Our wedding reception consisted of a glass of sherry in his study. It was there that I was attacked by a sense of urgency that was as visceral as hunger pangs.

"We've got to go now," I announced before my bride could finish her sherry.

"Go? Go where?" Samuel looked blank.

"To Cuernavaca. We need to be on the morning train. With a little luck, we'll be in Mexico City before Rodolfo realizes what's happened. Then we'll head north to Chihuahua."

"Why Chihuahua?"

How can you be so dense? I wanted to ask.

"We're joining the revolution!" Isabel told him, her face glowing like candlelight.

"What?" Samuel turned on me. "Are you out of you mind? You can't take your wife to war!"

"I'll protect her." I put my arm around Isabel as if to demonstrate the point. All the while my doubts grew at the pace of Jack's overzealous beanstalk.

"It's all right, Samuel. I'm not afraid," Isabel murmured happily.

"We need to go now."

"The roads are not safe these days, especially after dark! Your getting here safely is a miracle. But miracles are a gift from God, not something we can have on demand."

We weren't swayed.

"Please don't risk it!" Samuel tried again. "Stay here tonight. We'll figure something out in the morning—"

"No. We've got to put more distance between Rodolfo and us."

"It's the middle of the night. Your horse will stumble—"

"Get your head out of your missal, padre. There's a full moon out. You can read by it!" I gathered up our few belongings. "Thank you, Samuel!"

"I'm telling you, it's dangerous!" Samuel blocked the door.

"Not nearly as dangerous as Rodolfo and me shooting it out in the morning."

"You're being absurd."

"Make no mistake about it. If he tries to stop us, and he will, one of us will die. So we're leaving. Now."

Samuel sighed and stepped aside.

He was right, damn it! What is it about saints in training? Are they given brief flashes of foreknowledge to humble the rest of us? Or is someone like Samuel just maddeningly more sensible than I'll ever be? We had just reached the outskirts of the Xochimancas hacienda when riders appeared out of the shadows and surrounded us. Falco skittered nervously from side to side. I drew my gun. I had the impression that they were initially as startled as we were. However, their ten or twelve guns calmed them considerably.

"Where are you headed?" one of the gunmen demanded.

"Cuernavaca," I answered as calmly as I could.

"Hand over the gun."

They drew closer. As I could not hope to hold off all of them, I aimed my gun at one specific man. Even now I'm not certain how I knew that he was the leader. It worked. It stopped the others. The standoff continued for minutes that seemed hours. The leader put away his gun. I could see in the moonlight that he was a youngish man, maybe in his thirties. He had the casual stance of an accomplished horseman.

"Where are you going at this hour?" he asked calmly.

"To join the revolution."

"The revolution my ass!" someone heckled.

They laughed.

"Get his gun, Emiliano," one of the men insisted.

"Seeing that you're outnumbered, we'll need to relieve you of your gun and of your horse," the leader observed.

Before I could respond, Isa spoke up. Her voice was like a little nightjar's among these guttural whip-poor-wills. "Please. We just got married an hour ago and need to get away while we can."

The leader drew closer in spite of my gun. He studied Isabel for a moment. Doffing his hat, he smiled, "Then allow me to congratulate you both! Put away your guns, boys!"

"Thank you." She smiled. I felt the tension in her body relax, but I was not about to be duped at her expense.

"As a wedding present, please allow us to escort you to Cuernavaca," the leader offered with maddening gallantry.

"Thank you, but that won't be necessary," I spoke with studied calm.

"I insist. The roads are full of marauders."

I tightened my grip on my revolver. "How do I know we can trust you?"

"Because I give you my word." The man must have understood my dilemma and added, "Emiliano Zapata is always true to his word!"

If he had pledged anything but his honor, I would have been forced to die fighting to save Isa from them. Clearly, our wedding night was not going as expected. But then, is anything ever quite as we imagine it? Here I was, the wayward son of a powerful and hated plantation owner, being escorted by the very man who was soon to wage war against my family and others like us. I hear even in this prison that hostilities have erupted again, that haciendas and towns are being burned to the ground, plantation administrators nailed to doors, rebels and Federals alike strung on trees and telegraph poles. But that night gallantry still traveled our nation's roads. I holstered my gun. What choice did I have? We traveled together in silence. When we saw the spires of the cathedral of Cuernavaca, the sky was suffused with an orange-pink tint that would have pleased Cadwallader's garish taste. Our escorts left us in the outskirts of town. Zapata touched two fingers to the brim of his hat in deference to Isa. Then he and the other horsemen rode off.

We were alone. I released my tension.

"Samuel's right! I can't take you with me! You've got to stay here with your grandfather where you'll be safe."

Isa turned to face me. Before I could say another word, she pressed her lips to mine. If I had seen all that lay ahead of us—love, adventure, murder, imprisonment, and despair—if I had glimpsed even the shadow of the monster that my passion for her would unleash, or if I had remembered the garden of my childhood with the clarity of scent or taste, I might have been able to stop it all, to gallop back to the safety of San Serafín with her in my arms, whether Rodolfo took her from me or not. But it was too late. I had tasted the fruit—not just of her lips, but of freedom. The church got it wrong, it seems to me. Is it really a sorrow that humanity lost the garden through sin? How else are we to grow and learn? A child can trade the terror of the unknown for the security of its mother's arms, content to remain there. But can the adolescent? The adult?

I kissed her as if I knew all that we were trading. Perhaps I sensed that even if I had known where it would all lead, I still would have chosen to leave paradise—as energetically as a child breaking free from the confinement of the womb. Or perhaps I had already sensed in Isa's arms that paradise is not a geographical place and never had been. Even now, I would change nothing.

Together, we boarded the morning train and headed for the war.

Sketch 14

LOVE AND WAR

CHANGING TRAINS IN Mexico City, we headed north to Querétaro, stopping there only long enough for a civil marriage. Two
days later we boarded another train and headed deep into the
sierras—north, ever north. We could have continued all the
way to Chihuahua to find Madero and his insurgents, but I was
far more interested in celebrating our nuptials. We got off in
the pink city of Zacatecas, that gem of colonial Spain. In case
Rodolfo were to feel honor bound to follow us there and shoot
me, we had to keep our whereabouts secret. Staying in Zacatecas could have been problematic. Eva and her Spanish fop of a
husband were normally there that time of year. They lived in a
fortress of a mansion that was almost as grim as San Justín. From
its lofty heights Pancho Comardo played at being a silver mag-
nate. Technically, he was in charge of administering the mines.
For this, Father allotted him a generous portion of the profits.
Since Comardo was savvy enough to hire a more capable administrator, he and Eva were free to live in style in Europe several
months of the year.

Comardo's presumed ownership of the mines also allowed
him to throw his weight around. Everyone knew him in Zacate-

cas. No one knew me. Even so, we would have needed to exercise much more caution had he been there. Eva would have posed no threat to us, but I could easily picture Pancho Comardo sending Rodolfo a telegram, just out of spite. Fortunately, Comardo was still cowering in Europe with his family, neither championing nor fighting against the revolution, merely keeping his thick neck safe. So we too were safe. I could treat Isa and me to the best suite in town, to candlelit dinners, and to walks along the city's terraced streets for one week, one perfect week.

After that we boarded yet another train and continued northward. As I was not about to put my wife in harm's way, I found lodgings for her with the family of a friend of mine whom I could trust, and thus began the first of several separations. I pressed on alone, catching up at last with Madero and his insurgents. I had made it! I was in the revolution! Yet all that I now wanted was to be with Isa. I considered defecting—all the more so when I had my first look around camp.

This was no professional army but the most motley assortment: shopkeepers hefting muskets from the colonial era, Yaqui Indians armed with prehistoric bows and arrows, school teachers and clerks shouldering fowling pieces, peasants wielding pitchforks and machetes, and city dandies fastidiously shining their shoes almost as often as they polished up old dueling pistols. There were almost as many women in the camp. The *soldadera,* a soldier's wife or woman, tended to be the most selfless of her gender. She was generally a poor woman rich in courage, whether her man fought for the Federal Army or the revolution. She suffered all the privations of camp life and more. A *soldadera* cooked for her man, cleaned his gun, tended to his needs and those of her children, nursed him if he was wounded, and buried him if he was killed. Some wore trousers and fought alongside the men. If Isa had seen them earlier, she would have insisted on joining their ranks, content to haul water from a river and cook my meals like any one of them or to fight alongside me. I couldn't have that. This was no life for any woman, least of all for my Isabel. So we endured our separations and feasted on those brief interludes when I could get away and find her, find her and love her.

The revolutionary army was the most disparate and pathetically unprepared group ever assembled. However, we were united in a common purpose: to end dictatorship in Mexico. I caught their fervor and forgot about defecting. Foreigners who were fired up by idealism or the simple desire for adventure flocked to us, too. I remember Americans too numerous to mention. They came to us—not just from Texas and Arizona—but from Oklahoma, California, Minnesota, New York, and Massachusetts. I remember Germans like Oberbuscher and Lieber. Then there was Guiseppi Garibaldi, grandson of Italy's great liberator. Garibaldi and I discovered we could talk about war and poetry. With his perfect Oxford English and urbane manners, he made me think of Rodolfo.

And what of the man who started the whole thing? How do I describe Francisco Madero? He was the most unlikely of revolutionaries. When I finally met the great man, I was startled not only by his shortness, though I suspect historians will bill him as a giant, but by his gentlemanly demeanor. He had more of the well-stocked library to him than of the battlefield. Yet there's no denying that he was brave—no armchair general— and ethical to a fault, this son of the mighty Madero clan. He was a magnet, drawing to him the best of idealists and the worst of scoundrels—educated men like Eduardo Hay and crude cattle rustlers like Pancho Villa. But in my memory, the one that tops them all as scoundrel and revolutionary was Oscar Creighton. He had joined Madero just days before I did and quickly earned the nickname "The Dynamite Devil." Creighton was a wild man with a propensity for blowing up trains and bridges. He was fearless to the point of recklessness, but he got the job done. He also got himself killed that April. I read later that spring that his real name was Oscar Wheelock, and that he was wanted in the United States for bank robbery and embezzlement.

Into this wild mix were a few professional soldiers like me—men whose political idealism had made it impossible for them to continue in the Federal Army. It fell to us to try to turn the eager recruits into soldiers. When Madero was finally able to purchase American rifles, we began to look like an army. But could we behave like a disciplined one when the time came? I had serious doubts, yet I felt the old ardor burn in me: to free my country from tyranny, to die willingly for so noble a cause. *Dios Santo!* Was it only a year and a half ago that I was riding high on the crest of a nascent revolution, and that I was loved by the most wonderful woman in Mexico? How did I fall so quickly from those heady days of hope to the hopeless disgrace of this incarceration? How did I stray so far from the man I yearned to be?

~

During their morning run, El Brujo came up silently alongside Benjamín.

"In twelve days, no moon," he whispered as he sprinted ahead.

Then I only have ten or eleven days to finish the book! It's got to go out at least twenty-four hours before the escape.

Prisoner 243 knew he could not go to Cuernavaca to search for Isabel and plead his case with her. The police would easily track him there. Nor could he risk returning to San Serafín, which would also be targeted by the authorities. Instead, he would have to go north into the Copper Canyons with El Brujo and eventually to the United States. When he was safe, he could contact Isabel, but until then the memoir would have to speak for him.

On his runs Benjamín sometimes worked out the details for their escape: clothes for the arduous trek, money, false names, and any number of evasion tactics. Most of the time, however, he wrote mental drafts of the book and of the letter to Isabel that he intended to insert in the manuscript. Running. Composing.

Running. Escaping. Yet none of it meant anything to him if he failed to win her back.

She has every right to reject me, he reflected.

Yes, but she has an angelic nature and knows how to forgive.

Don't canonize her. She's a woman with a woman's enormous capacity to resent and to punish, his skepticism countered.

Still, he allowed himself to hope and to envision life outside the walls of the penitentiary, life in a small American city where they could begin again. He could work as a journalist. Or maybe he could work part-time and study ornithology as she had once suggested to him, back when despair over their financial ruin had robbed him of imagination. Now he let his imagination gallop unsaddled. He would let Isabel work as a teacher since she wanted to so much, at least until their first child came along, a little girl with Isa's blue eyes. He would rent a small house with a garden for them. He would embrace a life of hard work and simple joys and live with a grateful heart.

When he wasn't running and dreaming, he was working on the book, shaping from the past the man he had been, was now, and longed to become. Initially, he had opted to write it in English simply to safeguard his privacy. The last thing he wanted was for Mangel or one of the guards to read his most personal thoughts. Yet with each passing day, Benjamín realized that he had been writing it for Isabel all along, long before his turning point in the thirteenth sketch. Rereading "The Leap," he saw its flaws—the abrupt shift in narrative voice when his longing broke loose and he addressed her directly.

"What are you writing, boss?" Mangel asked him as he quietly stepped up behind him.

Benjamín jumped. "Damn it, Mangel! Don't walk up on a man like that!'

"Sorry, Captain. I'm just curious."

Benjamín pointed to an open book on his desk as he returned to his work.

"Birds. I'm writing about the ornithology of Morelos."

Mangel ignored the book, craning his neck for a look at the manuscript in progress. He mouthed a word silently and screwed up his face.

"It's in English." Benjamín spoke without looking up. "I've got to send this to an editor in New York in a week or so. Now get out of here and let a man work."

"Will it be published here in Mexico?"

"No."

From that day Benjamín doubled his efforts to sketch birds, inserting them in the margins of every page and on separate sheets of paper strategically scattered throughout the manuscript. He was conscious of a radical shift in his project, not just the ornithological sham but the book's very purpose and tone. What had started out as playful condemnation of himself and of Isa had morphed into an ardent apologia. *If she reads it she'll understand, and she'll forgive me,* he told himself when elated by the writing. When frustrated, he heard a different thought: *You're wasting your time. She'll never get past the cynicism of the prologue.*

No, she'll read the first few chapters out of morbid curiosity if nothing else. But how do I persuade her to stick it out to the end? he asked the nights when doubts lay heavy as bricks on his chest. *Even if she were to forgive me, how will we ever find each other? I'll be a fugitive for the rest of my life. Where in that vast country will we find each other? And what makes me think I can begin again?*

Stop! First, she'll never read it. Second, even if she does, it won't erase the past or restore the future. It's all pointless.

No. I'll get Samuel to hand deliver it and to beg her, out of simple compassion, to read it to the end. She'll read it, and she'll forgive me.

Forget the damn book! You'll have bigger problems when they discover what you and El Brujo are up to. Even if you do manage to climb the wall like spiders, you'll be caught and crushed. This time there will be no reprieve.

Running exorcised his doubts, at least for the two hours that he sweated in the cold predawn, outrunning his fears. Writing restored hope to him, and sketching birds gave him a sense of peace. All three helped him stay focused.

He and El Brujo understood that their daily run had to seem routine, boringly routine to the guards who only half watched them in the dim light. To keep down the cost of electricity— or to pocket funds—the head warden had ordered that only a third of the exterior lights were to be turned on between lockdown and morning. The wall with the toeholds was in shadow. Benjamín played out the scene again and again. On a moonless morning before dawn, he and El Brujo would leap onto the flat rooftop. With one agile motion, El Brujo had already managed to toss onto the roof a short rope that he had made by tearing two of Benjamín's sheets into strips that he wove together tightly. They would use it to let themselves down a side wall and run on swift, silent feet north to Toluca and beyond, vanishing into the mountains, all while it was still dark. They would avoid trains and roads, making their way on foot into the sierras, buying food in villages tucked deep in the middle of nowhere; they would walk for weeks, maybe months, but they would reach the Copper Canyons.

They'll never be able to track us in the canyons, Benjamín reasoned. *I'll lie low. Grow a beard, disguise myself, and head for the border. I'll write to Isa when I'm on the other side. Ask her to meet me. Samuel can give her money for her passage by train. Perhaps he can even escort her. Yes! Of course! I'll ask him. She must not think of traveling alone! Not in these times. But I've got to give him instructions cryptically. How?*

More strategizing. Another lap. Another tiny gouge.

Write to him in Latin. Praise Saint Anthony. Of course! I'll go to San Antonio! No! Too many Mexican agents there. If there's a bounty on me, I could get caught and sent back. Go deeper, deeper. But where?

And then a totally new thought came from nowhere.

The point is to find a place where she can be safe and happy—with or without me.

She has no family in the States. Where could she go?

Her old school in Pennsylvania. Of course! She has friends in Bryn Athyn—the Synnestvedts and others.

Another lap, another tiny gouge.

The escape, like the book, took on a new dimension for him. Even when reminiscing about his days in the revolution, which he sketched as quickly as the birds that now inhabited his memoir, the narratives inevitably led to Isabel. He wrote into the night, determined to capture just enough of the past to be able to explain himself to her—and to himself.

~

So what do I remember most about my time as a revolutionary—aside from its wild characters? That I pined continually for Isa; that I was always hungry; that growing a beard was infinitely easier than trying to shave without soap and hot water; and that war is tedious and monotonous most of the time, terrifying in brief flashes, and deeply troubling long after it's ended—even when your side has won. I was in few battles. Most of the time I was sent on diversionary forays whose object was to draw Federal fire while most of the troops headed north for the real battle. There was little glory and lots of discomfort.

I did get to fight in the Battle of Casas Grandes. When I heard that the Federal garrison was guarded by the Eighteenth Battalion, I feared the worst was finally coming true. I knew some of the officers. Mother had challenged me by asking if I would really be able to fight against former comrades, and I had answered boldly that I would if I had to. That hour was upon me. I dreaded it. Yet we tend to fear the wrong things.

We launched our attack at 5 a.m.—our eight hundred against some five hundred *federales*. They were well fortified, while we were out in the open receiving their machine gun fire.

It got worse. A mere two hours into the battle, Federal reinforce-ments arrived with mortars. Then all hell broke loose. I stopped worrying about the nuances of old loyalties. We were being cut to shreds. Even Madero was wounded. I'll never forget a com-panion who was standing directly in front of me, how he fell screaming as his intestines spilled onto the ground. In a matter of a few minutes, dozens of our troops lay dead or dying. The luckier ones were taken prisoner—among them my friends Sidney Severs from New York and Eduardo Hay. The wounded stood a better chance with the *federales* since they at least had a doctor and medical supplies. We had nothing.

Survivors had no choice but to run for it into the moun-tains. I found out later that the *federales* took 153 of our mules, over 150 of our horses, and 101 rifles. It was a disaster for our small army. Yet a mere month later, I was with the troops fighting the final battle of the war at Ciudad Juárez. Actually, there were two battles that ended the revolution—the offensive that Madero ordered on April 7 and the one on May 8 that he expressly *forbade*. Ignoring Madero's orders, two of our revolutionary jefes took matters into their own hands. Pancho Villa and Pascual Orozco broke the cease-fire by launching an offensive of their own. When the *federales* retreated into downtown Juárez, they pursued them, blowing up building after building. The garrison, comprised largely of conscripts, surrendered. By May 10 it was over. We had ended Porfirio Díaz's thirty-year dictatorship.

So Juárez—the first battle at Juárez—should stand out as my grandest day in the revolution. For a few minutes I even bor-dered on the heroic. But I remember another time with far more intensity.

It was earlier, shortly after our harrowing retreat from Casas Grandes. I remember waking up on the floor of one more ram-shackle boarding house—and there was Isa, standing in the doorway, a vision of beauty in the midst of squalor.

What are you doing here? How did you find me? I asked soundlessly, only half rising, afraid that speaking would wake me and end the dream. I could only stare at her. And then she was in my arms, her body pressed to mine, and we were making love in that squalid room. I never felt more alive!

We were together from then on, traveling from one encampment to another. The tent that I managed to get for us felt palatial because she was there. How did she stand it, the hardships and privations of that month or so? Mercifully, the revolution was finally brought to a halt. The treaty was signed, but with far too many concessions to the government. Who ever heard of the winners disbanding their own army while the enemy keeps theirs? Everyone complained, but disband us they did. So we headed home. There were victory celebrations in town after town. Isa and I ate and danced our way from Juárez to Mexico City. Flushed with victory, we entered the capital a few days ahead of Francisco Madero. We had defeated the mighty Porfirio Díaz, yet a far more formidable enemy lay in wait for Isabel and me.

❖ *Sketch 15* ❖

HERETICS AND OTHER OUTCASTS

Isa and I had thrived under the duress of separation, privation, and danger. Yet we now seemed unable to make our way in peacetime. Poverty proved more formidable than whole armies. We couldn't—no, that's not true. *I* couldn't cope with our sudden poverty. She took it in stride. When circumstances forced us to rent a room in a tenement in the city's east side, Isabel was enraptured by the *former* beauty of the room.

"Oh, Ben! It has a cupola! This must have been the chapel of the house long ago, or perhaps the library! It's obvious this was once a grand old house."

"Well, there's nothing grand about it now." I scowled at the peeling paint and drab colors.

I sputtered when the mattress sagged in the middle, thrusting us together into a narrow canyon, while she went into peals of laughter. When I came home from the *mercado* with crude earthenware dishes because they were the only ones I could afford, she cleaned them and carefully set them up on a shelf in our room as if they were the finest Bavaria and our mugs were Waterford crystal. While I pounded the streets of Mexico City in

search of work—work that would not dishonor me—she cheerfully washed our clothes on the patio with the other women in
the tenement. I was stunned to find her chatting with them.

"They are not your equals!" I fumed in English as I hurried
her up the stairs.

"But they're awfully nice! What's the harm in chatting as we
hang clothes to dry?"

I ignored her question until we were in our room. Then I
turned on her, my voice shaking with rage. "Never forget who
you are! Never! You're a Nyman now!"

"Don't be cross, Ben."

"Those women are not fit to be your servants, let alone your
friends!"

"But in the camps—"

"Those days are over! We must all go back where we belong,
each to our own station in life. You are not to consort with such
people, do you understand?"

She burst into tears. I cringe as I write this, the more so
because it was only the first of many quarrels in those tense
weeks. It grew worse. The truth is that I was more afraid of that
tenement than I'd been at the Battle of Casas Grandes. When I
made her promise to stay away from our neighbors, I was trying desperately to hang onto my eroding sense of identity. On
the other hand, when I forbade her from going out alone, I was
genuinely trying to protect her. We lived in a such a rough barrio.
I couldn't bear the thought of her stepping out into those vile
streets with her sweet trusting way and being accosted. So there
she sat in our room day after day. How desperately lonely she
must have been! Yet I honestly believed I was shielding her from
dragons as our situation worsened.

In terms of career, I had returned to the capital victorious
yet no longer part of a victorious army. With my family connections, I thought I could get a government post in the interim
administration of President Francisco León de la Barra. But the
administration was essentially *porfirista.* The old guard wanted

no part of me. Neither did the Federal Army. By defecting, I had burned my bridges with them. My best hope lay with the triumphant *maderistas,* but they had not yet taken possession of the country. Our idealistic leader insisted on running a true election. Everyone knew he would win by a landslide, but that would not happen for several more months. I only had enough money for one more week, two at best if I could elude our landlady.

I began calling on members of the extended family. We had no relatives on Father's side and few on Mother's. Those few, as I discovered, had fled to Europe at the outbreak of the revolution. I turned to my godmother, Rosario Escandón de Torre y Landa, but she too was in Europe and her porter did not know her forwarding address. I grew despondent. In like measure, the holes in the soles of my boots widened. I knew there was no going back to San Serafín. How could I look my mother in the face after my betrayal—for what else could she consider it? Besides, I had little doubt that her disapproval of Isabel had solidified by now into outright contempt after our elopement. And I was damned if I was going to let Rodolfo see my desperation. So Father was my best hope. Mustering what courage and humility I could, I knocked on the great door of San Justín. Eufemio Rosarito peered at me through a grated peephole.

"Don Benjamín!" He seemed more surprised than glad to see me.

"How are you, Eufemio?"

He nodded slowly but did not unbolt the door.

"I've come to see my father."

"Pardoning, don Benjamín, but I have my orders."

"What orders?"

"Not to admit you, begging your pardon, sir."

"That's ridiculous! Tell my father that I need to see him."

He started to back away. "No! Wait! Please, Eufemio! What's this about?"

He answered with a pained silence.

"Is it because I joined the revolution?"

"Yes, sir. But he's even more upset that you married a heretic, begging your pardon."

"That's absurd! Wait! Tell him I can explain everything!"

Moments later Eufemio returned to the door. I struggled to speak calmly. "What did he say?"

"I'm sorry, don Benjamín. He told me to tell you—" The old man looked away.

"What?"

"He has disowned you. Pardoning, but he asks that you never come back here again." Eufemio closed the small window in the door with a finality that left me reeling.

It felt like a blow to the stomach. When I could breathe more evenly again, I started to walk back to the city.

Then I'll make it without him! He can go to hell!

I raged inwardly, yet I had to keep wiping tears off my face. Isa cradled me in her arms when I told her. She understood that I was struggling with more than the loss of an inheritance.

"I'm so sorry, my darling!"

I let her rock me gently.

"We have each other. We don't need him," she murmured, and I nodded mutely. "We'll be all right. I'll get a job as a teacher. After all, I did get *some* training in Pennsyl—"

"Do you think so little of me?" I jerked away. "Do you really think that I would let you support me?"

"Only until we're back on our feet."

"And have people say that the wife of Benjamín Nyman supports him! Never! Never suggest such a thing again, do you hear me!" I was shouting. "It's disgraceful that you would even—"

"There's no disgrace in honorable work! Lots of respectable women work!"

Now she too was shouting.

"Maybe in the United States. But this is Mexico, and no upper-class woman works! It's unthinkable!"

"But I want to. I can't go on being locked away. Ben, I'll go out of my mind . . ."

She was sobbing, her whole body shuddering with despair. I had never seen her like that. Her distress brought me up short. I vowed to make it up to her, to change our lives. That afternoon I took her to the Alameda Park, where flowers, trees, and outdoor concerts are free. The First Battalion Military Band was in fine form. I remember they played Verdi and Bellini. Isa and I strolled arm in arm in fine apparel, as if we had a home on Reforma Avenue and an army of servants preparing our dinner. I bought her a cup of coffee. I couldn't afford a cup for myself. She kept sliding it back and forth between us with an impish smile.

"Just one sip! I'm watching you, *capitán!*"

It's strange how a shared hardship can actually bring joy.

I set out again the next day, determined to tap into every contact that my name and rank made available to me. Where better than at the Jockey Club, where the most elite of Mexico's elite gathered? A club where men forged connections and discussed business over brandy and cigars. I timed my visit around lunchtime, when the club drew the most members. I couldn't afford a brandy, let alone lunch. But I figured I could quietly order a glass of iced water and make my rounds, taking vodka-like sips. When I arrived and presented my father's card, as I'd done dozens of times in the past, I was turned away.

I stepped back onto the sidewalk.

I'm nobody! I'm nothing!

The truth spoke with the brutality of a bullet making contact. My face was flushed, my breathing labored. I walked without purpose, needing the exertion just to keep breathing. Then I happened to run into Federico Casamayor. We had never figured out if we were second cousins once removed, third cousins not so removed, or simply cousins through wishful thinking. I had been schooled from childhood to refer to his mother as *tía* Sofía—Aunt Sofía—and to him as *primo* when they came to live with us for a few years at San Serafín. During those years, Federico, Samuel, and I were inseparable. Since they both had the good sense to acknowledge me as the leader, we had few quarrels and many adventures.

"Good gracious! Is that you under that beard, Benjamín?"

Federico stared up at me, eyes smiling. He had one of those faces that never quite outgrew childhood, his features minimally altered across the years. He was still round-faced and pug-nosed, and looked almost as guileless as Samuel; his dark hair remained rebelliously curly. Federico stood beaming at me through boyish eyes.

"I like the moustache," I said, returning the compliment, though the facial hair in question was barely more than a pencil line above his lip.

He thumped me on the back and drew me into a tight embrace.

"Have lunch with me, Benjamín!"

"No. I'm sorry. I can't."

"Come on. I must hear all about your exploits!"

He hailed a cab. "I can't, Federico. I don't have a penny to my name."

He knew better than most what the admission cost me. A shadow crossed his face. "Please let me take you to lunch, *primo*. Please."

It wasn't long before I was pouring out my story to him: my elopement with Isabel, our adventures in the revolution, my father's rejection, and my financial ruin. Federico always was the most generous of listeners. Throughout lunch he watched me attentively.

"Enough about me!" I finally became self-conscious of my self-absorption. "Tell me about you, Federico. How are you? And how is your mother?"

"She's fine. She remarried, you know."

"No, I didn't know. What is he like, this stepfather of yours? Is he the pious type? Does he suffer from mad urges to genuflect eighty or a hundred times a day?"

"No." He laughed.

"Good! I like him already!" Now I was staring at the insignia on Federico's uniform. "You've obviously done well for yourself, Major! The uniform suits you."

He grew solemn again, which seemed uncharacteristic of the Federico that used to play pranks with me. "I heard that you had joined the revolution. I was stationed in Querétaro. The whole time I had the nagging fear that one day they would ship me north and I would find myself having to fight you. It became a recurrent nightmare."

"But here we are, cousin, sitting at the same table!" I smiled. "Friends for life, whatever life does to us."

He motioned to the waiter for the bill. "Shake on it."

"On what?"

"Friends for life whatever the politics of our poor country. Shake on it!"

I extended my hand and felt him press a thick coin into my palm. It was a *centenario*, a hundred-peso gold piece. A private in the revolutionary army generally earned no more than two pesos a week. This was a fortune.

"Thank you, cousin, but I can't accept it."

"Then consider it a loan. Don't argue, man. Take it for your wife's sake." He leaned toward me, lowered his voice, and spoke quickly, as in our old conspiratorial days. We might as well have been eleven or twelve again, but the stakes were higher now.

"Listen, Benjamín. Word has it that the Federal Army is going to be kept intact after Madero takes over. Now, I can't promise you anything, but I might be able to pull some strings for you. My immediate superior is a man who can be talked into many things if given sufficient—"

"Persuasion?"

"He has expensive tastes. Let me see what I can do. Give me your address."

"You don't want to go there, even if you had a battalion to back you."

Federico wasn't smiling. *That bad, is it?* his eyes seemed to say. Knowing my pride, he didn't push the point. "I'll need a week. Let's meet at the Alameda at noon."

"All right, but you make it all sound so easy, cousin. Haven't you heard? I'm a traitor to the army. A pariah."

"I've learned not to believe everything the papers report."

"What report?"

"Your father's rant, of course."

"What rant?"

I could see him tighten his jaw as he looked away, then back at me. "I'm sorry, Benjamín. I thought you knew."

I returned to Isa more discouraged than ever, but at least now I understood why so many doors were closing on me. Father had published a letter in the newspapers titled "Sons and Other Traitors," an exposé on the deteriorating values in the army with me as a case in point. Not content with that, he had written to anyone who might possibly consider giving me a position in the military or in the government, expressing profound shame for my profligacy and traitorous nature. I was an outcast.

❖ *Sketch 16* ❖

TREMORS

I DIDN'T WAIT for Federico. I had no doubts about his good intentions, only about his ability. I was still thinking of him in terms of our shared boyhood, when I so easily outdid him at every game. How could I have known how very adept the affable Federico had become at playing politics? If I had known what progress he was making on my behalf, I never would have hatched the desperate scheme of masquerading as Samuel. Taking matters into my own hands, I resolved that I would trick Father into seeing me—and let "Samuel" plead my case.

"I'll be back late, so don't wait up for me," I told Isa and ducked out before she could ask questions.

Hidden under the stairwell was a package guarded by a boy of nine or ten. I paid him the twenty *centavos* I had promised and set off for San Angel. In a dark, secluded spot I put on the cassock and began the disastrous masquerade.

My plan was simple and well intentioned. But how does one claim good intentions and murder in the same sentence?

It was June 7, 1911—not quite 1 a.m. A few kilometers away, the lights of Mexico City glimmered like diamonds carelessly strewn across a blanket of the darkest hue. I remember that it had rained a few hours earlier. . . .

~

Benjamín described the fateful night, a little over a year ago, that he last visited his father. He carried his narrative all the way to the point when he entered what he termed his father's *lair*. And there he stopped, unable or unwilling to relive the encounter. He paced in the cell long after lockdown. It was clear to him that he needed to confront what had happened at his father's house. How else to exorcise it? Yet each time he tried to write about it, he tore sheet after sheet of paper, crumpling them in hands that shook.

I can't! Not yet, he finally admitted to himself.

It was two and a half days before Benjamín could resume his narrative, and then only by skipping ahead several hours. Now he only had five and a half days left to finish writing his book for Isa.

~

I got back from my father's house before dawn and climbed into bed without waking Isa. I was too agitated to sleep. Yet in spite of myself, I nodded off. I dreamed that she and I were at a station waiting on a platform. It was dark, and a thick fog enveloped us. There was no whistle to announce the approaching train, only its ferocious speed and mass. It bore down on us, jumping the track. Isa and I both woke up clinging to each other in our bed, only now the train seemed to be smashing through the walls downstairs.

"What's happening?" she cried out.

It took several seconds before I could grasp the reality. "It's an earthquake!"

Isabel's carefully placed pottery flew to the floor, shattering on the tiles. The bed stand overturned, sending my pocket watch clattering onto the fragments of clay and glass.

June 7, 1911, will always stand as the most bizarre day of my life. Three events converged in its twenty-four-hour span: my father's death, the destruction of portions of the city, and the triumphant entrance of the hero of the revolution. When the earthquake stopped, I remember feeling grateful to be alive. What did it matter that I'd been disinherited, or that my father didn't care one fig for me! I made love to Isa on our sagging bed that was now covered in chips of plaster. *I have everything!* The thought sang exultantly in my head, in my body.

The city proved amazingly resilient. By afternoon it seemed to have dusted itself off. The wounded had been taken to hospitals, the dead to morgues and funeral homes. The capital could now turn its attention to lavishing Francisco Madero with a hero's welcome. That same day there was a wake for my father, a long-forgotten hero of a forgotten war. Since none of the family even knew that Isabel and I were in the city, no one notified us. Unaware of his death, we joined the city in its passionate reception of "the apostle of democracy," as Madero was known. More than a hundred thousand people thronged the train station and the sidewalks, balconies, and rooftops. Isabel and I stood among them, waving small tricolored flags. The cheering was deafening. Our spirits soared with hope. Even I forgot our poverty for a few hours and celebrated with the crowds well into the night. When we met up by chance with two fellow revolutionaries we had known in Chihuahua, we all went out to dinner at the Sylvein, which I was able to afford thanks to Federico's generous gift. Later that evening, great fireworks lit up the sultry skies. Isa and I relished every moment. Meanwhile, families of the old guard continued paying their last respects to General Lucio Nyman Berquist, presumably a victim of the earthquake.

The next morning my father was laid to rest in the Cementerio Francés, where most of the city's elite like to bury their dead. I wouldn't learn about his death nor the funeral until days later, even though I had allowed myself the luxury of purchasing a newspaper. Isa and I pored over the headlines, photographs, and articles about the extraordinary reception the city had given Francisco Madero.

"I'm keeping this one. It's a historic edition!" she smiled, carefully storing the newspaper in the trunk that held our clothes. It had not occurred to us to look at the obituary section.

Several days later I met my cousin Federico in Alameda Park as previously agreed. He embraced me with marked intensity.

"I'm so sorry about your father!"

"Because he's finally lost his marbles? Or because he thinks he's a monk? Don't be. I've named the old Swede an honorary member of the crane family: the great *Grus fanáticus.*"

Federico thrust his jaw forward the way he always did when tense. "I'm so sorry, cousin! There's no other way to tell you than outright. Your father was killed in the earthquake."

Federico seemed destined to be the bearer of bad news. I heard him but could not quite take it in, merely nodding as if he were informing me about the upcoming elections or the price of beans.

"I didn't know where you live, so I kept checking here at the Alameda, hoping to run into you. I'm so sorry, Benjamín!"

I had him take me to the gravesite. The mound was covered with wilted flowers. We stood by silently as a gardener raked them up. There was a marker with a number. No gravestone yet.

"Are you sure about all this?" I asked in disbelief.

"Yes." He placed a hand on my shoulder as if to steady me, but I noticed his hand was shaking almost as much as mine.

When I returned alone to my lodgings, I had Isa find the newspaper that she had carefully stored away. Silently, our faces close together, we read the obituary. One line stood out above them all, a line I had to read more than once in order to take in its full meaning: "General Nyman Berquist is survived by his wife, the most esteemed Manuela Vizcarra de Nyman and their children, Rodolfo Nyman, Countess Eva Nyman de Comardo, and Father Samuel Nyman Vizcarra." There was no mention of me. They had written me off. The page blurred.

Isa embraced me. "Oh, my darling!"

I clung to her and sobbed like a child for the family I had lost. When I was calmer, she stroked the hair off my hot forehead. "You must go to your mother."

"No! They can all go to hell!"

But I was the one in hell.

Oh, Isa! What would I have done without you? When they all abandoned me, you alone stood by me! How could I have forgotten that? How could I have let a photograph, a blurred one at that, turn me against you? How could I have been so *vile* as to believe the appearance when I knew your goodness? Yet hasn't that always been my way? From earliest childhood I have always been quick to reject rather than risk being rejected, to believe the worst when I had the choice to see the best. Oh, my dearest Isa! What would I give to be able to go back in time, even into that slum! What higher dream than to live humbly, simply, always by your side!

~

Benjamín and El Brujo ran and plotted. Only four days to go.

"I can feel the earth under my feet," the shaman whispered.

"How is it?"

"Soft and wet. It rained," El Brujo added as his feet skimmed the dry, cold tiles.

Benjamín sensed that his friend was sculpting the prison walls into the steep sides of the canyons.

"And do you see your wife?" he asked good-naturedly as they paused in a stairwell.

"Yes. I see her." The Tarahumara yielded one of his rare smiles. "She's looking up from the fire pit as I enter the cave."

"What does she say?"

"Nothing. Her joy is as intense as pain."

They set off again, and Benjamín let himself imagine such a look in Isabel's eyes. Perhaps when he met her train somewhere in the United States, perhaps as far north as Philadelphia. She would step onto the platform with his memoir clutched to her chest, her eyes intently seeking him in the crowd, her face lighting up at the sight of him. No words, her lips forgiving him as she pressed them to his—the speech of lips saying all that needed to be said.

On the eighth lap he thought of his twin and of his mother.

I'll write to them from the States. I must remember to release Samuel from his vow of silence. He can tell Mamá about my recovery, but I must not tell either of them of my whereabouts, at least not right off. For now, let my escape be my gift to her, the clearest assurance that I am not as damaged as I have let her believe. Forgive me, Mamá!

Benjamín continued to write and to sketch birds—everything from common tree swallows and mourning doves to purple-throated caribs and the Demoiselle cranes of India. The birds were fillers whenever words clogged to a trickle or came to a total standstill. After losing himself in the contour of beaks, wings, and feathered breasts, he would return to words with the exhilaration of flight. Lately, in his absorption, he gave little thought to the fast-approaching escape attempt. Two weeks earlier, however, he had arranged for El Brujo to cut off his long hair. The idea was to help him blend into the crowd once they vaulted over the prison walls.

"Brujo!" he had said expansively after sharing a gourmet dinner with him and the bodyguards, the Sunday dinners being a kind of once-a-week ritual that solidified his power over them. "Brujo! It's time you stopped scaring people around here with that mangy mane of yours," Benjamín bantered good-naturedly. "You need to look the part if you're going to sit with fine gentlemen like us!"

El Vago smiled his deceptively inane, toothless grin; El Manco laughed outright; Mangel hunched his enormous shoulders forward and grunted good-naturedly.

"Mangel, see to it that this worthy gentleman gets a haircut from the prison barber first thing tomorrow morning!"

Benjamín dispensed the necessary money that was always in ready supply thanks to Manuela, who supplied it; to Samuel, who notified their banker to hand deliver it monthly to Benjamín; to the locked compartment in Benjamín's desk that kept the money safe; and to the bodyguards who guarded the desk *and* its owner.

"Here! For your cigarettes." He tossed in extra for the bodyguards, carefully cultivating their dependence on him. So persuasive was the weight of the gold in his hands that Benjamín Nyman tended to forget his own dependence. Confident in the protection and comfort that his family's wealth provided him, he often strayed into the dangerous illusion of self-sufficiency.

❖ *Sketch 17* ❖

THE SUMMONS

By the middle of June 1911, I no longer cared about political reform, my hero Madero, or any other revolutionary. Money dominated my waking thoughts and sleepless nights—money and Isabel. If there was anything the least bit noble in my soul, it was the genuine regret of having condemned my wife to a life of poverty even worse than she had known with her grandfather, if that was possible. Yet all that was about to change. I should have known that Federico would be true to his word. Two days after he showed me Father's grave, he arranged an interview, via hefty bribes, with his immediate superior. Colonel Saldovar Cantú was *de pocas moscas,* as they say—even house flies were not attracted to him. The man was as dry in manner as the deserts of Sonora. He sized me up silently. Then he came straight to the point.

"I don't much care what side you fought on, so long as I don't have to explain to my superiors why I would admit Benjamín Nyman back into the ranks. You can have your old commission back, but only as Captain Benjamín Nieto—and only as long as you honor our business agreement"—by which he meant giving him a hefty 60 percent commission from my first month's pay.

"Why the name change? What if someone recognizes me?"

"Then I'll boot you out for your deceit."

"Nieto is a fine name," I told him without further hesitation.

"And you'll have to get out of the city. In about thirty days I can post you to a small garrison in Mazatlán or in Mérida."

Mazatlán was little more than a fishing town on the Pacific coast. I quickly calculated that the capital of Yucatán could offer Isa and me a degree of sophistication. Unfortunately, I was known by a number of people in Mérida. "I'll take Mazatlán," I told Saldovar.

"Then I'll have the papers drawn up. Report to me on Thursday, *Capitán* Nieto."

That very morning Federico took me to his tailor and I was fitted for two uniforms. "Consider this a wedding gift from me."

"No, *primo*. You've already done too much! I'll pay you—"

"Not this month. I know what that bastard is charging you for your commission. Tell you what, just promise to pay for my funeral at Gayoso when my time comes!" He laughed.

I was in fine spirits when I kissed Isa. "How would you like to live by the ocean in about a month's time?"

"What ocean?" she asked, laughing. I don't think she believed me.

"Why, the great Pacific! None other would do for you. So put on your hat, Mrs. Nieto! I'll tell you all about it over coffee at the Alameda!"

I'd been reprieved. Employment and having an income again—however measly after paying Saldovar—had set my derailed life back on track again. The first noticeable change was in our diet. We could now afford to add chicken once a week to our rice and beans. I even felt secure enough to lift the ban on the neighbors, allowing Isa to converse with the women as she did our laundry in the speckled sunshine of the patio. After all, this was all temporary. We would soon start a new life in a place where the breezes smelled of salt and where sea lions lounged on the rocks of nearby islands. We just had to endure the barrio for about four more weeks. So long as no one recognized me, I could start a new life with a new identity. I began to sketch sea birds and to tell Isa about pelicans.

"To impress the ladies, a male points his bill-cum-pouch up to the heavens like so." I pointed my chin with its scraggly beard upward to the peak of our room's cupola and strutted like a pelican for her.

"Oh, yes! I see what you mean! Who could resist such a . . . what did you call it?"

"A bill-cum-pouch!"

"Then come nest with me!"

She laughed as I chased her down the stairs, to the amusement of the laundresses in the courtyard.

But before my dreams of sea birds could be fulfilled, the past intruded once more. As I came home from duty one day, Isa greeted me with the news that we had been summoned to the reading of my father's will. I felt a shock run through me.

"There's no point."

"Rodolfo says you must."

"Rodolfo was here!" *He saw how we live!* My pride clamored. Then my mind leaped to the image of Isabel having to confront him alone.

"It's all right." She reached for my hand as if reading my mind. "He was here only a few minutes."

"How did he treat you?"

"With perfect civility. He just said that you must go to San Justín on Friday at ten in the morning. That was it. Then he left."

I could have asked how he found us, but what did it matter? It was over, the simple life that I was just beginning to appreciate.

My reawakened pride insisted that we make the right impression on the family. I lavished a hefty portion of Federico's gift/loan on outfitting Isa—not merely with black taffeta but with the finest silk day dress that the Palacio de Hierro could furnish on such short notice. I would let my Federal uniform and my new beard and moustache speak for themselves. My dress uniform included all the finery: gold braiding, epaulettes, and a plumed, tri-cornered hat. Timing our arrival so we would be the last, I had the closed cab pull over a block or so from my father's house. Only when I had seen a carriage pass us with the family crest on it, and a second one with the Comardo coat of arms, only then did I alert the cabbie to drive us the rest of the way. When he drew up at San Justín de los Moros, I smiled wanly at Isa.

"San Tristín de los Loros!"

"What was that?" she murmured.

"Saint Sad Sack of the Loons, my name for the house after my father transformed it into his personal monastery."

She was fidgeting with a fold in her gown. I pulled on my gloves and inspected her. With her new Gainsborough hat perched at an angle, she rivaled the Tsarina Alexandra herself and anyone in any court of Europe for sheer elegance. Why then did I not feel the confidence of a tsar? I hesitated inside the coach. When Isa pressed my hand, I opened the door and helped her down.

A stranger demanded my name at the door.

"Where's Eufemio?" I asked the new porter.

"The old man? He left for his pueblo. Your name, sir?"

Captain Nieto, I almost said, but caught myself. "Captain Benjamín Nyman Vizcarra," I answered in a bold, clear voice.

At that moment I cut the rope anchoring me to the man I might have become in Mazatlán or wherever else they chose to send me—a humbler man more content with his lot in life. Instead, I replaced him with the familiar, arrogant son of Lucio Nyman Berquist. Offering my arm to Isa, I led her through a dark passage that took us to the central patio. And there they were, a bevy of strangers—attorneys and notaries—and the family that had written me off. I felt Isa tremble. Or was it I?

I had resolved to greet mother with stiff civility. A bow and the words, "How are you, Mamá?" Simple. Restrained. Dignified. But Eva threw me off by running to me with outstretched arms.

"Benjamín!" She embraced me, sobbing. "Oh, Benjamín! Benjamín!"

I held her a long time. We were mourning our father. When I released her, she stared at Isa. Then she stepped forward and gave her a quick peck on the cheek.

Samuel was the next one to greet us, first embracing Isa quickly, almost shyly, then me. We clung to each other. By then the wall I had tried to construct had collapsed. Now we were both fighting back tears.

"How did Father die?" I asked Samuel. Federico had told me, but I was fumbling for something to say.

"God was merciful! He was struck by a heavy object and died almost instantly."

"A heavy object?" I was still struggling to regain my composure; to fill the awkward silence. "What heavy object?"

Samuel looked off for a moment, almost as if embarrassed. "A brass crucifix. You remember the one. It hung over his bed. The earthquake knocked it down . . . Eufemio found him moments later. Papá died instantly, Benjamín."

We were silent. Then I became aware of Mother. She neither rose nor beckoned. She waited for me to kneel at her feet—and I did just that.

"Mamá, I had no idea . . . I swear to you that I didn't know or I would have come to you sooner!" I could feel tears streaming down my face. "Please forgive me!"

My mother grasped me tightly. When she released me, she cradled my face in both hands. She seemed to want to say something, but instead drew me into a second embrace, ferocious in its love. After a few moments, I rose and Isabel stepped forward.

"I'm so sorry, señora—about everything!"

There was no embrace for her. "So! Has my son made an honest woman of you, Isabel Brentt?"

I put an arm around Isa in a protective gesture and answered for her. "Yes, we're married."

"If you can call a civil ceremony a marriage."

I stiffened. "We were also married by the church."

"But Isabel is not Catholic."

"She's a Christian, so a priest married us."

"What kind of a priest would do that? It's a blatant breach of ecclesiastical law," she continued with studied calm.

I wasn't about to betray Samuel.

"I don't know, and I don't care one fig about ecclesiastical law." I had donned anger again like a comfortable old coat. "Let me assure all of you that Isabel is my lawful wife. Rejecting her—"

"Then let me congratulate you!" Rodolfo stepped forward.

His manner was much more reserved than Samuel's but clearly conciliatory. After a momentary pause, he held out both arms to his prodigal sibling. We embraced. He even managed to embrace Isabel, quickly, stiffly. We were both in the fold once again. Only Father's death could have brought this about. I suppose it was his one true gift that day.

Pancho, Eva's husband, merely nodded at Isabel and me. Then, clearing his throat, he asked in his lisping Castilian, "Isn't it time we focused on what really brings us here?"

Sketch 18

READING OF THE WILL

How DO I describe my brother-in-law? The venerable Count Francisco Comardo Tejada del Renglón—Pancho to family and friends—was a tall, barrel-chested Spaniard from Toledo; a man both crude and refined; a man who fancied himself an aristocrat forced by life's vicissitudes to marry a woman of inferior rank; a middle-aged, balding fraud extraordinarily blind to his ordinariness. Convinced as he was of his superiority, he realized that he had overstepped the bounds of common courtesy with the crudity of his question. He hastened to make amends. With a self-conscious smile, the good count took out a neatly folded handkerchief from his breast pocket and wiped a stone bench in the patio.

"Doña Manuela!" He smiled at Mother.

"Thank you, Pancho," my mother responded with a regal nod. The small garden bench vanished under the flow of her black taffeta.

Samuel busied himself wiping off a bench for Eva and Isa. Comardo motioned to his butler to place the contents of two large picnic baskets on the stone table near my mother.

"Doña Manuela, could we offer you some refreshment?"

"How kind of you, Pancho. I suspect we could all use some fortification."

The butler, a Spaniard who was as punctilious as his master, set up a white linen tablecloth, a tray of canapés, and several bottles of champagne in a silver wine bucket with magnificent scrollwork. The ice bucket, made with silver from the family mines and crafted in our silversmith shops, bore only Comardo's family crest. We all chose to ignore the slight to Eva and the family. The butler served the ladies first. He then proceeded to the men, serving each according to his sense of social hierarchy: first his master, then Rodolfo, followed by Samuel, me, then the family's attorney, followed by the other attorneys and lastly the notaries. We sipped champagne in the most joyless of courtyards.

What must Isa have thought of my childhood home! The neglect of years shouted invectives into the morning light. Dead vines and shriveled bushes stood out in sharp relief against the smooth masonry. The fountain wasn't simply broken and silent. It was smothered in thick layers of dirt and desiccated leaves that completely obscured the Talavera tiles. We all gazed uneasily into the dusty, eerie emptiness of the cavernous house. Whenever the wind picked up, it rattled doors and windows that seemed to moan.

After about ten minutes, Mother rose. "The provisions of the will demand that we meet here in a house that has all of the discomforts of the sixteenth century and none of its charm. It seems that Lucio has played us one additional trick."

Mother spoke in the brisk, energetic fashion that has long characterized her speech. Her manner was as iron-streaked as the hair she pulled back in severe defiance of the softer Gibson look.

"In his monastic zeal, Lucio wasn't content with just stripping the house of all of its furnishings. Craving as much darkness as he could stuff into these rooms, he had every single lightbulb removed. Rodolfo and I can attest to this, since we inspected the house before you arrived. You'll be glad to know, however, that Lucio spared the plumbing. Now, if we had a lantern, which we do not, we could try to read the will inside. However, the empty rooms are as comfortable as tombs." She nodded over her shoulder. "Therefore, I suggest that we hold the reading out here in the patio, where at least we have the clean sky and some light."

Everyone agreed.

The family's attorney, the honorable *licenciado* Joaquín Gómez Perejil, put on his eyeglasses and cleared his throat. Instantly he had everyone's attention.

A priest entered the courtyard just then, a bull-necked man wide of girth. We knew Father Casimiro as the leech who had been living off father for the past fifteen years; we did not recognize the man who followed behind him. "Forgive our lateness," he mumbled to us all.

Rodolfo strode forward—to evict him, I'm sure. The parasite's attorney spoke up. "I am sorry to have to interrupt, señores. It is my duty to inform you that my client and I have the *last* will and testament of General Lucio Nyman, which as the date and notary's seal will prove, disqualifies all earlier documents."

Pancho Comardo jumped to his feet. "What is this? Who are you?" He pointed at the older priest.

"I am Father Casimiro, father confessor to the señor general," he answered with his hands folded across his stomach as if in prayer. The rest of us knew him only too well.

The wind picked up and moaned through the empty rooms. The lawyers carefully examined the documents and compared the dates. Two of the notaries also weighed in. Then Gómez Perejil, our attorney, gathered up his papers. "Ladies and gentlemen," he announced in a low, apologetic voice. "I am afraid that the *licenciado* is right. The will I was about to read is no longer valid. It predates the one you are about to hear. *Licenciado.*" He motioned to his colleague.

Father Casimiro's lawyer began to read in a monotone. When he got to the lines that left the bulk of our family's wealth to the Vatican, Pancho Comardo jumped up from his bench. "That's patently impossible! We have anti-clerical laws in this country that make it illegal for the church to inherit anything!"

"Which is why the señor general had the foresight to have me set up an account in Switzerland." The parasite smiled benignly. "For the express benefit of *la Santa Iglesia*."

Comardo flinched as if punched in the stomach. When he had somewhat recovered, he struck back: "You're lying! There isn't one bank in this country that would allow the withdrawal of excessively large sums!"

"Which is why I had to make a number of trips abroad," the cleric answered with a smile. "Six, to be precise. I have all the documentation. It's all here. The bank in Zurich and I have copies in triplicate of every single transaction."

"No! That's absurd! My father-in-law wouldn't leave his fortune to the church at the expense of his family!"

"The general was a pious man." Father Casimiro smiled indulgently. "Everything about this house proclaims that he lived and died like the humblest of martyrs for the glory of *la Santa Iglesia*."

"This is a fraud!" Comardo bellowed. Our collective anger and despair began to swell in oceanic waves.

"I assure you that this is a lawful document," the parasite's attorney said unemotionally. "It will stand up before any court of law. Now, if you wish to hear how the general has disposed of his properties here in Mexico, you must remain calm and allow me to finish."

An uneasy silence settled over the group. When the lawyer read the next lines, the family's rage was uncontainable.

"You're a thief!" Comardo shouted at Father Casimiro, who remained inscrutable as a Toltec warrior carved in stone. "You're a lousy, sanctimonious hypocrite! A schemer!"

"You waited until he was too senile to know what he was doing!" Now Rodolfo was shouting. "Then you got him to sign the properties over to you!"

"Not to me! To the church! I am merely the instrument of a higher will and noble purpose—to found a new brotherhood dedicated to the glory of God—"

"And the devil!" I muttered under my breath. In truth, I wasn't surprised by Father's final rejection.

"Everyone knows that my father-in-law was senile in his last years!" Comardo yelled in his high falsetto. "We can prove it! So that invalidates the will!"

Just then another attorney—I remember his surname was Tortugón, and indeed he seemed as sluggish as a sea turtle on land—roused himself. He had been napping as he leaned against a wall under the arcade. How he got past the porter is a mystery. Perhaps he was mistaken for one of the notaries or an assistant of an assistant! In any case, there he was like something out of a bad comedy, eyes bloodshot and words slurring as he held up yet another will with a flourish of his hand.

"Señores! Señores, if I may have your intentions, please . . ."

No one was listening. Comardo, Rodolfo, and our attorney clustered around Father Casimiro's lawyer, each one examining the date and the seal from the notary public. The date was undeniable: June 5, 1910. The other will was dated a full seven months earlier.

"Señores! I have a will dated February 27 of . . . of this year!" The drunken Tortugón waved a document. "*El sep-ti-mo vi-en-te fe-bre-ro—19—1911!*" He grinned amiably.

Rodolfo was the first to catch the import of his words and silenced the others. The lawyers regrouped and studied the new document. After a few moments, Father Casimiro's attorney shrugged. The priest turned as white as adobe. Then for the next harrowing moments Tortugón slurred his way through the will that deliberately disinherited Samuel, me, *and* Father Casimiro.

Eva was to get the mines—Minas del Rey—and Rodolfo was to inherit San Serafín lock, stock, and barrel: the sugar refinery, the trains, and all the land. The Mother Church could have the cash assets in Father's bank account in Mexico City and San Justín in the bargain.

"It's a fraud!" Father Casimiro yelled. "I gave the general fifteen years of my life! I cared for his soul as none of you ever did! I protest!"

Pancho Comardo's eyes glowed like torches in the darkest of mines. In a fit of rapture, he grasped Eva's hands and kissed them. Rodolfo embraced Mother.

"You will always be the mistress of San Serafín!" I heard him reassure her. "It's your home all the days of your life. Count on it!"

Father Casimiro stormed out, trailed by his attorney. The champagne flowed.

Isabel hugged me. "We're free," she whispered intensely. I nodded. As I think back on it, on some level I was actually relieved not to have to be grateful to Father. I could make a clean break. I was free to be my own man. Taking her hand, I guided us toward Samuel.

"Well, Father Samuel, we are duly chastised!" I couldn't resist telling him. "I married a heretic and you dared to be a diocesan rather than some eremitic monk!"

He didn't smile. He studied me closely, assessing the true sentiment behind my levity. I think he was bracing for an explosion. Or perhaps he wondered how Isabel and I would survive. "It's all right," I tried again. "Now I have no choice but to become a great general!"

Moments later I was congratulating Rodolfo with a hearty Mexican embrace.

"Anything you need, you have only to ask for it!" He seemed sheepish.

Before I could respond, another lawyer stepped out of the shadows.

"Señores! Your attention, please!" He spoke with authority.

We all turned and had our first look at Tomás Tepaneca, the man Mother would later accuse of being Isabel's lover. He had the bronzed, aquiline features of an Indian. A true Tlahuica, according to Mother. He was small in stature, thin, and I suppose handsome, if I'm honest.

"I am the *licenciado* Tomás Tepaneca." He spoke with quiet confidence.

Did Isabel's hand tremble in mine? Or do I imagine it, knowing now what I know?

"It is my duty to inform you that I have in my possession the absolute last will and testament of General Nyman Berquist. On Tuesday—"

"Don't be absurd," Pancho Comardo cut him off. "Montalvo! The man has no further business here. Show him to the door."

The butler started forward.

"We can read the will here or in court!" Tepaneca spoke sharply.

Comardo called off his man.

"On Tuesday, June 6, 1911, on the very afternoon before his death, the general requested that I draw up his last will and testament. I drafted the document as he commanded, here in this house. The señor general signed it, and it was duly notarized by the notary public, Raúl Bravo, whom you see before you. We are prepared to testify before any court of law to the validity of this document."

The day before my visit! The day before our fight! My mind was racing. *Then he might have changed his mind about disowning me, or why bother to draw up another will!*

Mother, Rodolfo, and Pancho inspected the date and the seal on the document. After much clamor, with the family attorney weighing in, Rodolfo nodded somberly.

"Proceed, *licenciado.*"

Tomás Tepaneca read in a bold, clear voice, and once again I was prisoner to hope, my earlier resolution shoved aside. I trailed along, sifting through the legal jargon. I grasped that the Vatican was still getting the lion's share—something that no longer surprised anyone. Perhaps we were all too numb, or we were desperately trying to transform our hopes into realistic expectations. We knew collectively that sharing the mines and the plantation would be enough to ensure the leisure of all our days on earth. So we waited breathlessly. And then we heard the only sentence that mattered—the one that changed our lives:

"I, Lucio Nyman Berquist, being of sound mind, do hereby convey San Justín de los Moros, Minas del Rey, and San Serafín, in their entirety, to Isabel Brentt, granddaughter of Cadwallader Brentt of Cuernavaca, Morelos."

Sketch 19

SHOCK WAVES

There was a stunned silence.

"There must be a mistake!" Mother gasped. "That can't be right!"

Eva reacted more dramatically. She simply stopped breathing. Rodolfo was the first to reach her.

"Eva!" When her face started to take on a blue tinge, Rodolfo slapped her. "Eva! Breathe!"

Her eyes had the wide, raw terror of a zebra caught in a lion's stranglehold. Mother sprang forward. Tossing out the champagne bottles so that they shattered on the stone patio, she grabbed the ice bucket and flung its contents of crushed and melted ice into her daughter's face. There was a sharp intake of air, followed by Eva's hysterical sobbing.

"Why, Papá? Why?" she cried uncontrollably, articulating for the family its collective pain and disbelief.

Isa stood rigid as the dead vines. Pancho Comardo took several steps toward her, his voice shaking as much as the finger he waved in her face. "I don't know how or why this has happened, but I'm going to expose you!"

I stepped in front of her. "Anything you have to say to my wife, you will have to say to me, if you have the guts!"

Comardo backed off and turned to the others. "Are you going to accept this? Hand it all over to her? *To this opportunist?*"

I leaped at him. Rodolfo struggled to pull me off him.

"Steady, Benjamín! We all need to stay calm!"

By now Comardo was sobbing uncontrollably.

"Stay calm!" Comardo blubbered. "For *seventeen* years . . . seventeen years, I've administered the mines! Have I ever once failed this family? Have I ever once, just once, failed to uphold my end of the deal?"

I released him.

"No one is questioning your dedication, Pancho." Mother spoke without looking at him, her face rigid as the iron grates on the windows. "This is a surprise to us all—"

"A surprise!" His eyes almost bulged out of his head. "A surprise!" The word reshaped his despair into rage. "Need I remind you that when I married your daughter, when I gave her my name and my title, your husband promised me the mines! Instead, I got nothing! Nothing!"

I lunged at him a second time. Grabbing Comardo by the throat, I slammed him against one of the courtyard pillars—

～

Benjamín stopped writing. The face of a gaunt old man faded in and out of Pancho Comardo's round face with its double chin. Caught in the overlap of memories, Benjamín Nyman remembered the surprising scrawniness of his father's neck under his fingers and the thickness of Pancho's bulging Adam's apple. The images bled into each other. His hands trembled; his breathing stuttered.

My God! I am a murderer! A brute who strikes out mindlessly! A third image rose out of the stillness: Isa's face the one time she visited him in prison. He saw once more the shock and disbelief in her eyes when he grabbed her by the throat.

Tossing aside the pen, the prisoner clutched his head with both hands.

Hours later, when he awoke curled at the foot of his bed, the night silent and dark, the book drew him back to the desk, then onto the floor to search for the pen. He found it on the edge of a small purple pond that had dried into the rug. Turning on the banker's lamp on his desk, he read the last few lines of his manuscript—Comardo's rant aimed at his mother. In the silence of the sleeping prison, his brother-in-law's high falsetto voice spoke again.

～

"Need I remind you that when I married your daughter, when I gave her my name and my title, your husband promised me the mines! Instead, I got nothing! Nothing!"

Grabbing Comardo by the throat, I slammed him up against one of the courtyard pillars.

"Damn you, Comardo! When you married my sister you got *far* more than you deserved! You brought *nothing* to this family, you hear me! Nothing but your *decaying* name and your putrid arrogance!"

"Be still, both of you!" the family matriarch commanded. "Benjamín! Release him!"

I tightened my grip. "The next time I hear you speak so disrespectfully of my sister, I'll kill you."

"Benjamín! That's enough!" Mother commanded.

When I released him, his hair was disheveled and his neck visibly bruised. He shook himself. "Eva. We're leaving."

"Please!" Isabel pleaded. "I don't want to be the cause of all this!"

But you are, their looks answered. No one spoke as the butler packed up the wicker baskets. The clinking of shattered crystal filled the silence. Comardo's breathing was labored—so much so that I allowed myself the fantasy of Eva's sudden widowhood. He staggered onto a bench and mopped his face with his handkerchief. Forgetting that he had used it earlier to wipe off a seat for Mother, he drew a smudged line of dirt across his nose and cheeks.

"Why her? Why Isabel Brentt of all people?" he gasped, his face red and dirt-streaked. A small vessel in his left eye had burst, pooling blood under the dark pupil. "Who is she, anyway? And who the hell is her lawyer?"

"He's not my lawyer," Isabel answered quietly.

I remember looking into her face. "Isa, do you know this man?"

"No." She answered quickly but without looking me in the eye. She lied, but I now realize it was not from craft or malice, but from sheer mortification. "Ben! I didn't know about any of this! I swear it!"

And that I do believe. She simply looked too stunned.

Still sobbing and bedraggled, Eva threw her arms around mother's neck. "Mamá! What's going to happen to us? What will become of my children?"

"Have courage, daughter! We're in God's hands!" Mother murmured, embracing her with fierce tenderness.

Isabel approached them with tears streaming down her face. "We all know this is a mistake. A misunderstanding. We'll work it out any way you like."

Pancho Comardo turned about sharply, a desperate hope igniting his eyes.

"Of course! Thank you, Miss Brentt! Thank you!"

"*Señora Brentt de Nyman.*" I spoke with slow emphasis, my hands curling into fists along my sides. Comardo caught himself and smiled at Isabel. "Pardon me! Señora! Though of course it's Isabela now that we are all family! May I call you Isabelita?"

"Yes, of course," she murmured in a voice husky from her own tears.

Pancho Comardo turned to the others. "We can draw up a new will right here, right now. One that reflects what the general wanted when he was in full command of his faculties. Isabela can sign it and set everything straight!"

"Not so fast!" I glared at Comardo. "First, my wife's name is Isabel. Second, we have to work this out as a *family,* calmly and carefully."

"What is there to work out? Sign over the mines that your father promised me, and do what you like with the rest. But let's do it now, while we're all here. We have no shortage of attorneys!" He gave a short laugh.

Tepaneca stepped forward. "Our legal task today is to honor the will as it is written. My colleagues will agree that changing the provisions of a will is not something that can be done quickly. There are legal procedures."

"I'm afraid I have to agree with the *licenciado,*" the family's attorney added quietly.

"They're right." I nodded. "Rest assured, Isa and I will see to it that there is a fair distribution—"

"Will you now!" Comardo cut in as he reached for Eva's arm and pulled her from Mother. "Don't you understand? There *is* no Isa *and you.* That scrap of paper says it's all hers now. So, Isabel, I must appeal to you and to you alone to act honorably, as conscience dictates."

Mother had been studying her daughter-in-law. Then she began issuing orders. "We'll settle this in San Serafín. We leave today, so I want all of you at the station by no later than three o'clock."

"That's impossible, Mamá." Eva gazed up from her handkerchief. "I can't possibly be packed—"

"Leave it. You have everything you need there. Three o'clock sharp, everyone. Is that clear? We're going to work this out calmly, not in the heat of passion. Rodolfo, inform Guzmán that we'll need the train."

Pancho Comardo gave his mother-in-law a look of utter incredulity. "You expect me to take my wife and daughters into

Morelos after all that has happened there with the damned revolution! I'm not insane."

Rodolfo and I both started forward, fists clenched—not because there wasn't some sense to his concern. The revolution *had* been violent, particularly in Cuautla and other nearby towns. It was Pancho's tone that was such an affront—to our mother and therefore to us. Samuel quickly interposed himself between us and our target. "It's only natural to feel uneasy about returning to Morelos," our peacemaker prompted. "A lot has happened there recently."

"Firstly, we're not going to Cuautla," Mother responded as she pulled on her gloves. "Secondly, the revolution is over, Pancho. And thirdly, Madero and Zapata are fellow revolutionists, *euphoric* with triumph. Despite his family's wealth and social position, Madero seems to have a penchant for peasants. There will be talks and cordial visits between him and Zapata. So actually, there's no better time to travel to Morelos. We must capitalize on their friendship while it lasts."

"Maybe you have forgotten the haciendas that revolutionaries and other thieving renegades burned to the ground, not to mention the families they murdered, señora! "

"I have forgotten nothing, Pancho. I am simply reading the times. God has granted us a respite with this interim presidency of de la Barra. Thank God, he is one of our own!"

"Do you seriously believe that this temporary peace guarantees our safety? That the rabble has suddenly gone back to being law-abiding citizens? They're armed to the teeth and believe they own the future now!" Comardo mustered a mirthless laugh.

"I don't know what the future holds, Pancho. What I do know is that for the present we can all assemble safely in San Serafín, and that is what we need to do—as a *united* family, where we can all fit under one roof."

"First, there are papers to sign." Tomás Tepaneca spoke quietly.

Mother fired a hard look at him. "There will be no signing of anything today!"

"No, Mother. We need to follow through and keep it all legal." I spoke firmly. "Then we'll be free to do the right thing."

Cupping my face with both hands, Mother kissed me gently. "All right." She then kissed Isabel. "Until later, daughter." With that one word, *daughter,* clearly etched into the noon day, Isa had just been accorded the status of a family member. Turning to the rest of us, Mother reiterated, "Remember! Everyone be at the station at three o'clock sharp! You too." She turned to Tepaneca. "You and *el licenciado* Gómez Perejil must travel with us. Naturally, we'll pay for your expenses at a hotel in Cuernavaca." She paused. "Actually, we could accommodate you in the hacienda, if you would do us the honor of accepting our hospitality."

Tepaneca, with his suit and city trappings, seemed schooled in the rules of civility. He must have known that Mexicans of our class rarely consort with men of his class, let alone house them overnight in our homes. Did he suspect her motives? Was he determined to enforce the terms of the will for his own devious purposes? Or was he simply intent on protecting the wishes of his recently deceased client?

Whatever his motivation, Tepaneca accepted her offer.

Most of the family left as Isabel began signing the documents. Only Gómez Perejil, Tepaneca, and I remained to witness the moments that turned a pale and unhappy American girl into the sole heir of both the Nyman and Vizcarra fortunes.

"If you'd be so kind as to sign here, señora, and here," Tepaneca asked her with professional courtesy, spreading the documents onto the tile table now stripped of its linens and fine glassware.

I remember that she avoided his eyes. Did they know each other from years back? Mother's detective determined shortly afterward that Tepaneca grew up in Cuernavaca. It's a small town. Given that Isabel was allowed to play in its streets with the humblest of children and that he looked to be about her age, it *is* distinctly possible that they had known each other since childhood. Or was he scrutinizing her with simple curiosity as the object of a family's resentment? No. His gaze was too intense for mere curiosity. Certainly it was the gaze of a man aware that he stood in the presence of extraordinary beauty.

⁓

There was one moment when his face betrayed . . . In the silence of his prison cell, Benjamín Nyman struggled to recapture an impression, evanescent as a dream on awakening, chasing it through the labyrinth of memory and then suddenly tracking it to the very heart of the maze. There he saw it plainly. Yearning. Tepaneca's face betrayed yearning deep as a canyon. *He was in love with her. He'd probably loved her a long time.* Jealousy rushed up like a geyser. Yet just as quickly it spilled back into the depths from which it had surged. Prisoner 243 reflected with exquisite calm, *how could he* not *love her?*

⁓

I remember distinctly that Isabel's hand shook as she bent to sign the first copy of the documents that named her my father's one and only heir. When she had signed them all in triplicate, the small party headed out the front door in silence. As we stepped back onto the street, the porter came running after us. He was a young man who kept looking over his shoulder as if he expected to be ambushed from behind.

"I quit, sir!" he said to Gómez Perejil. "I've done my job. Please give me my pay."

Our attorney, who apparently had hired the man after Eufemio retired, began to object that he had not completed even a month. The porter planted his sandaled feet firmly and thrust his jaw forward. "There isn't money enough in all the world that could make me spend one more day or night here. Just pay me for three weeks, sir."

While Gómez Perejil paid the man his wages, Tomás Tepaneca locked the door behind us. Then he handed the key ring to Isabel. "Señora, the keys to your house!"

"I don't want them. I can't . . . Thank you."

Snatching them from Tepaneca, I offered them to Isa with a smile. "Take them, my darling. They're yours."

She gave them a quick burial in her small reticule, closing the bag with a sharp tug on the drawstrings. Moments later, all four of us were riding back to the city in the Gómez Perejil carriage.

"It looks like a *chubasco*." Tepaneca smiled pleasantly. The sky had darkened perceptibly.

I longed to be alone with Isa, far from prying ears. I needed to ask my wife for the answers my rioting emotions demanded: *How did you know my father? Why have you never told me that you knew him? What the hell was the nature of your relationship?* No. I had to stay calm, calm and civil in the confinement of the coach, working out for myself how best to handle the situation. Minutes later rain began to pelt the roof, softly at first, then with sudden ferocity, as if wind and rain were competing with my inner agitation. Fortunately, the racket discouraged conversation, but not the question that silently, persistently dashed itself against the interior of the carriage like a trapped dragonfly: Of all people, why Isabel?

Sketch 20

RETURN TO EDEN

WITH BRITISH PRECISION, our train pulled out of Mexico City at three o'clock sharp. We settled ourselves into the family Pullmans. I don't remember much about the trip except that a morose silence climbed aboard. Even Eva's children fell under its spell. Not a peep out of them. Comardo and Rodolfo left us for the smoking car with its leather club chairs. Mother said her rosary, the beads clicking against each other in the strained silence. Eva had changed into dry clothes, and her maid had managed to give her a fresh coif. Yet for the first time my beautiful sister looked haggard. Isa seemed intent on avoiding everyone. She sat beside me with a book, yet she rarely turned the pages. As for me, I could only stare at the landscape that shifted and blurred as much as my thoughts. When the walls of San Serafín came in sight, I tried to see the estate through the eyes of ownership, reasoning that what was Isabel's was mine.

I should have been ecstatic or, at the very least, relieved. My financial woes were over. I was now married to one of the wealthiest women in Mexico. Yet everything rankled me, beginning with my discussion with Isabel the moment we were alone in the bedroom assigned to us.

"I swear to you, I don't understand this any more than you do!"

"When did you meet my father? How?"

"Never!" Then she paused, her innate honesty forcing her to amend the denial. "Well, not in the sense you mean! I saw him once when I was a child and he bought one of Cadwally's paintings."

"So you did know him!"

"No, Ben! He was a stranger to me. Darling, I'm just as upset by this as you. I don't understand any of it. I'll do whatever you want. Give it all back . . ."

I should have been satisfied by the earnestness of her manner, by the quiver in her voice, by the way she wrung her hands and was fighting back tears. Instead, in the typical fashion of the spoiled creature I am, I stalked out of the room and left her by herself. I had a horse saddled. Within minutes I was finding fault with him too. It still galled me that I had been forced to sell Falco that spring. No horse was good enough now. My present mount seemed dim-witted and faltering at every step. I tried desperately to put Falco out of my mind. Riding to the crest of a hill, I could see a measure of what Isabel and I now owned. Kilometers of sugar cane rustled in the wind like a great ocean whose end blurs into a charcoal line against the sky. Behind me rose the compound with its many structures, all gleaming in the late afternoon sun.

It's ours! I kept telling myself. *Isa and I own every square . . . No! I don't own a damn thing! Comardo is right. It's all hers! In the end, I meant nothing to Father! None of us mattered!*

Was this his last cruel joke? It just didn't make sense! I knew better than any other mortal the depth of his hatred for her. *Why*, then? Why had he left it all to her?

There must be demons that specialize in inflating suspicion. If so, a veritable army of them went to work on my imagination. I returned from my ride more agitated than ever. Dinner that evening was a protracted ordeal. With Eva's young daughters seated at the table and with Tomás Tepaneca, the unwanted stranger, among us, we had to maintain a stifling conversation that spoke of everything except what was uppermost in everyone's mind. We alternated between superfluous observations and an oppressive silence. The moment the dessert dishes were removed, Mother turned to our unwelcome guest. "Well! Good night, Mr. Tepaneca. I hope you sleep well. We'll see you at breakfast."

She was dismissing him, along with the children, while allowing our family attorney to remain seated at our table. I almost felt sorry for Tepaneca as he rose with as much dignity as he could muster. Nodding to my mother, he let himself out into the tranquil night. We kept our conversation tethered as the children kissed each and every one of us good night. Only when assorted nannies had come to scoop them away, only then did we finally set aside all false pretenses and burst free. The Battle of Redistribution was on.

Isa excused herself from the table. I don't doubt that her nerves were every bit as frayed as ours. She at least had the good sense to go to bed, as the rest of us should have done. But no, we Nyman Vizcarras always think we have to settle our differences *inmediatamente*, without the benefit of reflection or time to cool tempers. We argued heatedly, since no one could agree on anything. As I think on it, Mother's proposal may have been the best one: to divide the estate and the mines into shares that would be handed out equitably. That seemed reasonable. But what was equitable? Comardo was a one-note crow, cawing for sole ownership of the mines over and over until I was ready to throttle him. Rodolfo, as the eldest, believed that he and Mother should run the proposed family corporation. Isa and I would be granted any bedroom we liked in San Serafín. At one point I had to fight the impulse to jump up and tell them all—except Mother—to get out of my house.

To Samuel's everlasting credit, he stayed on to act as a referee. Everyone in the room knew that he was the only one there who didn't care about the inheritance per se. Yet I knew that he was reeling from Father's rejection as much as the rest of us. To salve our wounds, Rodolfo and I uncorked more than one bottle of brandy. Samuel abstained; Mother and Eva broke down and drank with us. I don't know about the others, but certainly by the time I went to bed, I was roaring drunk. I don't remember if I walked up the stairs or climbed them on all fours. I woke up the next day in the canopied bed, still fully dressed and with a massive hangover. Isa was gone. When I had bathed and made my way downstairs to the nearest coffee pot, I began making inquiries. None of the servants knew anything—or they weren't saying. One of the grooms in the stables admitted that he had saddled up two horses at dawn—one for Isabel, the other for Tepaneca—and that they had not yet returned from their ride.

"Where did they go? In what direction?"

No one knew anything. By midafternoon, everyone knew everything. Benjamín Nyman's wife had run off with her lawyer.

In her haste to leave me, Isa had left behind her trunk with just about all of her worldly possessions. I doubt that she had any money with her. I followed her to her grandfather's house in Cuernavaca. The old gringo pointedly refused to allow me to cross his threshold.

"Isabel doesn't want to see you."

He punctuated her refusal by slamming the window's shutters in my face. I camped on their doorstep, enduring rain and the curious stares of the neighbors. When my short supply of patience ran dry, I stood on my horse and vaulted over the wall onto a flat rooftop. Seconds later I dropped down into Cadwallader Brentt's small courtyard garden. It was dusk by then, but there was still enough light for me to take in the bizarreness of that house. Every wall, from top to bottom, was an artist's canvas. Each was painted a different color, bright and garish. Indian warriors and maidens from another time, jaguars, monkeys, and parrots fairly leaped from the murals as if to bar my path. Just then a flash of motion in the upper corridor caught my eye—Isabel hurrying into her bedroom.

"Isa!" I yelled.

I headed for the garden stairs. Cadwallader Brentt, who was still on the ground floor, stepped out of the shadows and aimed a rifle at me. The tip of the barrel was less than four meters away. I remembered that the old boy had fought in the American Civil War. The muzzle loader looked ancient. As if reading my mind, Brentt half cocked it. "The gun's primed and still fires. Since my granddaughter does not want to speak with you, I suggest you leave now."

"Not without my wife!" I ignored the barrel and called up to Isa. I could see that the door to her bedroom was a Dutch door and that the upper portion was open. So I knew that she could hear me perfectly. "Get it straight!" I yelled. "I will not allow you or that lawyer of yours to besmirch my honor! Do you hear me, Isa? You're coming home with me now!"

"She *is* home," the old Yankee broke into my tirade. "Get out of my house!"

I ignored him.

"Isa! How dare you treat me—and my family—in so despicable a way! What did I do to deserve this? Is it because I got drunk last night?"

I leaned into the silence.

"I only get drunk when I'm disinherited." I tried to laugh.

I became acutely aware of the droning of insects. "Talk to me, Isabel! I'm warning you—"

"And I'm warning you, Nyman. Get out of my house."

I was aware again of the rifle. Had he really loaded the thing or was he bluffing? The old man continued to aim the heavy rifle at me in perfect form, his military training suddenly coming to the fore, his arms surprisingly strong and unwavering.

"I'm going up there, Mr. Brentt. Please don't try to stop me." I spoke more softly.

He pulled the hammer to full cock. All he had to do now was press the trigger. *He won't dare shoot me,* I thought. Then I noticed that he was no longer aiming at my chest but lower.

"I won't kill you, Nyman. But take one more step and it will be the last time you walk on two legs." The old gringo spoke with chilling calm.

I left. Riding out of Cuernavaca, it occurred to me that by returning to Eden, I had lost Eve.

I remained in San Serafín for only one more night. In the morning I loaded a horse with provisions and headed into the hills. When I returned a full nine days later, San Serafín felt like a museum after hours. My footsteps were loud and obtrusive in the empty rooms.

"Where is everybody?" I asked one of the servants.

"In Mexico, sir." She hurried away. Moments later Valle Inclán, the hacienda administrator, came looking for me.

"Don Benjamín, they've all gone to the city. Your mother left instructions that you were to join them as soon as you got back. I can have the train ready—"

"Whoa! Slow down, man. I'm not going anywhere today."

I finished pouring myself a drink and dropped into a club chair. "Juana!" I called out. "Bring me some ice!" I took another thirsty gulp while stretching my legs as far as they'd go. "So what's going on?"

"Father Samuel has been arrested."

The servant girl brought the ice. "Arrested? What's he done? Given communion to Methodist missionaries?"

Valle Inclán did not answer right away. When I looked up, I had the fleeting impression that he was already savoring the reaction he knew was coming. Yet he quickly mastered the muscles of his face into the appropriate expression. "He's been accused of murdering your father. The trial started yesterday."

"Murder! The earthquake killed him! What the hell are you talking about?"

"I know. It's preposterous! But Father Samuel is known to have been the last person to visit your father."

"The damn crucifix fell on him!" I was shouting now.

"Yes, Captain, but you see, the autopsy revealed that the general was struck by the crucifix *twice*."

"Twice?" I let that sink in. "What autopsy?"

"The one your mother ordered when she had the body exhumed."

Thus began the nightmare of Samuel's trial.

I let my brother go through the ordeal because I was convinced that no one could possibly think him guilty of anything more grievous than stepping on spiders—and even those he tends to spare. Day after day I wore my army uniform and sat with the family. By then I had a thick beard and moustache. Samuel, by contrast, was clean shaven. Is that why no one in the court seemed to connect us as twins? And what of the family? Did none of them suspect anything?

Bribing my superior allowed me to take an extended leave of absence. So I was there, the guilty one, undetected though I sat in their midst. To be fair, I did not think of myself as guilty of murder back then—only of deception. The day before the sentencing, I sensed what was coming. So I shaved off the beard and moustache, bundled up the priestly cassock that I had worn that fateful night, and brought it with me to the trial.

God knows I am guilty of many things, but not of letting another man take the blame for me.

～

Benjamín Nyman's pen hung suspended over the page. *Isn't that exactly what I'm about to do? Escape and leave Mangel and the others holding the bag? They'll be blamed or used as scapegoats. But if I let them in on the plan, I'll blow the whole thing for El Brujo. I can't—*

Benjamín froze. Somewhere in the prison, a man was crying out in a frenzied voice.

✦ *Sketch 21* ✦

THE ENDING

PRISONER 243 RELIVED the beating in all its terror. With every cry from that other man, he felt the blows, again and again, until he could no longer separate himself from that other victim, terror engulfing them both, blurring lines of illusory separateness. Between sharp intakes of breath, he became both victim and horrified observer.

"I'm the son of General Lucio Nyman Berquist!" he remembered shouting at his attackers, as if that could possibly deter demons.

"And I'm Calixto Contreras, son of the devil!" The guard had laughed as he and the other two clubbed him into submission.

Prisoner 243 remained hunched over, clutching his head, flinching with each cry, crying with and for the latest victim. *God in heaven! Help him! Help me!*

It finally grew quiet again. Benjamín remained in the same posture, halfway between terror and prayer. Slowly, he looked up and wiped his face. Then anger jolted him to his feet.

I've got to get the hell out of here!

He stayed up most of the night. The book had to be finished by morning, before 9 a.m., when the mail for the day left the prison. That would give the book less than a day's head start from the escape. He had to finish it, but he had no idea how. He reread the last line over and over: *God knows I am guilty of many things, but not of letting another man take the blame for me.*

Wonderful! Should I expect Isa to forgive everything simply because I didn't let Samuel go to prison for me? What is that moment of honesty compared to my brutal mistreatment of my father and of her? So where do I go from here? Decry once more the murder I never intended and will regret to my dying day? Bemoan the marriage I destroyed and learned to cherish only by living in a prison? Beg her forgiveness for whatever it is that I did or said the last night that we were together?

The torment was that he could remember nothing beyond the downing of brandy after brandy and waking up hours later to find her gone.

She endured poverty and isolation and my temper. What finally drove her away? Was it because she had never seen me drunk? Did she fear that I might become like her grandfather? Was that it? I know that I didn't lay a hand on her; even drunk I would never stoop to hurting her . . .

Remembering how he leaped at her here in the penitentiary, his hands murderously tight around her throat, Benjamín Nyman groaned deeply. In the sullen silence of the night, he acknowledged that he could no more vouch for his drunken self than for the sober counterpart when aflame with jealousy and rage.

Dios Santo! Who am I? What am I?

He gave up searching for the lost memory of that lost night, determined instead to create closure in the memoir—to end the story he had originally written for his brother but that had been for her all along—to end it in a manner that would persuade her to forgive him. But how? The last line in his book sounded increasingly self-righteous to him.

Is this how it ends—with a vain boast? What is Isabel to make of the abrupt, self-laudatory ending?

Samuel! How do I ask her forgiveness? His ardent question flew blindly across the valleys that separated them.

Keep it simple. He remembered his twin's advice. *Truth speaks in simple words.*

Dropping down a space on the page as the only transition, Benjamín Nyman added a letter to Isa, disguising it as the final three paragraphs to his book:

~

Beloved, I love you and always will, yet I have wronged you every step of the way. That day in my cell, you came to me with nothing but generous intentions, and I repaid you with brutality. I was half crazed with jealousy and despair, but that neither explains nor justifies my despicable behavior when I do not fully understand it myself. Yet here I am begging you to forgive me. Only that, Isa. You owe me nothing, you who gave me everything.

I have been wrong about everything, but most of all about you and Tomás Tepaneca. I don't know how long you have known him or under what circumstances, and it doesn't matter. It's clear to me that he loves you, perhaps even as much as I do. I don't know how or why the fates made him my father's attorney, or why my father left everything to you, or why Tepaneca kissed you on the lips. No, that's not true. I know all too well why he kissed you. I see it in that grainy photograph: *his* longing, not yours; *his* desire, not your betrayal; *his* arms around you, not yours around him. *Dios Santo!* Why was I so blind to what I knew in my heart? I know what marriage means to you—its sacredness, its eternalness. That is why you were willing to try again, to come to me even here in this wretched prison. Ah, my love! What would I give to take back that day and recast it for you with love and the most profound gratitude!

And what would I give to meet you there where you first learned to think of angels and spirits and feel my spirit transformed by your smile.

~

Sometime in the course of the night, Benjamín fell asleep hunched over his desk. A few hours later he awoke with a start. All about his feet were the crumpled-up balls of his efforts, like large pieces of hail. It was time for another run, the last one before the final one. He kept the run short—barely an hour. Feigning sickness, he returned to his cell, showered, and resumed his dash to the last page. By 8:35 a.m., twenty-five minutes before the day's mail was scheduled to leave the penitentiary, he had made two key additions to the manuscript: a note to Samuel and an entreaty to Isabel that he disguised as the dedication page, replacing the original dedication he had written to Samuel.

No! Don't be too clever! Write it so she'll notice it! Let form draw her eye to it.

Reaching for a sheet of paper, he recopied the dedication:

Beloved, if as your Swedenborg notes, birds are like thoughts,
Accept these as the flocks I have gathered for you alone.

There wasn't time to proofread the other two items. Prisoner 243 wrapped the memoir in the brown paper from the latest delivery of the Sylvein restaurant. Tying the manuscript with string, he addressed the package to Samuel and personally took it to the mail room. Mangel and El Manco, who had posted themselves outside his door, jumped up and followed him as always. The postal official, a surly man with pinched cheeks and a nasal voice, stared at the package as if it were a large spider and he were trying to decide whether or not to step on it. He decided to stomp.

"Open it."

Benjamín undid it carefully. The official stared at the title page. Benjamín had sketched a trogon in the right-hand margin.

Paradise Misplaced
Observations from the Aviary
By Benjamín Nyman Vizcarra

"What is it?"

"A book on ornithology—birds." Benjamín flipped through a number of pages to show him his many sketches of trogons and other species scattered throughout the manuscript. The official wrinkled his brow as he read the title aloud, superimposing Spanish pronunciation onto the English words.

"Pa-rah-dee-say Mees-plah-said. What the hell is that?"

"It's English for 'Bird of Paradise,'" Benjamín smiled. "I've written the whole thing in English for a friend of my brother. . . . He wants to publish a book about Mexican and Central American birds." He grew increasingly inventive.

"What's this?" The official pulled out Benjamín's note to Samuel.

"A memo to the editor."

Da librum uxori meae,
quam pessime iudicavimus.

"What's it say?"

Benjamín hoped that his Latin would say to his brother: *Give it to my wife, whom we have judged wrongly.*

"That the book is finished and ready for the printer."

The official wet his fingers as he continued to leaf through the manuscript. Sometimes he mouthed words, all of which were as unintelligible to him as Chinese pictographs.

"The editor needs the manuscript as soon as possible," Benjamín tried hurrying him along. "He will pay me soon, but I will pay you now for being kind enough to mail it today." He spoke with exquisite Mexican politeness and adroitly dropped another two gold coins onto the table.

The official pocketed them, but he continued to thumb through the pages as if looking for contraband. "What kind of a *pajarraco* is this?"

"It's a cormorant."

"I never saw a duck like that! You're not much of an artist, are you?"

Actually, the pen and ink drawings were skillfully executed.

"I try. Now, if you'd be so kind . . . I need to repackage it. I see that the mailman will be arriving any minute now. My editor and I would be most appreciative if you would see to it that it leaves in today's mail."

"What's the rush?" The official smirked. "Let the gringo editor wait."

Another two coins found their way onto the counter as the prisoner proceeded to rewrap the manuscript. "For your kindness in helping us meet the printer's tight schedule, you can count on a commission when the first edition is printed." He smiled.

"How much?"

"Ten pesos gold."

"Fifty."

"No. I don't have that much."

"Then I guess it will be delayed a bit."

"Never mind, then. You're right. Let the bastard wait."

Benjamín Nyman scooped up his package and headed toward the door.

"Thirty, then!"

"Twenty-five," Benjamín answered coolly.

The official grunted in agreement.

Outside in a sunlit courtyard that smelled of urine, Benjamín smiled to himself. *I would have given the greedy bastard a thousand pesos in gold!*

That evening he surprised his bodyguards by inviting them to sit at his table for dinner along with El Brujo.

"Is it Sunday already?" El Vago squinted.

"No. It's a special occasion." Benjamín knew he risked raising their suspicion. He went ahead anyway. "Sit down, gentlemen! We're celebrating tonight!"

No one argued. Chairs scraped noiselessly on the oriental carpet of the splendid cell.

"What are we celebrating, boss?" Mangel asked as he eyed the tantalizing boxes from the Sylvein.

"That I finished my book. Then again, maybe we need to celebrate Vago's saint's day."

El Vago twitched. He was about to protest that it wasn't until November, but a whiff of burgundy sauce silenced him. Benjamín leaned back, tipping his chair onto two legs.

"Everyone knows that today is San Vagubius's day! Vago, you first."

The men laughed, eagerly plundering the boxed meals. The taciturn El Brujo even smiled once. Watching his bodyguards, even Mangel, whom he deeply distrusted, Benjamín was assaulted by a sense of regret.

How can a meal compensate for a betrayal?

The question plagued him. Yet he played his part, eating, laughing, and swapping jokes.

"I just remembered that El Manco has a saint's day coming up soon!" Mangel announced, remembering to wipe his mouth with his napkin as he had observed Benjamín do a hundred times. "San Manco-*maniático!*" Everyone laughed. "Maybe the saint will send him a whore as a present!" From there, the conversation turned bawdy.

Sleep was difficult that night—not so much because Benjamín feared being shot in the morning as he tried to escape, or because he might be recaptured and tortured, though these thoughts jogged alongside him, but because to him everything, the very purpose of his life, depended on Isa forgiving him.

But will she read it? Have I made my regret and longing clear? Or will she see my self-deprecating Edenic story as nothing more than a taunt? Some cynical Voltairean account for my amusement and her debasement?

His restless mind ran for hours, until sleep outran him.

Suddenly a guard was unlocking the cell as he did every day, only this time Benjamín was utterly unprepared.

 *Sketch 22*

THE LAST RUN

He was still in his pajamas. With heart pounding like an Aztec drum, Prisoner 243 slipped out of his pajama bottoms and into the pants he had set aside for the escape.

"Move it!" the guard grumbled. "I can't stand here all morning."

There was no time to get out of his pajama top. Grabbing his jacket and quickly ramming his feet into his shoes, he headed out the door sockless.

It will be all right! The top is blue. It will look like a shirt, Benjamín assured himself.

As usual, it was dark and dimly lit at this hour, with only half of the outside lights on. Benjamín tried to calm his breathing. The chill morning air of the high central plateau crystallized it into soft plumes. He started off at a slow gait, conscious of how strange it felt to run in shoes. He would have preferred running barefoot like El Brujo had taught him, but he could hardly hope to blend into the city in a suit and bare feet. He spotted El Brujo in the opposite corridor. They met halfway and quickly shared a gourd of *iskiate*.

"On the seventh lap," the shaman whispered.

Benjamín nodded. They set off, backs straight, feet barely touching the floor. As agreed, they were both going to make the run with shoes on. Details. It was all about the details.

After the second round, El Brujo paused just beyond an orb of light to take off his sandals. He was going to make the arduous journey to the Copper Canyons, hundreds of kilometers away, on bare feet. That's when it dawned on Benjamín that the shaman was not wearing the pants and shirt that he had provided for him.

"What are you doing?" he muttered when he caught up to him inside a stairwell. "Why aren't you wearing the clothes I gave you?" El Brujo ignored the reproach and sprinted ahead.

He sticks out like a damn scarlet ibis!

Their careful planning was already unraveling. By the third lap, Benjamín's sockless feet were as agitated as his thoughts. Removing his shoes, he stashed them in the dark stairwell alongside El Brujo's sandals, but he intended to retrieve them just before the final lap. He would tie them together and hang them around his neck before leaping onto the wall. His agitation grew.

During the fourth lap, Benjamín thought about El Vago with his inane jokes and gap-toothed smile; he reflected that El Manco, thief and murderer that he was, tried living by a code of honor anchored in loyalty to friends; and then there was Mangel, crude and gruff, the epitome of self-centeredness, a man ferocious as an enormous mastiff that has been long abused. By now Benjamín could no longer pretend to himself that it didn't matter what happened to these men. They were fully implicated in the escape. He knew with the certainty of each footfall that the guards would vent their rage on them.

For reasons that he could not fully understand, Benjamín Nyman suddenly felt it as impossible to betray his fellow inmates as to betray his own brothers. By the fifth lap, it was clear to him that he was not going to add more remorse onto his shoulders, but, above all, that he could not allow El Brujo to venture into

Mexico City as a fugitive dressed in the white loincloth and the bright red shirt of a Tarahumara.

When they reached a stairwell and were momentarily out of sight of the guards, he pulled off his jacket and the pajama top. "Put these on," he whispered. "I'm not going."

"Come with me."

"No. I have a debt to pay. Put them on. There's no time to argue."

The shaman pushed his hand away.

"Brujo, go home to your wife and children."

That broke the impasse. El Brujo pulled off his tunic and shirt, but there was only time to exchange tops. They were off again, men in mixed garb—the Tarahumara in a blue pajama top untucked over his loincloth, Benjamín in tailored pants and the Tarahumara tunic and scarlet shirt. At the next meeting in the stairwell, they finished the trade and were off again, each in the other man's clothing.

Halfway down the stairwell, the Tarahumara came to a full stop. Benjamín passed him and stopped a few steps down. They knew they could only pause for a few seconds without arousing suspicion. El Brujo removed his *koyera,* the scarlet strip that kept his hair out of his face. With utmost solemnity, he tied it around his friend's head. Then he bounded across the courtyard with Benjamín a short distance behind.

When they took the stairs for the seventh lap, Benjamín let him get considerably ahead in a ploy to split the guards' attention, assuming any of them cared enough to watch their monotonous run. He reached the far end of a corridor just in time to see the Tarahumara leap onto the wall, his right foot finding the lower toehold, his left foot the second gouge in the wall. It all happened with astonishing speed and agility. Then he was on top of the wall and over it.

No shots rang out. No one noticed. Benjamín ran to the wall and slapped it with his right hand. Then he set off to finish one last lap. The morning breeze fanned him, the ends of the *koyera* rising and falling on the nape of his neck.

They'll probably beat the crap out of me.

Maybe.

It's the last run they'll ever let me take.

True.

"Hey! Where's the rich guy?" a guard called out.

Benjamín realized he had just been mistaken for El Brujo. He couldn't see the man's face, but neither could the guard see his. He slowed his pace but kept his back turned.

"In his cell, puking."

"Then get back in yours!"

Still keeping his back turned, the prisoner waved amiably to the faceless man and obeyed. When he cast a quick look over his shoulder and realized the guards were more intent on their conversation than on him, he ducked into his own cell. Catching sight of himself in his dresser's mirror, Benjamín Nyman paused and took in the measure of the Tarahumara who stared back.

He pictured El Brujo running all that day and for days afterward without stopping, unstoppable as his calloused feet carried him northwest deep into the sierras, home to the labyrinthine canyons that none knew like the Tarahumaras. He remembered a saying El Brujo had taught him: "When you run on the earth and run with the earth, you can run forever."

What about Isa? How will we ever find each other now?

With the book. She'll read the book, his heart told him.

He suddenly remembered a mating pair of trogons in his mother's aviary, back when he was a small child and his father still loved life. He remembered that the male managed to get out one night, and that he hovered insistently outside the cage to be near his mate. In the morning he was easily recaptured by the keepers. When Benjamín heard about the failed escape, he had run crying to the aviary.

"Why are you crying?" his father had asked, his face hand-some with gentle concern, his eyes bright as the Morelos sky overhead.

"Because I wanted the trogon to be free!"

"He is."

"No he's not! He's in there!"

"Where he has chosen to be."

Standing by the open door of his cell, Benjamín Nyman glanced back at the wall that might have led him to freedom, and he felt his spirit soar.

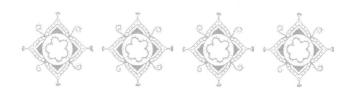

ACKNOWLEDGEMENTS

THE IMAGE OF the writer who works in total isolation is a fiction. Then again, fiction does tell its share of truths. So yes, I did work alone inside the silence that heightens the clicking sound of a keyboard or that watches morning light morph and vanish into nightfall. But to say that I wrote *Paradise Misplaced* alone is hardly accurate. I had readers like my father, who braved a full draft of the manuscript in its bawling infancy, and readers who saw it grow from adolescence to adulthood, from work in progress through a succession of drafts to the final one.

A very special thanks to my daughter, Alex, who was my sounding board and first editor. Attentive listener that she is, she sat with me by the lake as I spoke my book to her. As each chapter took shape, she read it with a careful eye for narrative and the nuanced word. My deep appreciation to Lisa Hyatt Cooper, who took time from her translation work to read substantial portions of Book 1 and of the upcoming Book 2 of the trilogy. The physical act of printing and mailing chapters to her as I completed each one kept me wonderfully motivated. Warm thanks to Jess Rose, whose sensitive reading reminded me of the power of the implied over the explicit, particularly in the crudity of language among prisoners. As the classics demonstrate so powerfully, art is above all an *interpretation* of reality, a vehicle whereby metaphor and imagination create worlds.

Dr. Stephen Smith read the full manuscript in its later stages and gave me valuable feedback, not just as a physician but as a prolific reader, as did Dr. Robin Larsen, who grasped the psychological implications of Benjamín's journal writing as a vehicle for spiritual healing.

I'd like to thank my editor, Morgan Beard, who kept track of time within the novel, precisely at those points where it tended to bolt away from me. Her advice in this and other matters helped see the book to its final form, assuming that final is no more a fiction than fictional finality.

And lastly, I'd like to thank my character Manuela Nyman Vizcarra, if mine she be. On a summer afternoon when I was describing the eve of Benjamín's departure for the revolution, she stepped in forcefully and totally subverted my dramatic tone with the first cup that she flung at the quarreling brothers. I laughed out loud. What could I do but let her lead?

QUESTIONS FOR DISCUSSION

1. The entire book is written from Benjamin's perspective, first from a third-person limited point of view, and in the second half of the book through first-person narrative. We see all of the other characters and events in the story mostly through his eyes. Is Benjamín a reliable narrator?

2. How does your perception of Isabel change in the course of the book? How would you describe her?

3. Why do you think Isabel chose Benjamín over Rodolfo?

4. Isabel's acceptance into, or rejection by, the Nyman family hinged largely on the way she spoke. Does that seem odd to you? Do we make those kinds of judgments in our own society?

5. To what extent does Benjamín define himself by his family's social status? To what extent does he rebel against it or repudiate its values?

6. How far should a mother go to keep her son safe? Do Manuela's good intentions justify her act of keeping Benjamín a prisoner to prevent him from joining the revolution?

7. Is Father Samuel a strong character or is he essentially weak-willed?

8. Does Benjamín have a religious sensibility? Does he believe in God?

9. Why is it that journal writing can be so powerful a tool for self-realization? How does the act of writing the memoir change Benjamín's view of his relationship with Isabel? Of himself? If he had not written it, do you think he would have made a different choice at the end of the book?

10. Why do you think that Lucio Nyman left his fortune to Isabel?

11. Why do you think Isabel left Benjamín following the revelation that she was the heir to the Nyman fortune? Were Manuela and Benjamín justified in their assumption that she and Tomás Tepaneca were lovers?

12. Throughout the story, Benjamín relies on his family's wealth and status to keep him safe and comfortable. When deprived of this after the end of the revolution, he was desperate to get it back. Now that he is in prison and his safety depends on it, how do you think he would react to losing it a second time?

13. Aside from the proper technique for running, what does El Brujo teach Benjamín?

14. How does Benjamín's moral character change over the course of the book?

THE REVOLUTION IS FAR FROM OVER . . .

Follow the adventures of Benjamín, Isabel, and the rest of the Nyman family in books 2 and 3 of the Mexican Eden Trilogy

Book 2: FLIGHT OF THE TROGON

As the Mexican Revolution of 1910 heads toward a darker, more violent period, many wealthy Mexicans flee to Europe while humble villagers find themselves trapped between contending armies. Imprisoned for murdering his father, Benjamín Nyman seeks redemption through a brotherhood of criminals; one of his bodyguards is given the order to murder him; and a prostitute inspires love in one of his fellow convicts.

Outside the prison walls, an honest priest is forced to maintain an elaborate lie; a young lawyer sets off on a quest to find the truth about General Nyman's death; and Benjamín's mother self-righteously punishes his wife, Isabel, whom she holds responsible for her son's misfortunes. In the midst of chaos, Isabel and Benjamín Nyman struggle to find each other.

Unwilling heir to the Nyman fortune, Isabel discovers that a will is not just a legal document, or even the tenacity to survive brutal isolation or to hope for the freedom to love again. In the silent recesses of her heart, she discovers that the will is the person itself.

Her inner journey begins in Benjamín's prison cell on a hot summer day in August 1911, the second day of his twenty-five-year sentence. Believing that Isabel has betrayed him for another man, his psychological wounds and fierce temper at their worst, he attacks her. She flees from him in terror, only to discover new terrors outside the prison walls—and new wonders within her spirit.

Book 3: PLANTING EDEN

DEEP IN THE Mexican sierras, the citizens of the ancient city of Zacatecas feel protected by its natural isolation. Yet its very isolation is what the Countess Eva Nyman de Comardo most hates about the city. She disdains its provincialism and fears the sense of entrapment that her fortress of a mansion inspires in her—until she falls in love with a man who is determined to stay in Zacatecas despite the distant rumblings of war. Eva persuades her husband to postpone their return to Europe and begins a secret campaign to free herself from her loveless marriage. When she writes to her brother Samuel to enlist his help, the priest sets out for Zacatecas, intent on saving her from the perilous path of adultery, divorce, and possible excommunication.

What neither he nor Eva nor any of the citizens can know is that the revolution is rolling inexorably toward them. Nor do the brother and sister realize that one of their own siblings is riding with the horde that will soon descend on them.

Zacatecas is about to become the scene of the bloodiest battle of the Mexican Revolution—and the site of deep internal battles.